# Angels of Armour

A.C. MARSH

Cover Art: Fantastical Ink
Proofreading: Phoenix Book Promo
Formatting: Phoenix Book Promo

*For anyone like Ella,*
*That lives their adventures through the pages of books.*

# CHAPTER ONE

The last few tables of hungry patrons were going to be leaving soon and then she would be free. Well, almost free. She was crazy if she thought that her grandma would let her leave this restaurant without having something to eat first. She wished this were one of those days where they would leave the restaurant and grab something to go on their way home, but no. Leo was stopping by just after closing time so that told her all she needed to know. Not that she didn't want to see her brother, she had missed him dearly when he'd moved out of the house, but all she wanted was a book, her favorite arm chair and her dog curled up by her feet. She sighed to herself, wiping her clean rag over the same spot of the counter, just for something to occupy her hands while her mind wandered. She couldn't help but think that she needed something to change. She was at a stalemate in her life and was in desperate need of some sort of adventure. She wasn't exactly the adventurous type, her friends would probably describe her as sensible and safe. Although she knew that there was nothing wrong with that, she couldn't help but wish for something more. Since she had split with her long term boyfriend six months ago, she had been dipping her toes into the waters of change. First it was different hair, different clothes, saying yes to more things, working on her confidence. The changes were small and the progress was slow but she could certainly feel the change within her.

The little bell above the door rang and her eyes snapped up to see who was entering. People didn't usually come into the café so late, the store/deli side of the business had closed hours ago. The man who entered the room was of average height and he was wearing a black scarf pulled up high over his face to try and shield him from the rain but his auburn hair did not fair so well with droplets clinging to the curls like diamonds. He strolled confidently over to a table and slid into the seat casually. There was something graceful in the way the man moved, his arms and legs were slender and as he pulled the scarf from around his neck she saw the freckles that were splashed across his cheeks. He was the complete opposite of what her type would be but she could not deny that the man sitting in that chair was undeniably gorgeous.

She approached him and he looked up at her with a polite smile. "Just to let you know, the kitchen's closed," she said kindly.

"Am I in time for a cappuccino?" he asked.

Ella nodded. "Sure thing," she said. "I'll be right back." His voice was softer than she was expecting but it had a richness to it that left her feeling a little shiver of pleasure dancing over her skin.

She jumped slightly when the door to the kitchen opened and her grandma Elena stepped out looking tired.

"Marcella, the kitchen is now closed," she said, rubbing her hands on a towel that she always had thrown over her shoulder.

"Please Nona." She looked all around, checking the auburn haired man twice, making sure that no one seemed to be listening. "Please don't call me Marcella."

Her grandmother fixed her with an exasperated stare. "Oh of course, mia regina, it's only your *name,*" she countered with an eye roll, but she seemed to see the distress on her granddaughter's face and looked around the room. She spotted the man with the auburn hair and appeared, to Ella, to narrow her eyes.

"Kitchen is closed," she said again, nodding slightly towards the man.

"I know. He only wants a coffee." She turned and got to work on the cappuccino.

"Well, he hasn't got long to drink it. We're closing in twenty." She seemed to take the details of the stranger in and then with an evaluating look at Ella, she went back into the kitchen.

As Ella made the coffee absentmindedly, she had used this coffee machine so often she thought she could probably have made the drink with her eyes closed, she wondered what was wrong with her Nona. On a bad day, the woman usually greeted regulars like family and newcomers warmly enough that they soon became regulars. Her Nona was a beautiful woman, her hair was grey but there was still streaks of the dark brown almost black hair that she'd had in her younger years. She was smaller than Ella, dainty looking and much less wrinkled than a lady of her age should be. Mal had asked her time and time again for her skincare routine and Elena had always brushed her off, telling her that good Italian cooking and SPF was her secret. She was usually an extremely positive and cheery person but lately she had seemed stressed and tired. She

4

was nearing retirement age but still worked her ass off in the café. Deciding that her Nona was likely tired and looking forward to closing up, she delivered the drink to the startlingly beautiful man.

"Can I ask you a question?" he asked, nodding his thanks for the warm coffee.

"I'm new in town and tomorrow I have to find the public library. I just wondered if you'd be able to give me some direction of where I'm headed?" She smiled. He was certainly asking the right girl, she had been in that library every week since she was seven years old.

"Of course!" she exclaimed. "From here, you carry on to the end of the street, take a left and halfway down that street, opposite the elementary school is the library." He looked out of the window and down the street that she had indicated.

"Perfect thank you, I really didn't want to be late my first day at work." He let out a breathy laugh. She paused, she felt a little flutter of excitement at the thought that there was possibly a gorgeous man in front of her, who engaged her in conversation and must love books enough to work at the library.

"You're going to be working at the library?" she asked, her eyes slightly wide.

"Yes," he said with a chuckle. Studying her face carefully he gave a little sideways smirk.

"I'm sorry," she said, "you just don't look like the normal librarian we would get in there." Her mouth went dry when what can only be described as a feline grin crept over his features.

"What do they usually look like?" he teased.

"Well, you know, clothes that smell like moth balls, suits in every shade of brown, glasses like magnifying glasses..." she reeled off, barely thinking about what she was saying. She stopped herself from continuing the strange and probably offensive list.

"When I lived in Michigan, I got myself through college by working at the college library and I fell in love with it. Changed my major to literature and worked there ever since. Until I moved here." He smiled at the sense of wonder on her face.

"I don't think I've ever seen someone so enraptured about working in a library." She felt a warmth creep up her neck.

"Sorry, I just love books and the library is one of my favorite places to be. I'd love to work there but I know I'd get nothing done, I'd just want to sit and read all day." She chuckled slightly.

He brother Leo had been the one to point this out to her when she was looking for a job. Her Nona had automatically offered her the job here, not even offered really, it was expected of her to start work at the café and when Nona wanted to retire the beautiful café would be passed to her. As it had been for generations, ever since her Italian family first came to the United States and bought the café. It never changed hands except from mother to daughter. Her own mother had worked there and she would have taken over from Nona by now, had she still been here. Inwardly, she had been reluctant to take the job, telling her brother she wanted to apply for the library. He looked as though he had understood her desire to get away from the café, but there was a softness in his eyes that told her all she had needed to know. That Nona would have been devastated. So he'd tried to make light of it. *You'd get fired on your first day, he'd told her, laughing. You'd spend more time pulling books off of the shelves than putting them back on.* So she took the job working with her Nona. The stranger was looking up at her, his smirk had twisted into a genuine smile.

"Then I'm sure I'll be seeing you again. Soon." She nodded, mentally scolding herself for replying so quickly and with so much enthusiasm.

"I'm Lucas," he said, boldly, holding out a hand. She took it in hers, noticing that his hand covered hers almost completely. His hands were soft.

"Ella, nice to meet you," she said, dropping his hand.

"It's *very* nice to meet you, Ella," he muttered as she turned to walk away.

She smiled to herself, swinging her hips a little more than she normally would have done as she moved to the next table to provide them with the check.

***

When Lucas had left, he said goodbye to Ella and sent her a disarming grin that made her stomach flutter nervously. She saw the last table out of the restaurant and rushed to slide the bolt across behind them. She took another look around at the small space. The café could have been much bigger if half of the space wasn't used as a Deli counter with Italian meats, cheeses, desserts and Gelato. They had a small range of different authentic Italian pasta's and flours etc. but most of their money came from the meats and cheeses in the winter and the Gelato in the summer. The café itself had a large counter, a high tech coffee machine, some freshly made cakes and desserts in glass casing and a chalkboard menu on the wall behind showing the day's specials. She stood against the counter, staring out over the room.

There were only around ten mahogany tables of different sizes, each with a small glass vase with a few fake red roses sitting on the edge of the table, with the salt and pepper shakers nestled in front of them. These were surrounded by an assortment of mahogany chairs. The navy walls should have made the room look too dark with the dimmed lighting and dark hard wood flooring but somehow it looked like a comfortable and cozy sitting room, rather than the dungeon it could have been. The pictures on the walls showed beautiful Italian artwork of angels and saints. Although their family weren't religious, there was something about the imagery that had always intrigued her, ever since she was a small girl. She closed the airflow on the log burner to let the flames stop and embers settle and set about clearing and cleaning the last few tables. There was a knock on the door a little while later that she assumed was Leo, so she opened it with a smile. This fell immediately as she saw it wasn't her brother. It was Will, Leo's infuriating best friend, who happens to be their family's next-door neighbor, grinning down at her. He raised his eyebrows at her expression as he stood waiting to be let in.

Will Baker. They'd been friends once, when they were kids. He towered above her by almost a head height and grinned his bright white smile. She noticed his almost black hair was slightly damp with drizzle and a droplet of water was sliding down his temple. She had the mental image of reaching up and wiping it away and her hands clenched to stop herself. He had his usual black coat on, the collar pulled up around his neck to keep away the wind and rain but she could still see through the small gap at the front. There was a hint of the black lines that covered much of his arms, back and chest. She felt a thrum of something in her veins, she had always tried to trick herself into thinking that all she felt for him was annoyance and sometimes disgust.

She was pretty sure that he was up to some shady shit, he had a 'second job' that he never spoke about, everyone else but her family and her few close friends appeared terrified of him and if the rumours were to be believed, he wasn't shy about people knowing he was a criminal. She didn't really believe half of what she heard because as much as she wanted to hate him and his shady business, she knew him. He was a good guy. She had witnessed with her own eyes him helping old Mrs. Clarke from down the street into her house with groceries, she knew he went to putty when he saw a cute puppy and as much as she teased him for being a player, she had only ever seen him be kind and gentlemanly to and about women.

His hazel green eyes danced with amusement as she settled her face into a glare.

"You're not Leo," she said stupidly. He snorted.

"Thank you for your accurate assessment Captain Obvious, he asked me to meet him here. I'm joining you for dinner." Her eyes had narrowed at the insult but she stepped aside. There was no point in trying to deny him. He was Leo's best friend and for some reason, her Nona also seemed to adore the moron. He moved past, unable to stop his arm from brushing against her in the small space of the entryway. She shuddered where his coat was damp. With the log burner going Ella had learned very quickly just to wear a thin t-shirt to work no matter how bad the weather was outside.

"Joy," she muttered under her breath and wiped at her black t-shirt. He grinned as if he'd heard.

She hated that she stared at him but she couldn't help herself. Even though Ella was tall, he towered above her by at least a head's height and as he took off his coat, she saw the black t-shirt he wore beneath stretch over his broad chest. The black swirling of his tattoos traced his well muscled arms and she stared at the sphere with strange patterns that was tattooed on his thick, tanned neck. She swallowed and tried not to think about how it might feel to kiss that neck. He hung up his coat on the rack along the wall and his t-shirt rode up slightly, showing a strip of tanned, taught skin and Ella quickly moved her eyes to the next table to be cleared, deciding she definitely needed to get laid soon. As much as she wanted Will, she wouldn't ever let herself go there and she was sure he would never be seriously interested in her. He would make suggestive comments and flirt with her sometimes but with the intention of either embarrassing her or annoying her.

"William!" Elena all but shouted, moving into the restaurant area, opening her arms wide to give Will a hug. With eyes rolling so hard she thought they might fall out, Ella went back to her cleaning duties.

The next time the door did receive a sharp knock, it was Leo that stood before her.

"Hey Ells!" he said, walking in and giving his sister a brief but tight hug. Leo and Ella had always been close; ever since they were little she knew that he would protect her. That bond had been proven when their mom died.

"Hey." She gave him a little squeeze. "Willy's back there with Nona." Leo clicked his tongue at her.

"Please stop calling him that."

"He calls me worse."

"You two drive me crazy, I wish you were twelve again and went back to having a crush on him, it would be much less tedious." She shushed him and swatted at his arm.

"I've never had a crush on that knuckle dragging..." Leo shot her a glare. Any time Ella or Will got close to really insulting each other, one look from Leo that said *you're going too far* usually stopped them.

They had been close as kids, but it had changed, so now she was left to endure him alone as her family and friends all seemed to love him but he grated on her in a way that she couldn't explain. The biggest reason that she couldn't stand her brother's best friend was because he tried to tell her what to do. Nona and Leo both knew it was pointless to speak to her when she was so riled, but to wait until she was a little calmer. Will however, told her no. He told her what she was doing was stupid, told her what she didn't want to hear. Only those close to her knew how stubborn she was, how quick she turned to anger, while everyone else seemed to wait for her to cool down before trying to reason with her, Will just told her plain and simple. Usually, although she would never in a month of Sundays admit this to him, he was right. Obviously, this made her hate him even more. Everyone else in her life seemed to think that the pair were perfect for each other and none of them were shy about letting either of them know about it. She knew that although she may want him more than she would ever care to admit, she could not live with not knowing about his second job; his secrets irked her enough as it was. It also helped that he usually went for girls who were, for want of a better word, completely gorgeous. Her mind wandered about how far she was from his type as she finished cleaning the last of the tables.

She untied the apron from around her waist and pulled her long hair from its tight bun. She hated wearing her hair up because it gave her headaches but with hair that almost reached her waist, there was no way she could wear it down while working in the café. She ran her fingers through her hair, looking in the mirror to check she didn't look like she'd been electrocuted and saw her light brown hair shimmer with the new honey blonde highlights that she'd had added only a few weeks ago. It had taken a long time for her friends to pull her out of her stupor since her and David had split, and Mal, whose mother was a hairdresser talked her into changing her hair for the first time in her life. She couldn't believe how much it had done for her self-esteem. Slowly, she started to come back to herself and to her great shock she'd even been convinced to go and spend some of her hard earned cash on a new wardrobe. She had some pretty daring items of clothing now that she wasn't sure she would ever wear but sure had a sense of danger knowing they were there and had even stopped buying clothes two sizes too big for her. So what if her hips were wider than some girls, or if her stomach wasn't completely toned and it jiggled a little.

David was a terrible boyfriend and a really shitty person, he'd always make little comments about Ella's appearance, about her body, her skills in the bedroom, how she kissed. Now that she was out of the relationship she could see that he was trying to wear her down, so that she would believe no one else could possibly want to be with her. She ran a hand across her stomach and pulled her t-shirt down slightly, making sure her belly was covered. She caught a pair of golden hazel eyes staring at her. He was leaning against the counter with his arms crossed over his chest. He looked at her with an appraising glance and when his eyes met hers in the mirror, she raised an eyebrow and smiled but instead of his cocky side grin that she was expecting, his brows furrowed together slightly and his lips seemed to point downwards. Her relationship with Will had changed when she and David split up, this is why everyone thought there was something there when there definitely wasn't. There were more glances filled with tension, their sniping turned to harmless and often shameless flirting, it became a game of who could make the other more flustered or who could wound the other's ego quicker but when they argued for real, when he tried to tell her what to do, these arguments were worse. Their friends and family had taken to leaving the room if they got into it. Ella couldn't back down from a fight and Will had a maddening ability to stay calm, stoic and quiet. If she got under his skin enough that he reacted, people practically ran out of his way. She thought of the light of his eyes, the vein that stuck out in his neck when he got truly angry and a thrill of excitement shot through her. She'd never admit it but arguing with him was one of her favorite things to do. He turned away to speak to Elena, still frowning. She'd paused, a hand still in her hair and the other still on her belly but she let them fall softly to her side. *What was that about?* She took a seat at the table that Elena had prepared and waited for the others to join her.

"Leo," she said loudly, passing Will, who had sat in the seat next to her, the breadbasket with a sweet smile. "How's work going?" She saw Will's eyebrows rise as she moved her hair to look at her brother.

"It's okay, I mean, I don't think my work is something Nona wants us to discuss at the dinner table," he said, looking at her with a smile. Leo worked in the local hospital, he was still a resident, not long out of med school but he seemed to enjoy it.

It meant that Ella hadn't been able to spend as much time as she usually would have with her brother for the last few years but it hadn't worked out badly for her. Her and Blake, her childhood best friend, had found a solid group of friends in her last few years of high school. She had no longer needed to use her brother as a social crutch.

"Definitely not," Elena said firmly. Surely thinking about all of the awful stories of being vomited on or covered in blood by the end of his shifts.

"Have you finally decided what you want to do for your birthday Ella?" Leo asked. She jumped slightly.

"It's not for another month," she said, half shrugging. She was the youngest of her friends and so was the last to turn twenty-one. You'd think, with it being such a big birthday that she would have been excited, want to go to as many bars as she could and get as drunk as was humanly possible but the thought of it made her want to curl up in bed and hide until she was at least thirty. It didn't help that when Blake had turned twenty-one, he seemed to distance himself from her and only now was she starting to feel their relationship return to normal after three months. She didn't want to push him to speak about what was bothering him, he would tell her when he was ready but she was curious.

"I'm sure Mal is organising something truly horrible," Will said. Leo shot his friend a look. Ella smirked. He may be Will's best friend but Ella knew that her brother had a soft spot for her female friend. He found her sweet and saw her as a good friend to Ella, keeping her grounded when she got too hot headed and boosting her when she became sad or insecure.

"I don't mean it like that." He narrowed his eyes at his friend. "But ya' know, it's not like Ella likes doing anything fun." Her spine straightened and her hand clamped around her fork.

"I'm sorry Will," she said with ice in every syllable. "I just don't find getting as drunk as I can and trying to sleep with anything with a pulse as interesting as you do." Elena frowned at her but Leo snorted into his arm, trying to hide his grin. Will shot him a withering look and turned to Ella.

"Jealous?" He smirked.

"Of you trying to sleep with half of the population of Illinois? No, can't say I am." She took another bite of food and almost choked on it as he retorted.

"That you're not one of them." He grinned as she coughed up the bread that had been sucked to the back of her throat. Elena's eyebrows rose but she was looking resolutely at the food on her plate.

"Honestly? It's a religious experience." Everyone looked at her like she'd suddenly sprouted another head. That spoke French.

"What?" Will asked, looking completely bewildered.

"Well, it means there must be a god out there somewhere, someone sure is listening to my prayers." Leo laughed a deep bark and Elena huffed a laugh into her wine glass.

Will grinned at her with a light in his eyes that quite plainly said *game on.* She so wished that the bolt of electric energy didn't shoot through her as he did.

# CHAPTER
# TWO

W ill and Leo had left to go to Phoenix, a bar they often frequented so they could have a drink so Ella and Elena headed home. Ella was more than happy to see the face of her Alsatian Ruby peering at her from the living room doorway. Ruby was more than a pet to Ella; she was without a doubt her best friend. Even before Blake. There was no one she trusted more. She'd ignored Ruby's advice only once and went on a date with a guy that Ruby had growled at when he'd come to pick her up. She got halfway through the meal before deciding that she wouldn't ever do it again.

"Hey Ruby," she said, walking towards the dog and scratching her behind the ears. Ruby licked her arm in greeting and wagged her tail.

"Ella, I'm going to have a bath and I'll be going straight to bed," Elena said warily. Ella frowned, she hadn't seen Elena this tired in a while.

"Sure thing Nona." She smiled and watched her grandma climb the stairs. Although it was nearing eleven, Ella wasn't ready to settle down for the night. She went into the kitchen, smiling slightly at the clatter of paws that she heard from behind her. She made herself a chamomile tea and sat herself in the little nook of the kitchen, where they had managed to fit a booth surrounding a large table, remembering where she had left her book earlier before she had left for work. She drummed her fingers on the cover of the book, thinking about what Will had said earlier. *Does he really think that I'm not fun?* Sure they often clashed and they always made fun of each other but teasing and fighting were better than indifference. She had always been the sensible one until someone pushed her too far. She wouldn't stay out past curfew or go out and buy a fake ID to get into bars. She never threw house parties when Elena went to visit her friends a few towns over and if she ever bothered to go to a classmate's house party, she had always left early when it got too rowdy. That didn't make her boring; it just means that she preferred to spend her time with people she found worthy. Life was too short to spend time with people you don't like, doing things that make you feel uncomfortable. She groaned and put her head in her hand. *I'm boring and safe and I never do anything that scares me. Even my boyfriends have been safe.*

She was opening her phone and calling the number before she had even thought about the lateness of the hour.

"It's way past your bedtime," said the voice of Mal. Mal, Malaika actually but only her mother called her that, was a ray of complete sunshine in Ella's life. Her beautiful black curls that formed a big afro bounced along in her wake as she almost skipped around, beaming at everyone with a full smile, round glasses that didn't make her look at all like a nerd, but like a scholar. She usually wore something bright like yellow, orange, pink and always managed to look stylish. She was a little shorter than Ella but she was more curvaceous and a lot more confident with it.

"Don't you start," Ella muttered.

"Uh oh. I know that tone. That's a I've seen Will and he got under my skin voice." Ella rolled her eyes but sighed in defeat.

"Am I boring?" she asked without pre-amble. There was a long pause.

"MAL!" she said loudly sounding offended.

"I'm sorry sweetie, you know I love you and I

don't think you're necessarily boring but you don't take risks, you're dependable, people can rely on you and that's part of your charm." She tried not to huff at her.

"Why can't I be dependable and interesting?" she almost whined.

"Hey, I never said that you weren't interesting. You're feisty." Another word that Ella hated.

"That's just a nicer way of saying I'm a bitch," she pointed out.

"No, I can say you're feisty and a bitch," Mal said. Ella paused but then sighed.

"Are you upset because you worry other people think you're boring or are you upset that Will said you were boring." Ella actually growled.

"I'd be just as upset if you or Blake had said it." She knew that wasn't true, but she ploughed on, hoping that her too observant friend didn't notice that.

"Except I did just say it," Mal pointed out.

"Shit."

"When are you going to accept that you're head over heels in l–" Ella cut her off.

"I am not in love with anyone, least of all Will. He may be pretty but he's an ass." Mal laughed.

"Girl, he's more than pretty and he's only an ass to

you. He's pulling the pig tails in the playground." She'd heard her friend make this argument too.

"That whole saying is stupid, allowing a guy who treats you like shit into your life cause it means he really likes you? Try being a decent human being and getting my attention instead and besides." She continued as it sounded as though Mal was considering interrupting her. "If you think that Will sees me as anything other than Leo's annoying little sister, you're wrong."

Mal's voice seemed to soften. "Is that what you think? Is that why it's easier to fight with him?"

"Jesus Mal! Stop trying to analyze everything that I'm saying. He's not into me and I'm not into him. Besides, I met a cute guy today," she said, thinking back to the auburn haired Lucas. She hadn't originally planned to tell Mal about the man she had met earlier but if it got her off of the subject of Will, she would wield it.

"You did? Did you get his number?" she asked, sounding interested.

"No but he works at the library," she said with a mischievous ring to her voice that Mal must have heard.

"You're not!" she said laughing.

"I am! I'm going to the library tomorrow and I'm

going to give him my number. Take that for boring."
She felt quite smug until Mal laughed.

"My baby is all grown up and out there finding
herself a MAN!" Ella laughed but bit her lip.

"And I need your help to try and catch him." Her
heart squeezed slightly with the bravery that would be
needed.

"Oh now I'm interested."

"You should be. Meet me at the mall tomorrow
about one?" she asked. "We have an outfit to buy." She
knew that she needed the moral support and Mal's
keen eye for this. Mal squealed with excitement and
agreed to meet her at the mall at one.

---

T he rain was bouncing off the pavement as
she walked, her umbrella fighting against
the wind that whipped her long hair around
her face. If she had been sensible this morning, she
would have tied it up but knowing that she was going
to see Lucas, she decided to style it carefully instead.
That had been a complete waste of time. She made it
up the stairs and into the alcove in front of the door of
the library where she took down her umbrella, shaking
as much excess water out of it as she possibly could and

ran a hand through her mostly dry hair. Looking in the reflection of the glass door, she was happy to see that she didn't look too bedraggled and windswept and she pulled the door open, walking into the spacious room.

She took in a big breath, like she did every time she entered the library and let the scent of the books fill her. It was much more than a library to her. It was a secret doorway into hundreds of different worlds. She had begrudged Will implying that she was boring but she couldn't really disagree, she spent so much time with her head in a book to get away from the horrible monotony of her life. She could go and flirt with Mr. Darcy, join a pirate crew and sail the seas, find a lover in a small town bakery, live in a castle with a prince or become an assassin or a trained warrior. She had all of the excitement with none of the risk. Would she have liked something to happen in her life that excited her? Yes! But if it didn't, she would be quite content to live vicariously through her favorite characters.

She found herself wandering aimlessly to her favorite shelf searching through the titles, trying to find something new to read when a voice behind her made her turn.

"I wasn't expecting to see you quite this soon." She turned to see Lucas and her mouth went dry. He looked so out of place but at the same time like he had been here forever. His white shirt clung to him, he was lean but well muscled if his sturdy arms were anything to go by, the shirt sleeves were pushed up to the elbows and a smattering of freckles covered his forearms. His black dress pants and polished shoes seemed at odds with his messy hair; he left his deep copper curls untouched by product, like he knew he would spend most of the day running his hand through them. Unbidden into her mind was an image of her hand running through them and she blushed slightly.

"I had some books to return and I thought I'd come along and make sure you found your way here." She smiled at him. He leaned against the bookshelf and gazed up and down at her without an ounce of shame.

"I'm glad to hear that you worried on my behalf." Her smile was almost feline when she replied.

"Well, I have a very good standing with the librarians here, I wouldn't like them to think badly of me." She moved closer, under the guise of looking at more books. When she was almost next to him she faced him again and his eyes were roaming her face. He looked awed.

"I'm sorry if this is too forward of me," he said in a deep almost whisper. "But you're the most beautiful woman that I have ever seen."

She paused, not expecting to hear him say such a

thing but she had put on her game face the moment she saw him. Giving herself a mental pep talk she reached into her coat pocket and pulled out a piece of paper with her number on it.

"As long as it's not too forward of me to do this." She tucked the piece of paper into his pocket. He was fighting against a smile.

"Not at all." He huffed out a breath and Ella had to stop herself grinning in triumph.

"So what're you looking for?" he asked her. "Except me." She let out a surprised chuckle.

"So much for worrying about being forward huh?" she asked. "I'm not sure what adventure I want to go on next." The tip of his tongue flicked out to lick his lips and he gestured for her to follow him.

"I think you should read this." He pulled a book off of the shelf and she raised her eyebrows at him. There was a cover of a man with an open shirt, holding a sword and swooning with a damsel in distress whose dress was very low cut.

"Is this the kind of book that you read, Lucas?" she teased.

"No," he said, his voice so low she moved slightly closer to be able to hear his next few words. She felt his breath hit the shell of her ear as he spoke. "This is the kind of book I want you to be reading when you think of me." She closed her eyes at the tingle in her skin and he pulled back. Her breath came fast as she felt excitement crawling up her spine, her brain feeling fogged with lust and she would have pushed him further into the stacks to show him just what she thought of him but she didn't fuck almost strangers in libraries. Not ones that she wanted to be allowed to visit again at any rate. "I'll call you, see how you're getting on with that book." He smirked as he backed away, turning out of the stacks and into the main area of the library.

Her back hit the shelf lightly as she took in a deep breath. Her skin was hot and her mind was fuzzy. The way that he'd whispered in her ear and made her shiver with lust, she had to give herself a second to gather her thoughts.

She chose a few more books to check out with the scandalous one that Lucas had suggested. The librarian at the desk eyed her curiously. She put her hands on her hips and shot a glare at her. Surely a librarian should be a little less judge-y about other people's reading preferences. As she filled her bag with the books and turned to leave she spotted Lucas across the room. He raised his hand in a farewell and she smiled at him, raising her own and, surprising herself at her own daring, sent him a wink before striding confidently out of the door.

Out of the door... but into the rain. She paused, trying to detangle her umbrella from her bag without getting too soaked. When she had finally got the umbrella up and over her head she wanted to turn, to make sure Lucas hadn't seen but she didn't think she could stand the shame if he had. Deciding she would rather not know, she walked back to her car, throwing the books and her umbrella into the trunk and checking her watch. She was running late to meet Mal but when she told her friend about how well her visit to the library had gone, she was sure Mal wouldn't be angry.

She was right. They sat in the Starbucks, quiet considering it was lunch time and Mal had wanted to hear every detail.

"Ella!" she had squealed when she told her what happened.

"You and Lucas are totally gonna have book sex!" Ella snorted into her latte and coughed slightly.

"Excuse me? Book sex? What does that even mean?" Mal rolled her eyes and leaned closer.

"You know, giving each other book recs to see who can find the hottest sex scene until one of you explodes and jumps the bones of the other." She said this as if it was a well-known fact.

"Who do you have book sex with?" Ella laughed but her eyes widened when Mal grinned at her.

"I don't have book sex. I have cocktail sex." Ella made a face.

"That sounds so gross." Mal laughed and sipped her extra-large Frappuccino.

"She recommends sexy sounding cocktails and I drink them, then I look up other sexy cocktails and ask if she knows how to make them. She almost dropped the bottle of tequila she was holding when I asked if she could get me a slippery nipple." An older gentleman who passed their table looked alarmed. Ella sent him an apologetic look but couldn't help giggling along with Mal.

"So, who is she?" Ella watched her friend closely. Mal loved hard, she rarely made an effort with someone she wasn't serious about. Mal shrugged.

"She runs the Phoenix bar. She doesn't often work behind the bar but I've caught her a few times and it's just a little bit of fun. I'm sure she's straight, the amount of men that drool after her every night." Giving her friend another once over she nodded. Mal had a complicated relationship with her sexuality. Finally deciding that she likes whomever she likes and anyone who didn't like that about her could pick themselves up and walk away. Like everything Mal did, she did it with grace and confidence. "Anyway enough about me, what about Lucas?" Ella was ripped from her thoughts.

"What about him?" Her friend rolled her eyes.

"Are you gonna see him again?"

"I don't know, it's down to him I guess. If he calls me and asks, I'll say yes." She smiled.

"And this isn't just one of those things that you'd do to annoy Will and Leo?" Ella glared at her friend.

"I don't choose to go on dates to get a rise out of people Mal," she said sharply. She might go on dates to get over some people, like David and a voice deep, deep inside her head whispered *Will* but not to annoy them specifically.

"Okay." Mal nodded. "So the point of asking me here?" she said, changing the conversation again.

"Yes!" Ella said, sitting up straight in her chair and gulping the last of her luke-warm coffee.

"I want to do something so un-Ella-like for my birthday." Mal's eyes widened in surprise.

"Like what?"

"Like a party."

"Say what now?"

"A party. You know. With balloons, clowns and

cake, lots of people. Although I hope mine will have less clowns and balloons and more dirty dancing and tequila."

"I know what a party is," she said with a huffy breath. "I just didn't know that you did."

Ella's shoulders stiffened.

"Like I said, un-Ella-like. I want to do something fun, wear something that I would never wear, drink more than I would ever drink. Then, even if I hate every moment of it, at least I would have tried it, right? I'm nearly twenty-one years old and I have the personality of an old spinster and the situation of a teenage girl," she said, running a frustrated hand through her hair.

"Situation?" Mal questioned.

"I'm single, I work practically part time in my Nona's café, I still live at home and I have never been to college." Mal's eyes softened and she reached out a hand to rest it on Ella's own.

"You staying home with Nona isn't something to be ashamed of, you don't want to leave her in that big old house all alone and god, we both know she would never sell it." Ella laughed and nodded her head in agreement. There would be absolutely no way Elena would ever sell the house or the café and she also knew that her Nona wasn't going to be around forever, that she is getting more and more tired as the months go by. If Ella had to stay and learn every inch of that business ready for when Nona wants to hand over the keys she would. College be damned.

"It could be worse, she could be like my mom and Grandma, forcing me to go to a college I don't want to go to, to study a subject I don't want to study." Mal looked down at her own hands sadly, having taken hers off of Ella's. Mal had always wanted to be a fashion designer. She took art classes behind her mom's back because her mom had always wanted her to use her remarkable brains to do something worthy, like a lawyer or a doctor. Mal was currently studying business and she hates every minute of it. Ella's heart twinged for her friend.

"I guess you're right, I should count my blessings, sorry sweetie. I'm saving money, I have more free time, I'm not stressed all the time. It just gets boring sometimes. I feel like I'm constantly waiting for my life to start."

"I know the feeling." The girls looked at each other and started laughing.

"Now," Mal said when the giggles had subsided. "I remember you saying something about an outfit?"

They had been in every single store in the mall. At least once, some of them twice and Mal loved every second of it. Ella however was starting to feel her nerves were waning.

"This is a stupid idea, I'm going to turn up and people are going to think I look like a clown," she said, flicking through the racks of beautiful, different brightly colored dresses.

"You will not look stupid, you will look like a phoenix being born from the ashes," Mal said fiercely.

"Phoenix... do you think you could talk to your bar friend who owns Phoenix and ask her if we can rent a private space for my party?" Her friend's eyes looked a little weary.

"I don't really know her that well. We haven't spoken much, past all the sex on the beach and the slippery nipples." She sighed as Ella snorted in a laugh to herself.

"I'll ask Leo to find out for me, he's in there enough." She nodded.

"I can't wait till you can start coming out with us more! Do you know how frustrating it is having to sit there while Sam and Blake blatantly ignore the fact that they're in love with each other, occasionally catch a glimpse of Will dancing with some goddess on the dancefloor or Leo–"

"I don't know what the end of that sentence is but I know that I do not wanna hear it," she said warningly. She fished her phone out of her coat pocket and sent a text to her brother to ask about the party at Phoenix. The comment about Will had made her stomach flop in a way that she didn't want to think about too hard when she felt a buzzing in her hand. She jumped a little, looking at her phone to read the message.

*It's Lucas. It was nice seeing you again today, I'm sorry if I came on a little strong. I don't really know what came over me.*

A smirk slithered onto her face and Mal looked to read the message over her shoulder.

"He even types sexy. Look at all that punctuation and capital letters. Uh." She winked at her and Ella laughed loudly.

*It wasn't too strong, it was just enough.*

She was surprised at her own daring. This is the first time she had properly flirted with someone and they didn't make a joke out of it or make her feel like an idiot for it. Lucas made her feel different. David had always said she had been too intense. He blamed all of the books she read, saying it gave her 'unrealistic expectations of men.' He didn't agree when she said the same thing about women in porn but she always knew she would never win an argument with David. He was right, about everything, all of the time. God she was glad to be rid of him, no matter how much it hurt at first.

*Good. Have you started that book I recommended?*

Her cheeks heated and she turned away from Mal, walking towards a section of deep blue, red and emerald dresses.

*Not yet, out shopping for a dress to wear to my birthday party.*

She was about to put her phone away when it buzzed in her hand.

*When's your birthday?*

She paused. She would wait until they've seen each other a few times before she thinks about inviting him to her birthday.

*Next month, October 5th.*

She thought of how excited she was to be getting into fall, she loved the colors of fall, the browns and the oranges. Dark copper hair and deep brown eyes flew into her mind and she cursed herself. She wanted to be confident but wary. She had been used too many times.

*I'm sure whatever you pick you will look delectable.*

Angels have mercy this man was something else. She loved a good adjective. Could she possibly have the gumption to not only accept his compliment but also take it further? If this scared him off, she decided, then he wasn't worth the effort.

*I assure you I will. Maybe if you're lucky you might even get to see it.*

She hit send and immediately lost all of her courage. She turned her phone off of vibrate and put it back in her pocket, promising herself that she would spare herself the horror of looking at the reply until she was alone.

It was then that she spotted it. It was the perfect mix of old fashioned corset with sexy satin material and a sweeping skirt that slit up to the mid-thigh, the rest swooping around to reach her knee. The emerald green satin slipped through her fingers as she touched the skirt of the dress. The cap sleeves hung in the same swag as the skirt and even Ella, who barely knew how to dress herself knew that this was one of those once in a lifetime dresses. This was the dress.

"Holy shit Ella," Mal said, coming up behind her. "Try it on." She didn't even attempt to argue. She found her size and walked purposefully towards the dressing rooms, Mal bouncing excitedly behind her. When she came out of the dressing room and saw the look on Mal's face, she knew she had made the right choice.

"You look phenomenal," she whispered. It wasn't very often that Mal was speechless. Ella turned to the long mirror in the corridor and took in a breath that made her chest heave. The corset bodice tightened further and she let out the breath in a laugh.

"I love it." She pulled her hair down from her messy bun that she had thrown it into halfway through the day and Mal let out a little squeal.

"Buy it. Buy it right now." She put a hand on her hips.

"I am but I'm going to look for one more dress." Mal looked at her like she was insane.

"What for? This is it, this is the birthday dress."

"Oh it is, but I think I'm going to be asked on a date soon, so I'd like to have something in the wardrobe to wear..." She trailed off with a wink at her friend and smiled to herself as she strutted back to the changing room. She found another dress, a simple, little black dress that hugged her shape and made her feel sexy as hell. It didn't have the same punch as the green dress but if he played his cards right, Lucas might get to see her in both.

# CHAPTER THREE

hen she got home she threw her bags into her room and headed down to the kitchen to the smell of something delicious being cooked. She poked her head around the door to see Elena adding the finishing touches to what seemed to be meatballs.

"Nona that smells amazing." Ella walked into the kitchen with Ruby hot on her heels.

"And it's almost ready, did you have a good day?" she asked as she plated up the meals. Ella nodded, moving to the refrigerator and pulling out the jug of lemonade. She grabbed two glasses and took all of them to the table. As Elena brought the food over and Ella poured out the drinks, she spoke. "I decided that I'm going to throw a party for my birthday, kind of.

I'm trying to get a private booth at the Phoenix bar if I can rent it." She saw her Elena's eyebrows rise.

"Really?" she asked. "This isn't about what Will said last night is it? You know he doesn't mean it, you two just like to get under each other's skin." She smiled almost sadly at her Nona, she was pretty sure Will was her favorite and he wasn't even her grandkid. "No Nona, I've been getting my confidence back, ya' know, since David and it's something I want to do. I'm an adult now, I need to grow up sometime." Her grandmother smiled at her, eyes softening.

"You're growing into such a beautiful young woman Marcella." She doesn't even correct her as she watches her bring the plates over and lays a plate of heaped spaghetti and meatballs down.

"Thank you," she said to Elena, and she knew that she had known that Ella had said thank you for the compliment and the food.

They talked as they ate. Ella had almost mentioned Lucas at the library but at the memory of the look on Elena's face when he had entered the café last night, she decided against it. She cleared away and once everything was clean she ran up to her room to get the dress to show to Elena. She felt slightly embarrassed of the silver sheen of tears rimming her Nona's eyes.

"That was your Mama's favorite color, you know."

She had her hands clasped over her heart and Ella's own gave a little flutter at the thought.

"I didn't know that." Ella didn't know a lot about her mom. She had died when she was so young that the memories she had with her are faded and distorted by grief. She didn't want to think about her mother so she excused herself and took herself back up to her room. Putting the dress into her wardrobe she turned and saw Ruby sat on her bed. She pushed everything else off of the bed and onto the floor and crawled onto the bed, lying next to Ruby who rested her head on Ella's stomach and huffed.

"You sound as tired as I feel Rubes." She scratched her behind the ears with one hand as she picked up her phone from the nightstand.

She opened her messages; she had a few from Mal, Blake and Sam, one from Will and one from Lucas. Her mind wandered back to the last message that she had sent him and she opened the message with a sinking feeling.

*I would count myself as very lucky indeed.*

Her stomach came shooting back to its proper place as she grinned stupidly at the text message. She flicked through her other messages. It was rare that Will ever text her more than a few words so when she saw that she had to click on the message to read it fully, curiosity took over and she opened it.

*I've spoken to Lyra at the Phoenix bar, she's happy to let you have a booth for the evening. Before I confirm it with her I just wanna make sure. You're doing this because it's what you want right? Not because I called you boring?*

She rolled her eyes.

*Believe it or not, not everything I do is because of something that you have said or done.*

She didn't have to wait very long for a reply.

*I know that but I thought I might have hit a nerve or something. If you want it I'll book it.*

She sighed.

*Yes, please. I'd like to book the booth. Just let me know how much it is and I'll go round with Mal and pay for it. Thanks.*

Ruby's eyes opened and looked at her.

"Yes I know, I just used manners with Will." Ruby let her eyes droop closed again.

*It's already paid for. Call it a birthday present.*

She sat up, Ruby making a noise of annoyance. She hit the dial button before she had finished thinking the thought.

"I'm so glad, I hate texting, it's so boring," Will's amused voice sang into her ear.

"Let me know how much I owe you," she said sternly.

"I told you, nothing. That's how a gift works." She clenched her fist.

"I appreciate the offer Will but it's not necessary."

"It wasn't an offer. You don't get to choose what I give you as a birthday gift."

"You are the most infuriating–

Ruby bounded off of the bed, jumping up onto the window seat in her bay window, barking and snarling at something outside of the window.

"What's going on?" Will asked, his voice serious now.

"I don't know, Ruby's spotted something outside." She looked out of the window to where the dog's attention was. "But I can't see anything, it's probably a squirrel or something."

"Stay away from the window," he said and she laughed

"Chill out dude, I don't think it's a sniper." She heard a growl of frustration, this time it came from the voice on the other end of the phone and not the dog poised at the window. A shiver of pleasure at the sound rippled through her.

"Just stay inside tonight, please?" It was his use of the word please that stopped her from snapping back.

"Okay," she said quietly. "If you wanna come over and canvas the garden and house before you sleep then make sure you knock quietly, Nona's asleep." Thankfully, he laughed.

"I don't think anyone in the street is going to be asleep if Ruby doesn't shut up." And she had to agree.

"Ruby, enough," she said in her deeper voice that told Ruby it was time to listen to a command and not normal everyday conversation. Ruby stopped barking but she was still on alert.

"I should not find that sexy," Will said and despite herself she laughed. She had to remind herself that these little comments were a part of the game they played with each other. The only reason he paid for the booth was to ease his own guilt for calling her boring and she was under no illusions that Leo hadn't had stern words with him about the comment.

"Gross. Goodnight Will." She thought for a second and added with an eye roll. "And thank you... for the gift."

"You're welcome." His voice was softer than she had possibly ever heard it. Then it snapped back to its normal, teasing tone. "Night loser." He hung the phone up before she could retort. She locked the phone and sat back on the bed. Ruby moved from the window to sitting at the door. She knew that whatever

Ruby had seen outside had spooked her enough that she would rather sleep guarding the door than in the comfortable bed. Ella laughed to herself; of course her dog would be as stubborn as she is.

---

Her eyes flung open and her upper body went with them, suddenly finding herself in a sitting position on her bed. Breath heaving, she felt a cold sweat across her skin, looking down she saw the glittering moisture in the moonlight. The hair that had fallen down, out of the bun she'd messily tied her hair into before she slept was sticking to her neck and face. She gasped, trying to get as much air into her lungs as possible and she felt a pressure on the bed as Ruby jumped onto the bed beside her. Ella placed a hand on the dog's comfortingly warm and soft neck, grateful for the presence keeping her anchored to the real world. Keeping her from falling back into the horror that she had woken from.

She'd had the nightmares most of her life, that's what happened when you went through something so traumatic at such a young age. Or so her therapist had told her but in the last few months, the nightmares were evolving. They were no longer based on what she remembered. She had been seven years old, Leo was nine. They'd been playing out a few streets over with Blake and his brothers and Leo had been concerned when Blake's mom had called them in for dinner as he realized their mom had not. They'd walked back to their house, holding hands as they always did. Leo was scared that impulsive Ella would run into the street. She remembered Leo pushing the door, it had been slightly ajar and she stayed behind him as he crept up the hall towards the kitchen. The house was silent, no barking from Tobias, no movement of their mom in the kitchen or of her singing softly to herself as she often did. The sight that had greeted them when they'd entered the kitchen had been one of nightmares. The flood of red covering the floor, the lifeless body of Tobias, his fur damp and stained and then she saw it. Her mother, led in the middle of the largest pool of crimson. Leo was pushing her back out of the door, telling her to run to the phone box down the street and call the police. She had known that her mom and their dog was dead, she didn't understand why or the implications of the way in which they were found.

She gripped a handful of fur lightly, listening to Ruby's pants as if to ensure herself that she was definitely here. Her mother's dog Tobias was to her mother what Ruby was to Ella herself. A companion, a guardian. A best friend. That image was horrible enough but now the images were changing. Every month that passed since her break up with David there seemed to be more and more details that her treacherous mind added to her horrors.

There was a man, dressed in black, his face in shadow, he had appeared in the dreams six months ago. It had only been a few weeks since her mind had allowed him to evolve into carrying what looked like a machete, with symbols and words etched into the blade that Ella didn't recognize.

Tonight, she had stayed in the dream longer. Watching the man in the shadows, blood dripping from his knife as Leo stood in front of her, telling her to run. The man had turned to them, eyes that were too dark to really see fixed on Ella and Leo and he had turned, run through the open patio doors. In tonight's dream, she had run to the doors, watching as the man ran. Faster than what would have been humanly possible. He vaulted the wall at the end of the yard and took off into the thicket of trees that was the start of the forest that started at their boundary wall. The forest itself was quiet, the wildlife rarely coming too close to the edge of the forest and the trees soon became thick enough that it would take a lot of effort to really penetrate the centre. The forest was huge and it would take someone who was skilled and knew the area well to navigate it without getting lost. As her heart rate began to slow she tried not to think about the forest, the man, the knife, Tobias or her mother. She looked towards her bedside clock to check the time and saw that her phone had lit up. She hadn't taken it off of silent when she had fallen asleep. Will's name flashed across her screen and she paused. The clock on her bedstand said it was 4.45 am. Why on earth would Will be calling her now?

"Hello?" she answered, voice rasped and dry.

"Ella, are you okay?" He sounded panicked.

"Yes, I'm fine, why?" There was a pause on the other end of the phone followed by a sigh.

"Can you come let me in?" Her eyes flew wide.

"Why are you here?" she squeaked.

"After Ruby acting funny and getting a weird feeling myself, I couldn't sleep. I needed to check on you." She was silent and after a beat or two he added. "And Nona." A slice of fear slithered down her chest landing icy cold in her stomach.

"I'll be two minutes." She tried to find her robe to throw over her pyjamas but looking around she decided she didn't have time, she tiptoed down the hallway and cracked open Nona's door, the icy sensation in her stomach lessened when she saw her Nona's face, sleeping peacefully. She watched just a moment longer to ensure she saw the steady rise and fall of her shoulders and ran silently down the stairs. Ruby was already waiting by the front door. Ella unlocked the door and pulled it open, Will was in his usual t-shirt and jeans and despite what he had said, he didn't look as though he had even attempted to get to sleep. She was just about to chastise him for making her worry when he yanked her arm and pulled her to him, enveloping her in a hug that stole her breath as their chests pressed together. Her annoyance with him fell away immediately. She couldn't remember the last time he had hugged her, probably not since they were children.

"I'm okay Will," she muttered into his shoulder and he tightened his arms slightly before releasing her, only enough to pull her back and look her over. She squirmed slightly, wishing she wasn't wearing her care bear pyjama pants and an all too revealing tank top.

"Will?" she asked questioningly and his eyes snapped to hers. "What's going on?" He moved past her and into the house without responding.

"Oh sure, come on in," she said agitatedly, following him back in and closing the front door quietly. He went into the kitchen and appeared to be looking all around. He opened the patio door and peered out, checking left and right before closing it again and she faltered, standing in the doorway. A flash of blood, a knife and a man in black flitted across her vision and she whimpered. He spun and came back to her immediately.

"What's wrong?" His voice was low and breathy, there was real panic on his face.

"Nothing," she said, hoping to sound defiant but in her own ears she could hear that the word had sounded nothing less than pathetic.

"Ella, please," he breathed out. "I don't care if you think I'm crazy or if you think you sound crazy, just tell me what is going on." She bit her lip. He'd always looked out for her, even when they weren't as close anymore but this was different, there was a sincerity in his eyes that she couldn't understand and his hands were shaking at his sides. There was no way he could know about her dreams, she had told Nona that they had stopped completely and as far as Leo knew, they were the same flashbacks of their mother's death that she had always experienced.

"You first," she challenged, brushing past him with a lot more bravado than she felt. She made her way to the coffee machine and set about refilling it. There was no way she was going to be able to go back to sleep tonight, not only because of the nightmare and Will storming in but since that hug, her entire body felt as though it was on fire and vibrating furiously. She gritted her teeth as she tried to think about anything other than his body wrapped around hers. *God,* she thought to herself, *I need to get laid.*

"I was concerned with how Ruby acted when we were on the phone earlier. I came home and did some skulking around." She rolled her eyes at him.

"I was only kidding when I told you to canvas the yard for angel's sake!" He narrowed his eyes.

"And she had a good reason to be concerned. I spotted a man lurking at the edge of the forest." The mug that she had picked up to pour his coffee into slipped from her hand as her mind went blank, the cup smashed on the tiled floor of the kitchen and she sank down between the broken shards.

"Ella?" Will was crouching in front of her, his hands on both cheeks, forcing her eyes to his. "What is going on?" She picked up her hand and saw blood from a cut on her palm, her hand had landed on one of the broken shards of porcelain. It was all too much. The sight of blood on the kitchen floor, on her hand, the knowledge that there had been a man at the edge of the woods. She screamed.

# CHAPTER FOUR

H e picked her up, she was still screaming and thrashing but he made sure she was secured as best he could and lifted her, moving her out of the kitchen and into the living room, placing her gently on the couch. Movement upstairs told him that her screams had woken Elena. Ruby had crawled onto the sofa and led atop Ella's body. She had almost immediately stopped thrashing. Ruby's muzzle buried into Ella's neck and he reached down to pull the stray hairs away from her neck. Ruby watched his every move but she knew that Will wasn't a threat to Ella. Elena entered the room.

"Will! What happened?" Ella whimpered and seemed to fall back into a fitful sleep.

"Ruby spotted something outside Ella's room

earlier, so I came back and checked the boundaries and found what looked like a man within the first few lines of the trees of the forest." Elena's eyes squeezed closed.

"But what set off Ella?" Will sighed and sat on the floor next to the couch. When she was feeling these emotions, it was difficult for him to stay away from her. It went against his very DNA.

"I can't be sure, because she never got round to telling me but I think she's been lying about her nightmares." He picked up her hand that had fallen off of Ruby, dangling off the edge of the couch and he held it in his. The cut had stopped bleeding, it wasn't deep but he held it in his own and let his power flow through him. When he moved his hands, the cut had disappeared.

"I told her that there was someone at the boundaries and she dropped her coffee mug. She fell to the floor and cut herself. She saw the blood and just lost it." Elena cursed quietly.

"She's breaking through the glamour, isn't she? She's remembering everything." Will nodded but a muscle ticked in his jaw.

"But she shouldn't be. She still has almost a month to go before her birthday. There must be something that's happened to kick into life her dormant powers somewhat." Elena frowned and took in a deep breath.

"There was a fallen, that came into the café." Will's head whipped up.

"Ella spoke to him?" She nodded.

"He was a customer, of course she spoke to him but surely his presence alone wouldn't be enough for anything to kick in a month early." Will sighed.

"I don't know, but it's time to call Magda again." Elena's eyes snapped to his.

"You know the warnings, William. If we continue to fight it so close to the day it's revealed, it can hinder her understanding when it comes. If we don't and she finds out early, there's a chance she will try and run from it. Without her powers snapping into place, do you really think she's going to accept it? Hell, do you think she is even going to believe us?" Elena put a hand to her head.

"I know that we can't tell her, but we can let her find out for herself." Will stood in one swift motion. He pointed at the pale woman on the couch.

"How is she supposed to work out something like this? And we have to sit back and watch her suffer like this for a month? You know I can't do that Elena. Even if I wanted to I am bound." Elena dropped her hand and gave him a glare.

"You do not have the final say here William. No

matter what she is to you, she is my granddaughter."
Will snarled and turned away.

"I cannot allow her to suffer for another month, it
will kill me." When she opened her mouth he added,
his tone softened. "You understand why Elena, more
than most." Elena seemed to deflate. "I know. I don't
take for granted how difficult this is for you." He
nodded and both of their eyes travelled to Ella, sleeping
almost peacefully with a restful Ruby protecting her
body.

"I'll call Magda, we will reinforce the glamour but
when it comes to telling her, William, just know it will
be difficult. Prepare for the worst." He let out a noise
of pain, but nodded.

"I'll call Leo, he should know." She nodded and
turned towards the hall. Will turned towards the
window and pulled his cell phone from his pocket.

Leo had answered on the third ring.

"You'll have to be quick, I'm on a night shift."

"It's Ella." Will noted that his voice sounded tired,
robotic almost.

"What's wrong?" Immediately, his voice sounded
strained and Will heard his footsteps as he was sure Leo
moved to somewhere more private.

"Ruby detected an intruder when I was on the
phone with Ella earlier. I did a boundary check and

found someone... or something lurking within the first few lines of the trees of the forest. Then about 4.30, I got a warning that Ella was in distress, so I called her again, she let me in. I was trying to get out of her what upset her so much but when I told her that Ruby had been right, there was someone in the trees, she dropped a coffee mug, she cut her hand. She sat on the kitchen floor, took one look at the blood and lost it. Crying, screaming, thrashing."

"Fuck," Leo said. It sounded as though he was moving again. "I've only got an hour left of my shift, I'm leaving now and I'll be home soon."

"Elena's calling Magda." There was silence.

"Is that... wise?" Leo questioned and Will gritted his teeth.

"We can't allow her to spend another month suffering."

"Are you worried about her? Or about you?" Leo's voice was cool and he clenched a fist in response.

"I can't believe you even have to ask me that." His teeth were clenched and Leo sighed.

"I'm sorry–" Will cut him off.

"It's fine, see you soon." He ended the call before Leo had even had time to say goodbye. He didn't want to upset Elena or Leo but neither of them understood fully what he went through. The fact that her in physical danger felt like someone was carving into his skin, when she was scared it felt like electric shocks bolting through him. The bond was there to make his job easier. To protect Ella, but it sucked. He was trying hard to stamp down on any other feelings for her, most he could blame on the bond that they shared but the elation he felt when she was finally free of the moron David was nothing to do with the bond. The heat that flooded him whenever she did something unintentionally sexy or when she was riling him up and calling him out on his shit. None of those things he could blame on the bond but one tug on his mind to remind him that the job always comes first.

Leo arrived only minutes after Magda. Will had barely closed the front door when it opened again. His best friend almost falling through the door. He grabbed Will and flung his arms around him, holding him tightly. Will allowed himself to sag into Leo's body.

"Thank you for being here and for doing what you do," Leo whispered and Will felt his eyes sting with the prickle of tears.

"No thanks needed, you know it's my duty." Leo pulled away and eyed his best friend.

"That may be so, but I know even if it wasn't, you'd still be here." Will nodded and swallowed hard.

He didn't want it to go so far that there was no chance of a friendship between him and Ella, because he couldn't do his job properly if she couldn't stand the sight of him but being so close to her and not being able to have her the way that he wanted was driving him crazy. So it was best to distance himself enough that he could stay in her life but not give in to temptation. That was what was best for everyone. At least, that's what he keeps telling himself.

He and Leo went into the living room. Ruby had finally moved away from Ella to let Magda get closer and upon seeing Will she came and sat next to him. He patted her head gingerly.

"I know buddy," he murmured to the dog, who licked his wrist in response.

Magda was muttering to herself and Elena was crouched next to her granddaughter, holding her hand. Leo had come behind his Nona and placed his hand on her shoulder.

"Will, are you ready?" Magda asked, eyes shooting to Will. Her dark skin was lightly wrinkled and her resemblance to her granddaughter was evident in her big warming smile and happy attitude. He nodded and moved forwards, standing between Magda and Ella. The hand that Elena wasn't holding was folded on her stomach and he reached out, holding it gently.

"Have you decided what you're going to do?" He nodded. He would weave the glamour into her mind that her dreams had been as normal, it wouldn't do anyone any good to take away her dreams completely, her memories of her mother's death. As much as he wanted to, there would be enough emotions and thoughts rushing back to her when she came of age, let alone the horror of how she and Leo had found her mother. Well, most of those details. Magda held onto his other hand and started to mumble in a language that was so old, he had no idea how she had learned it.

He concentrated and felt his mind connect to Ella's. He pulled away the memories of Ruby reacting last night, the rest of the nightmare, everything that had happened after. He replaced it with a bantering conversation discussing the Phoenix bar and her birthday. He allowed her to think she had dressed him down for swooping in and paying for it like he knew she had wanted to do. He felt his lips twitch at the false memories he infused to hers. The muttering stopped. The warmth that had tingled with the magic that flowed from Magda seemed to leak from him completely and into Ella. Magda dropped his hand and he watched as a peaceful expression fell across the girl's beautiful face. The immense relief that he felt was partly Ella's, connected as they were he could sense such things but some of that relief had been his own.

"And she will stay asleep for another few hours?" he heard Leo ask Magda.

"Yes, she won't wake until the memories Will implanted have really taken root, I estimate another 3 hours at least." Elena had let go of her granddaughter's hand and motioned for them to follow her into the kitchen. Leo and Magda left the room but Will and Ruby stayed. He bent and slipped an arm under her neck, the other arm going under her knees and he pulled her gently to him. He carried her up the stairs, Ruby present just behind him the entire time and when they reached Ella's bedroom door Ruby moved ahead and pushed it open with her nose. Will entered and set her gently onto her bed. She made a little contented noise and wrapped a hand around his arm. He stopped still and she let her hand slide down his arm, goosebumps following behind it. Finally her hand slipped away and she rolled away from him, facing the wall. He pulled the blankets up to her chest and brushed some fallen hair away from her face. Ruby clambered onto the bed, curling up behind her knees and Will nodded at the dog. He knew she would be safe with Ruby but it still took all of his considerable willpower to walk away from the bed and even more to close her bedroom door.

He gave himself a little shake and moved to the stairs, ready to join the others in the kitchen to discuss what to do from here.

When he walked into the kitchen, he saw Leo and Magda sat at the little nook around the table and watched as Elena brought cups to place next to a steaming pot of tea.

"Did she settle down okay?" Elena asked, turning her worried eyes to him. He nodded and moved to the table to sit next to her.

"Okay," Magda said, dragging one of the ivory mugs towards her. "Now what are we going to do with her? She can't keep having us mess around with her memories for the next month. There's obviously something triggering the power within her. We need to find out what that is and get rid of it, at least until she knows the truth." He watched as her wrinkled hands poured tea into four mugs and she started to hand them out.

"You said something about a fallen, one that came into the café and that she spoke to him?" Will asked Elena who was opposite him. She nodded, sighing warily.

"Well, she served him so I assume she must have

spoken to him but it was right around closing, I was shutting down the kitchen." Leo ran a hand over his exhausted looking face.

"Should we ask Blake and Sam if she's mentioned anything about someone new?" he asked. Elena smiled at him kindly.

"She won't tell them unless she has to, you know they're almost as protective of her as you and Will." Will fought an urge to snort in disbelief. He didn't think even Ella would agree with that one.

"Magda." She looked at her friend. "It might be worth trying to get something out of Mal. I think she's the only person she would tell if anything was different, if she had met anyone." Magda took a lengthy sip of her tea, smacking her lips when she finally put the cup down.

"I'll try, but lord knows that girl doesn't even tell me or her mama anything about her life, let alone Ella's." She licked her lips and set about pouring herself another smaller cup of tea.

"Even if she doesn't know this fallen and it's something else... shouldn't we be worried that there are fallen in the area? There's bound to be more right?" Leo pointed out. He was looking at his Nona but it was Will that answered.

"It's getting closer to her birthday. They'll know

that once she gets her power, even before she's trained, it will be a lot more difficult trying to get rid of her. They're going to be trying something before her birthday." Leo was clutching his mug so hard that he thought it was going to break apart in his friend's hand. He regretted not choosing his words more carefully but he had to be practical and level headed in these situations.

"Can we all agree that if it seems like she is close to finding out some things for herself, after tonight, we don't alter her mind again," Elena said. "It's bad enough that we've had to do it more than once, the thought of doing it again when she is getting so close to getting her power and especially when she should be on her guard."

"She doesn't need to be on her guard. This is literally the point of me being here." Will tried his best to keep his voice level.

"Yes, but you can't do that if she isn't letting us know what is happening in her life," she countered.

"I have my ways, and I know what you're going to say, that I can't watch her all hours but I can. And I will." He could feel Leo's eyes studying him. "But, you're right. She's going to be angry enough for all of us for lying to her for so long, if she finds out how often we altered her memories she will be furious and we do need her to trust us. There's going to be other people out there trying to get to her. I don't want her to have reason to pick someone else. Over her family," he added on the end. He could feel the eyes of his friend on him again. He knew that Leo had noticed the change between him and Ella and he wanted to avoid that conversation for as long as he possibly could.

"I'm going to move back home," Leo said suddenly. Will's eyes did swivel to his friends then. "We need Will to be here as much as possible and he can't keep trying to find reasons to stay around her, she will get suspicious."

"She doesn't hate me that much," Will muttered and Leo beamed at him.

"No, but it would make it easier. Plus, I'll be here to watch out for her too." He nodded curtly and Leo looked towards his grandma. "If that's okay, of course."

"You silly boy!" she almost shrieked through happy tears. "It's more than okay." He grinned at her and even Will let slip a smile.

He wasn't usually such a miserable bastard but the last few months had been the most stressful time of his life and it wasn't going to get better. Probably wouldn't even get better when they could finally tell Ella everything. When he wouldn't have to be a dick to her just to make sure that she was safe. He hated that he had to be that way with anyone, especially with her but she brought it out in him. That girl, he thought, was allergic to doing as she's told and never backed down from a fight. She made his blood boil in anger and then in the next minute, she would say or do something so incredible that meant his blood heated for entirely different reasons. But once she knew, he wouldn't have to be so hard on her, she could make decisions for herself without him trying to tell her what to do. He would be able to go from being her guard dog to her back up.

Every time he thought of throwing caution to the wind and telling Ella how he felt or pursuing her in any serious way, his mind went back to the job. His moral compass was somewhat south when it came to most things. He had no trouble destroying anything in his way, his reputation was that of a mindless killing machine, violent and merciless. When it came to her however, that compass was always pointing north.

# CHAPTER FIVE

T he shrillness of the ringtone pulled her from sleep with a jolt. She could have sworn she had turned her phone on silent last night but the sound of chirping birds coming from her night stand said otherwise. She glanced at the ID on the screen and the annoyance slipped away.

"Blake?" she croaked. She looked on her night stand and found a glass of water. She was mildly impressed with past Ella for getting something ready for the morning.

"Holy shit dude, are you only just waking up?" He laughed and his deep rumbling chuckle made her smile. There was a time that she wondered if she would ever hear that chuckle ever again.

"What time is it?"

"Almost ten am." She stilled. Holy cow, she had slept late. She wondered why Elena hadn't woken her up.

"I must have needed that sleep."

"Sam and I were wondering if you wanted to meet us for lunch? We called Mal but she's got lessons today." She raised an eyebrow.

"Am I second choice?"

"Technically third, I asked Sam, then Mal, then you." She let out a soft snort.

"You're a bitch."

"Always! Café in an hour?"

"Sure, see you there."

"Don't be surly with me Ella, you know you're my number one." She smiled again

"We both know that's not true…"

"Bye Ella," he said in a warning voice and this time she really did laugh loudly. She said goodbye and set about getting herself ready to go.

Blake had been her best friend since they were small children; he was huge, he looked like he could snap a person clean in half and if pushed, he would. But his nature was so much kinder than anyone she had ever met. When his parents died in a car accident, she thought she had lost the kind, sweet, funny best friend she'd had for years but then Sam, the literal angel came along. All bright blonde hair, ice blue eyes and sharp angled cheekbones had swooped in. Everyone in their high school had known that Blake was gay, no one cared and if they did they weren't brave enough to say anything to him. Sam arrived and the bullies must have decided he looked like an easier target. Ella, Blake and Mal had been walking by the old art building one day when they saw a small group of neanderthals from the football team pushing Sam around. Blake, who was on the team had started to walk over with Mal and Ella running after him when Sam punched the biggest and most annoying one right on the nose. Before the others could retaliate, Blake had shouted. They turned, took one look at him and hightailed it out of there so fast Ella was almost certain the pavement had smoked. Sam had looked at Blake and said "Thanks," and they were instantly best friends. From that day on Sam has been the grounding centre of their friendship. The first one you go to with a problem, when you need to be told the truth because as kind as he is, Ella thought, he would not dull his tongue to spare your delicate sensibilities. He helped pull Blake from a really dark place and Ella couldn't be more grateful to him. The question was, she thought as she ran a hair dryer over her damp hair, when were they going to admit the fact that they were completely and utterly in love with each other.

When Ella wandered into the kitchen pulling her leather jacket over one arm, she was a little surprised to see Will sitting at her kitchen table. His eyes flicked up to her and she paused in mid-air, her right arm half in the sleeve of the jacket.

"Hey," she said, tugging the jacket all the way on and moving to the coffee machine.

"Good morning Ella." His voice sounded weary, so she brought the coffee pot to the table and poured him another cup, sitting down opposite him with her own mug.

"Thanks," he said, playing with something on his phone. He clicked it shut and looked at Ella.

"You look nice," he said, eyeing her carefully and she paused, coffee halfway to her mouth.

"Thanks?" she said, not sure to trust this weirdly nice version of Will.

"I'm too tired to be an asshole right now, you're safe."

"Why're you so tired?" She opened her mouth immediately. "On second thoughts, I don't wanna know." He gave her a slight grin, with just one side of his lips pulling upwards.

"Not for any of those reasons you're thinking of. I

woke up early today and it's hitting me now, that's all."
She nodded. "But thank you, for assuming I'd be up all
night fucking," he said bluntly and she inhaled half of
her coffee up her nose.

"I didn't think that!" she said quickly. He raised an
eyebrow at her.

"Don't like to think of me with anyone else
princess?" he asked and she rolled her eyes. She did
notice though that his shoulders were slumped, his
eyes dull with tiredness. She wasn't stupid. This wasn't
lack of sleep tired. This was stressed and weary tired.
When she had recovered fully from her coffee entering
her system via her nostrils, she sent him a smirk of her
own. As much as he infuriated her, the thought of him
losing that utterly irritating 'I don't give a fuck'
attitude and a shit eating grin that told her he knew
just how beautiful he was, was unbearable. She could
play with him, keep that fire in his eyes from
spluttering out completely.

"I don't think of you at all." His eyes lit at the
challenge.

"Why do I find that hard to believe?"

"Believe what you want, I have plenty of other
things to occupy my mind even in the most... lonely of
times." Catching onto what she was insinuating his

tongue flicked out and licked his lip. Ella couldn't help but stare at it.

"Is it all of those romance books you read?"

"Maybe." She shrugged.

"And how many of those do you picture with my face?" More than she would care to admit, but there was no way in hell she was going to tell him that.

"Only the really, really annoying ones." He laughed and she grinned back.

"Well, just know that I'm better in bed." She laughed again.

"Sure you are champ." She sighed and looked into her cup. It was easy when it was like this. When they could have a conversation without wanting to throttle each other. Alright, those conversations almost always went straight to sex but that was just Will being Will. He was gorgeous and he knew it. It had been easy with them, when they were kids. Will, Leo and Ella, the three of them against the world, he didn't care that she was two years younger than them, he didn't care that their mother's death had made her meek and quiet one minute and angry and lashing out the next. It had been that way until Ella reached ten. Since that day by the river. Then he went distant, he stopped coming around so often, started to treat Ella like an annoying little sister that he had to look after, like it was a chore.

She knew he had a job he couldn't talk about, alongside the garage with his dad. That told her all she needed to know. Their relationship evolved the older they got, he was no less of an overprotective pain in her ass but sometimes he looked at her with a glance like a predator sizing up prey. There was tension, she never knew if he wanted to fight with her or if he wanted to... well. She wasn't going to let her mind wander there. Maybe he only flirted with Ella because they both knew it wasn't going to happen. So really, what's the harm in a little flirting.

"You okay?" he asked and she realized she had gone silent for a while.

"Yeah, I'm good. Just so you know I'm still pissed at you for paying for the booth at the Phoenix bar." He rolled his eyes.

"Get over it Ella. It ain't gonna change." She ground her teeth slightly.

"You're not my brother Will and I'm not twelve, you don't have to look after me."

"I should hope so, or that earlier conversation is fucked up in so many ways." He pulled a face.

"Will. I'm being serious." He looked her up and down slightly, studying her.

"I'm sorry if you think I overstepped a boundary."

"Thank you, so I can pay you back at least half?"

she asked as he stood up and took his coffee cup to the dishwasher. He turned around to face her before answering.

"Absolutely not," he said, winking at her and strolling right out of the kitchen. Ella made a shrieking sound of frustration and she heard a real, full laugh and the sound of the front door opening. She waited for the door to close and she let her annoyance float away. She smiled at his laugh and counted that interaction as a win for making sure that Will stayed the annoying and arrogant way she liked him.

# CHAPTER SIX

S he got to the café early, pulling her hood down and then yanking the scarf from around her neck. She may have been early but Blake and Sam were already sat at their usual table, right next to the counter. She walked over and plopped herself down in the seat, storing her bag under the table.

"Hey," she said, pulling a menu towards her. There was a silence and she looked up, seeing Blake and Sam doing their weird telepathy thing. It always freaked her out that even after knowing Blake for most of her life, she couldn't communicate with looks and small gestures like Sam could. Their bond was special. As much as Ella teased them, there was definitely something deep between them.

"What?" she snapped. Another look between them and she fought the urge to roll her eyes.

"You seem very... tense," Sam said quietly. His piercing blue eyes were assessing her. Her face turned hot. That encounter with Will was a win, but it had left her with some unresolved tension and that god damn wink.

Sam was still looking at her and she gulped. When she had first met him, although she immediately liked him, he had unnerved her slightly. His eyes were so blue that they were almost clear and his hair was so blonde she had thought that there was no way it could be natural, turns out it was. Every move he made was purposeful and graceful and every word he spoke was carefully considered. He seemed wise beyond his years and it had been that, which made him the one person to be able to pull Blake out of the black hole he was falling through when his parents died. Her eyes flicked to Blake then. His dark, thick eyebrows furrowed in a frown. His eyes were a melting pool of chocolate, his dark hair had grown, curling around his ears and neck, and his tanned skin looked even darker next to the deathly pale Sam. They made a strangely beautiful pair. Both gorgeous in their own right but together, they looked like fire and ice.

"Sorry guys, ran into Will this morning and well... you can imagine how well that turned out." Sam gave a tight nod but Blake gave a sympathetic smile.

"What did he do this time?" Blake asked. Blake had always been more likely to indulge her frustration with Will than any of the others and Ella very much enjoyed having someone to complain to but she wasn't going to be telling anyone that the annoying bastard had riled her up.

"Nothing really, he was just being Will. It's fine." She really needed to take a breath and let the thought of their conversation ebb away. She hoped Lucas did ask her out, she had a feeling he could definitely distract her from Will.

"Don't pretend you don't love arguing with him," Sam said, smirking at her.

"Yeah, I know." She sighed. They both looked at her astounded and she realized that the thought had actually come out of her mouth.

"Sorry, I'm just having a weird day. But, I'm here now." She took a big breath. "How're you guys?" she asks. They started to chat and Ella soon cheered up and when the talk came back to her birthday party, she started to get an excited flutter in her stomach.

"I need your advice," she blurted out suddenly.

The two boys looked at each other, looked back to her and Blake nodded.

"So there's this guy..." she started. Sam had paused while reaching for the sugar pot and Blake narrowed his eyes. "He's the new librarian down the street and we've been flirting." She wrung her hands in her lap.

"And you wanna know if you should invite him to your party or not?" Sam asked. Her mouth popped open.

"You belong in a circus," she said and he laughed.

"Ells. Go out with him a few times, if you like him ask him. Just don't drop it on him last minute." She nodded. Of course, that was the best way to do it. They ate while chatting about everything and nothing; their jobs, when they would be able to see Mal next, how Leo was doing at the hospital. It was easy conversation and Ella appreciated the relaxing atmosphere. They talked for a few hours, about Ella's birthday, Mal and the Bar owner, their plans for the next few days. Ella had always admired the flawless ways in which the two beautiful boys in front of her would interact with each other.

With everyone else Blake definitely gave off a 'I really don't give a shit what you have to say' vibe, but hung on to every word that uttered from Sam's lips.

Sam was blunt to the point of almost being rude sometimes but speaks with a softness and a fondness with Blake that she has never seen him use with anyone else. How they were both so oblivious to each other's feelings Ella did not know but she had told herself a long time ago she would never pry and let them figure things out for themselves. It was becoming painful to watch though. When they had finished there was the usual argument about the bill, Blake insisted on paying and Sam was trying to argue. Ella had offered and was given the dirtiest of looks from both chocolate eyes and those of ice. Once it was finally paid Blake sighed.

"Sorry Ella, we have to go." Blake stood and Sam stretched about to join him.

"No problem, I have a book waiting for me at home." She stood and hugged each of them in turn. She gave Blake a little extra squeeze and watched them out of the door.

---

"Nona?" she called. The house remained quiet so she went and picked up the book that Lucas had recommended and went to sit out in the garden, it was a warm afternoon considering the orange leaves on the trees. She nestled into the large garden chair and curled her legs beneath her, letting Ruby clamber up beside her and flop her head in her lap. It was a tight squeeze, Ruby wasn't exactly a lap dog but Ella had given up trying to explain that to Ruby. She opened the book, the fluttering in her stomach set off again as she started to read.

She was scrunching up her face, a fair few chapters into the book, almost halfway and she was sure that Lucas had to either have been joking, or had not known the contents of the book. The cover was deceiving, she thought, it may have had a swooning lady and an opened shirt man on the cover but the most scandalous thing that had happened so far was him seeing her right knee and it was more commentary of the period which the book was set. Her phone rang and she welcomed the distraction. She didn't like the heroine in the book. She was weak, feeble and whiny. The caller ID showed Lucas and the butterflies flapped harder.

"Hello?"

"Hi Ella," he said, his smooth voice warming her chest.

"How are you?" she asked, moving Ruby away and setting her book down on the rickety old garden table.

"I'm great, how are you? Have you read the book?" She cringed again.

"I'm good, thanks. Yeah, I have... Have you read that book?" she asked carefully. There was a beat of silence.

"Honestly? No. I felt brave so went to the romance section and picked the first one I found because I was terrified." She laughed at his worried voice. "Oh my god, it wasn't some weird fetish thing was it?" He groaned.

"No!" she said quickly, her face heating. "Nothing like that, it was just not a lot of romance at all, more social commentary on the Victorian era London." She heard his sigh of relief.

"Yeah, that is not what I want to remind you of me." She laughed again. "I'll make you a deal." She paused.

"I'm listening..." she teased.

"Let me take you on a date tomorrow night and I will buy you a book that has some actual romance in it." He stopped, waiting for her answer. She waited for an intrusive thought to tell her it was a bad idea, but none came.

"You don't have to do that, but I will go to dinner with you. It's a date." She could practically hear his grin as he spoke.

"Text me your address and I'll pick you up at seven thirty. We're going for dinner, it's a nice place but dress in whatever you're comfortable in." She smiled at the thoughtfulness but her mind drifted to the little black dress hanging in her closet.

"I have the perfect thing," she said, her voice full of mischief. He made a noise that sounded suspiciously like a grunt.

"Why do I get the feeling you're going to be a handful, Marcella Romano?" he asked and she smiled wide.

"You have no idea." She ended the call feeling triumphant. She could feel the confidence flowing through her. She couldn't imagine why someone as gorgeous and enthralling as Lucas was interested in her. There was something about him that was intoxicating and she was definitely going back for more. She had sucked in a big breath to cool the burning in her chest at the excitement she felt when she heard the front door shut from inside so she followed Ruby into the house, picking up the book from the old table on the way. She expected to see her Nona walking down the hall but instead she saw her brother moving towards her.

"Ella, I'm glad you're here. I need to speak to you."

She stopped and waited for him to reach her. "But first I need coffee." He nodded his head towards the kitchen and she followed him through, her worry lessening slightly. If he had time to have coffee, it couldn't be anything that bad. She sat down on the table as Leo made them both a coffee and once he was sat he looked at her. His hands wrapped around his mug and he took a big gulp. His ocean blue eyes locked on to her steel grey eyes. He had inherited Nona's eyes, with their feeling of staring into a warm, inviting salty ocean. Ella on the other hand, had got her eyes from her mother. Steel grey and the same cold, gleaming stare.

"I've asked Nona if I can move back in." Her eyebrows furrowed in confusion.

"I thought you loved your apartment?" she asked. He nodded.

"I do, but I'm never there to enjoy it. I'm either at work, the café or here. I'm gonna move back here for a year or so, save up as much as I can so I can buy a place." He shrugged. She grinned at him. "I take it you don't mind then?" He chuckled at her.

"Not in the slightest. I've missed you." His eyes softened.

"I've missed you too, short stack." She rolled her

eyes at her childhood nickname, she wasn't particularly short and really only a few inches shorter than her brother. It was Will, Blake and Sam that all reached over six feet tall but she was always a short, scrawny kid, with thin arms and legs. It wasn't until puberty hit her like a tonne of bricks that her shape changed to mirror her mother's; well, she thought, the puberty and all the pasta.

"It does mean Will might be around more though," he warned with a teasing voice. She huffed a laugh.

"I came downstairs this morning to find Nona gone and Will sitting here with a cup of coffee, so I don't think it'll change that much." Leo's eyebrow rose.

"And the house was still standing when you left?" She thought back to the conversation they'd had this morning and she felt a distinctly warm sensation creeping up from her chest to her neck.

"He may be an asshole with secrets that I will assume means he has some seriously screwed up morals but I'm starting to understand what everyone is saying. He does it cause he cares." She sighed.

"You know, that day on the lake–" She stiffened with her cup almost to her mouth. "I know you don't like talking about it but just hear me out." She continued her swig of coffee, welcoming the bitter burning taste as memories flashed through her.

*S*he had called to Leo but he hadn't heard her. He and Will were right up on the bank looking at something in their hands. She was getting bored, and found herself going to the edge of the dock, looking over the edge into the dark water below. She could have sworn she'd seen something silver glinting in the water and bent, only slightly forward to see closer. One of the boards of the dock was loose, she lost her footing and tumbled into the cold water. She felt the pain of the cold the moment she hit it and she opened her mouth in surprise, water filled it quickly and she tried to take another breath. Arms flapping and legs kicking but no matter how much she tried she never broke the surface. She saw a disturbance in the water next to her and she felt arms around her waist before her vision went completely black. When she had awoken she was on a gurney, Leo was crying beside her and Will was stood with another EMT, a foil blanket around his shoulders and soaking wet. His eyes met hers and she saw the terror in his eyes.

"He does care about you Ella, not just cause you're my little sister, or because he's our neighbor. When you were led there and you weren't breathing..." His hands shook a little as he placed his own mug on the table. "When Will did CPR and it didn't seem to be working at first, the terror in his face and the sound that he made... it wasn't human Ella." Tears started to well in her eyes and she swallowed hard. "It's his business but there's a reason he pushes you away. Why he keeps you at arm's length and a big part of it is the terror that he felt that day. . . If anything were to happen to you, he would be just as terrified. Maybe even more so." She nodded. She knew what her brother was implying but she wasn't sure that she could allow herself to even think these things might be true because if she did, she would find herself deep in a rabbit hole she was not sure that she wanted to fall down. She thought of her date with Lucas and her gut twisted guiltily. She did like Lucas, he was attractive and funny, he made her feel confident enough to flirt back. She wanted to at least pursue Lucas and see where it went. So the box that she usually kept Will inside remained untouched.

Although, she was done sniping with him. Will wasn't an option for her, no matter how much she wanted him. She wouldn't put Lucas, a beautiful, sweet man who actually showed her interest, on the back burner for Will.

# CHAPTER SEVEN

S he thought she had given herself more than enough time to get ready for her date with Lucas, yet here she was, trying to wedge her feet into a ridiculous pair of high heels and put earrings in at the same time. Although Lucas had offered to pick her up at first, she told him she would be more comfortable meeting him there. Not that she didn't want him to pick her up but that her family were a lot to deal with and it was safer for him. She grabbed her small black handbag and rushed out of the room. Leo had started moving his stuff back into his old room and he and Will were currently sat in the kitchen eating pizza.

She walked into the kitchen and they stopped talking and looked at her. Will started coughing and

Leo thumped him on the back, grinning at his sister. She chanced a small smile back.

"You look beautiful," Leo said as Will gulped down a glass of water.

"Thank you," she said. Will put the glass down on the counter and looked back up at her. His usually golden eyes were strangely dark and he braced his arms on the counter in front of him. The muscles in his forearms tensed and she watched the movement of the inked skin.

"Where's he taking you?" Leo asked, as if to remind her he was in the room too. She frowned a little. Her brother and Will had been a little too okay with her going on a date. Not that she wasn't a grown ass woman who could do whatever the hell she wanted but they usually at least asked some questions.

"We're going to the Rose." It was a swanky wine bar that served excellent tapas and fabulous cocktails.

"Fancy," Will said, finally moving his arms to cross over his chest, which was puffed out slightly and Ella had to fight not to roll her eyes.

"Is he picking you up?" Leo asked and she laughed.

"Absolutely not, not with you two and Ruby here, the poor man would be lucky to get out unscathed." Will flashed a deadly grin full of sharp teeth and wicked promise. "And if I don't leave now I'm going to be late." She went to turn.

"Do you want a ride on the bike?" Will asked and she laughed, a proper laugh.

"Uh huh, and how would that work?" She gestured down at her very tight dress. The tip of his tongue darted out and flicked across his bottom lip as he looked down at the dress again.

"And I'm not sure that would make a good impression. Arriving to a date on the back of a motor bike, driven by a man who looks like you." Will scowled.

"What's that supposed to mean?" Leo saw the light in his sister's eyes and averted his own. This was either going to be brutally harsh or borderline indecent and he clearly wasn't comfortable with either outcome.

"It means, William, that you look like most girls' idea of a 'one to many tequila's' kind of bad decision." Her head tilted as it was her turn to look him up and down. Her eyes seemed to get stuck on his thick neck as she saw a swallow raise his Adam's apple. "But thanks for the offer," she said in her usual tone and this time she did turn away and walk out of the door. She stifled a laugh as she heard their following words.

"Fucking hell," Will groaned.

"Dude, that's my fucking sister."

"Sorry, but... fucking hell." There was a thud and she heard Will say, "Asshole." She didn't know what her brother had thrown at him, but she was very disappointed she wasn't there to see it.

———

L ucas had been waiting for her outside of the bar when her cab had pulled up outside. He looked amazing with his copper curls slightly styled but not too much. He was wearing dark pants and a fitted white shirt with a black blazer. There were silver rings adorning his long, slender fingers. His shirt was open a few buttons and she saw a peek of tanned, freckled skin.

"Hey Ella, you look delicious," he said, kissing her on the cheek and she felt her face heat immediately. She had needed to talk herself into wearing the dress. It was skin tight and a year ago Ella would have never even looked at it. It hugged her curves and as much as she tried not to worry about the fact that her stomach wasn't flat, she still felt herself clasping her hands in front of her, holding her purse to try and hide it. The moment Lucas had said those words she stood a little straighter. He really did find her attractive.

"Thank you, you don't look too bad yourself." He

smiled and gestured her into the restaurant in front of him. The host took them to a table, she eyed Lucas with interest and Ella found herself glaring at the back of the woman's head. She sat at the table and took the menu from the host. She smirked when Lucas took the menu from the host without even glancing at her. His eyes were on Ella and it seemed that's where they were going to stay. The host walked away rather sadly after telling them that their server would be with them shortly. Ella gave her a little smile but when it wasn't returned she grinned again. It wasn't often that Ella found herself the cause for other women to be jealous.

"I believe I owe you a gift," Lucas said, taking a book out of the inside pocket of his coat and sliding it across the table to her. She put down the drinks menu and picked up the book. She read a few lines of the blurb and felt that heat rush to her cheeks again but this time, there was a pool of warmth low in her stomach too. She put the book in her bag and bit her lip. She looked up at him and Lucas was smirking at her.

"You really didn't have to," she said, smiling back.

"I really did, I need to make my point." He quirked his eyebrow at her and she laughed slightly.

"I can't wait to read it." His eyes glinted with mischief as he opened his own drinks menu.

ANGELS OF ARMOUR

"Order whatever you want, don't worry about price or embarrassment. If you wanna order the most expensive drink there is, or if you want a beer, I don't care either way." Her eyes softened. This was the second time he had made it clear to put her at ease over something that he didn't even know if she would be worrying about. He was making a real effort to make her aware that whatever choice she made would be fine by him.

"Well I definitely won't be ordering beer for another month, I'm only twenty," she confessed. He looked up at her and frowned.

"I'm sorry, I didn't realize. How about you have one and then stick to soft drinks?" he offered. "If they card you, just say you forgot it and you'll have a soda." He winked and she smiled. Her stomach dropped at the thought of being carded but she nodded. She didn't drink very often. She'd grown up being allowed wine with meals, it was the Italian way but never had she drank underage in public. She was about to refuse when a little voice popped into her head. *Don't be boring.* She found a sickly sweet sounding cocktail and gave her order to the server. He ordered scotch and a bottle of water for the table.

"That cocktail sounded like a cavity in a glass, I bet it's delicious." She laughed softly.

"I'll let you have a taste." He swept his eyes to her.

"And the cocktail?" Her eyes flew open in shock. A shiver danced over her skin, leaving goosebumps in its wake. She sucked in a breath.

"I'm sorry, I seem to find myself wanting to make that beautiful blush crawl over your face." She rolled her eyes.

"Game on." She sat back and pulled a mask of sultry deviousness over her. She may have felt like a gibbering wreck on the inside but there was no way in hell she was going to show that to him.

His eyes widened in surprise.

"You're going to be a handful I fear." He leaned back arrogantly in his chair, the picture of male beauty. She smirked at him and he bit his lip.

"Tell me about yourself, you mentioned a brother?" he asked, his eyes raking over her.

"Yes, Leo. He's training to be a doctor." She sat up a little straighter at the change in conversation and ignored the well of need pooling in her.

"Wow, impressive." He looked into his glass. "What about your parents?" Ella bit her lip. "I'm sorry, if you don't want to talk about it I understand." He rushed, sensing her hesitation.

"It's just... a little heavy for first date territory," she said carefully. She didn't want to tell him her depressing past on the first date. He smiled at her sadly.

"Understood, whenever you're ready." Her heart squeezed at the kindness in his voice and the softness of his eyes.

As they ate they spoke about pretty much everything else; books, movies, music, what their favorite food was, their jobs, their lives. She found out that Lucas had picked up and moved from Michigan, he had very little family but Ella didn't pry into what that meant. Not when he had been so understanding that she had not wanted to divulge on her family issues. When the food was done and the conversation was winding down, Ella looked towards the other side of a bar where there was a small dancefloor, filled with couples slow dancing.

"Would you like to dance?" he asked. She turned to look at him.

"Would you?" she replied. He smiled, a genuine smile, no smirk or wicked grin.

"I would like... almost nothing more." Ella playfully rolled her eyes. She couldn't help the flutter in her chest and tried her hardest not to blush.

"Well, dancing is a much more appropriate activity for a first date." He chuckled as he stood, offering her his hand. She placed her bag on her shoulder and put her hand in his. He left a wad of cash on the table which more than covered the cost of the evening and a generous tip and guided her towards the dancefloor.

The moment they stepped onto it, he pulled her to him and her body landed flush against him. He placed a hand at the small of her back and one still in the hand he had held, she placed her free arm around his neck. He smelled like expensive cologne. She wondered for a moment just how well the library paid its employees but then another scent filled her senses. The smell of smoke, burning wood, like a campfire. It wasn't unpleasant but she couldn't understand where it was coming from. It appeared to be Lucas himself. She looked up to his face and saw he was looking down at her, eyes hooded and as her eyes reached his, he pulled her even closer to him. They were moving slowly and their bodies didn't part for an entire song. He gently moved them around in a circle and Ella was genuinely enjoying herself. There was no conversation, no flirting, no awkwardness, just contentment at being in his arms. As she was manoeuvred around and faced the bar, she went suddenly stiff and deathly still. Will was leaning against the bar, talking to a girl who she didn't know. She was gorgeous, blonde, figure to die for and he was smirking at her. Will and the mystery girl were stood together, talking closely. She closed her eyes.

"Are you okay?" Lucas asked, pulling back a little. He turned and saw what she was staring at.

"You know him I take it?" Lucas asked, looking him up and down, a steel cold face replacing his soft, warm features.

She was on a date! She was dancing with Lucas, she had no right to get jealous but she had every right to get angry. He knew this is where she was going on her date. Showing up to check on her was one thing but this...

"Unfortunately yes." Lucas relaxed slightly. "He's my brother's best friend and he seems to think he's also my guard dog. I'm going to go and get rid of him. I'll be right back." He nodded and stepped aside. She rammed her bag down onto a table on the side of the dancefloor and stalked towards the bar. Will caught her eye and he muttered "Excuse me," to the girl he'd been entertaining at the bar, coming to meet Ella half way.

"What the fuck Will." She folded her arms and Will looked her up and down.

"I know what it looks like princess, but I promise, I'm just here on business." She rolled her eyes.

"I didn't realize that picking up bimbos at a bar constituted as work, or whatever shady shit you're into." Will narrowed his eyes.

"She approached me and..." A look of realisation hit him. "You're jealous." She widened her eyes at him.

"Are you insane? I'm pissed that you thought it was okay to come to the place where you knew I had a date. Get over yourself," she scoffed but he was smirking at her.

"I had to come here. I asked my boss if he could send someone else and he said no. I had no choice, I notice you only noticed me when someone else was showing interest." She scoffed and went to turn away but he grabbed her wrist and spun her back around to him.

"You're here on a date Ella. You don't get to be mad at me for talking to a girl when I haven't said a peep about watching you in the arms of another man," he gritted out. She stepped back slightly.

"I don't appreciate being checked up on." She pulled her wrist away from him and he crossed his arms over his chest. He'd changed clothes from when she had seen him last and he looked disgustingly handsome. He was wearing a white button down shirt, tattoos visible beneath the white fabric and black fitted jeans.

"I promise. I'm here on business."

"Whatever, I'm going to get back to my date," she said, emphasizing the last word.

"Ella." She turned back to face him. "Be careful..." he started.

"No," she said, her voice shaking due to holding back tears. All she had wanted was this kind of attention from Will and now she was getting it while on a date with another guy who was treating her like a queen. "You don't get to do that." His eyebrows knitted together in confusion.

"Ella," he said indignantly but she held up a hand.

"We'll talk about this later." She turned resolutely, took in a big breath and exhaled. She walked confidently back to Lucas and dragged him back to the dancefloor, pressing herself against him once again.

They shared a cab home, dropping Ella off first and she prayed Will wasn't outside or anywhere near when she got home. Lucas had asked questions about Will for a good ten minutes after she got back, no matter how much she confirmed that he was nothing more than an irksome neighbor. She felt a pull of guilt in her stomach, he was much more than just a neighbor but Ella wasn't going to ruin her chance with Lucas for him.

"I had a really nice night," Lucas said simply. She smiled at him and nodded.

"Me too."

When they got to her house, Lucas paid for the cab

to wait a few minutes and walked her to the steps. He pulled her gently towards him, his lips were an inch away from hers when he muttered.

"Can I kiss you?" She had barely finished nodding her head before his mouth covered hers. It was a firm, searing kiss. She felt heat flowing through her and she moved closer, pressing herself slightly against him and he made a little sound. She opened her mouth slightly and he took the opportunity to deepen the kiss. Her breath caught as she tasted ashes and smoke on his tongue. She thought back to the smell she had identified in the bar. The kiss was becoming so hot, literally, she felt her lips burning. He pulled her even closer and she felt trapped in his arms. His mouth was branded against hers, his tongue pushing the taste of ashes into her mouth and when she pushed him back slightly, he yielded.

"Sorry I just... I've wanted to do that all night." His eyes opened and the brown was gone, they were almost completely black. She felt herself recoil slightly.

"Thank you," she stammered. "For tonight." He nodded.

"I'll see you soon," he breathed and it was her turn to nod. He pressed his mouth to hers in a farewell kiss that was over before it began and he climbed back into the taxi, holding up a hand in farewell as it pulled away.

Her hand went to her lips and she felt the heat still radiating from them. She climbed the steps and opened the door. The moment she was inside she kicked off her heels and ran her hands through her hair. She went straight up to her room, picking her shoes up and carrying them up the stairs with her. She opened her bedroom door and nearly screamed. Will was led on her bed, one hand petting Ruby who was laying next to him and one behind his head.

# CHAPTER
# EIGHT

"Will! What the fuck," she said, dropping her heels on the floor and kicking them under her bed. "What are you doing in here?" she asked.

"We need to have a conversation about what the fuck happened in that bar tonight," he said, getting up from the bed. His shirt was gone and he was back in his usual black t-shirt.

"I don't have the energy for this right now Will," she said, throwing her bag down on her floor. She was still feeling weird from the kiss with Lucas and she wanted to be alone.

"So we're not going to address the fact that we both acted like jealous idiots tonight?" he asked. She stopped and crossed her arms.

"You showed up where I was on my date Will!" she yelled, knowing that Elena was staying with a friend and they had the house to themselves as far as she could tell.

"I told you I was there on business."

"Fine, okay." She shrugged.

"What?" he spat.

"If you were there on business then fair enough, whatever, just leave." She was starting to shake. She turned away from him and ran a hand through her long hair.

"Ella," he said pointedly.

"What?" she said sternly, still facing away from him.

"What happened?" he asked, his voice softer than before and she ignored the way that voice made her whole body go on alert.

"Nothing, I'm tired." She felt him move closer to her, he must have been standing inches away from her and she turned slowly. She knew that he would be able to tell she was holding back tears but she was too tired to fight him anymore. When she faced him fully he looked her over, eyes lingering on her mouth and he snarled.

"Where is he?" She rolled her eyes.

"I'm fine," she said.

"Like fuck are you fine, have you seen your mouth? I'll ask again Ella. Where. Is. He?" She wiped a hand over her forehead.

"I don't know, probably back at his place by now. It's none of your business." She was looking at him confused as to what had set off his alpha male asshole attitude.

He pulled her into the en suite bathroom and turned on the light. He pointed at the mirror and she gasped. The skin around her mouth was red and irritated, there was no mistaking it. It looked burned.

"Oh, I don't know what happened." But Will's face had a flicker of understanding.

He opened the top drawer of her cabinet and pulled out the first aid kit. He pulled out a cream made to treat burns and she cringed slightly. He put the lid of the toilet down and sat her on it. He remained standing, rummaging for something else and she realized she was essentially looking right at his crotch. She looked down at her hands until she felt strong fingers lift her chin. He had got down onto his knees and he pushed himself between her knees. The skirt of her dress crawled up her thighs at the movement but when he was as close as he could be, he looked her in the eyes. If she was able to think straight she might have been embarrassed by her body's reaction but seeing him kneeling between her legs, with her dress bunched up, made her core clench and she felt the heat between her legs.

"Just to warn you," he said in a strangely quiet voice, softer than she had heard him speak in a long time. "This is gonna sting like a bitch." He held up an antiseptic wipe and her eyes widened.

"Like hell are you putting that on my mouth."

"Ella, please. It's not bad. It'll probably be gone by morning but I need to clean it."

"I'll do it."

"Can you stop being such a stubborn dick for like five seconds and let me take care of you?" There was a growl to the tone of his voice and despite everything, a shudder travelled through her. She nodded. He started to move impossibly gentle over the red skin with the wipe. She hissed.

"I know princess, I'm sorry," he said soothingly. He thew the wipe into the bin. She felt a haze settle over her, like someone was trickling hot water from her head all the way down to her toes. A slight buzzing came into her head and she felt herself slacken. She felt drunk or like someone had disorientated her. She'd only had the one cocktail and as suggested, went onto soda after that.

"Will," she whimpered. "I'm not feeling too

good." She swayed slightly and he placed a hand on her arm to keep her upright. He locked eyes with hers. "I know Ells, not much longer." He took out the cream and rubbed it gently into her skin. It didn't sting as much as the wipe had but Will's hands on her were enough to make her feel even more dizzy. Her eyes flew open when he placed his hands on her bare thighs.

"Ella?" She looked down at his hands. Tanned, tattooed skin against the pale flesh of her thigh.

"Yes?" she whispered.

"You okay?" he asked quietly. She shook her head, she could feel panic rising in her.

"I only had one drink, I swear, I don't know what's happening." A sob escaped her and he pulled her from where she sat until she was sat in his lap across his knees. She wound her arms around his neck. She could feel the heat that was no longer just in her core, she felt like her blood was boiling with a thrumming rage of lust. In the back of her mind, she thought of Lucas but that thought didn't take hold. Not when she was wound so tightly around the man she really wanted. She could feel his cool skin on her bare flesh and she shuddered. She was pressed tightly against him, her dress pushed right up now.

"Shit Ella, you're hot." She let out a sound that might have been a sob or a laugh. "Not like that you moron, well... I mean, you're burning up." She felt it too. The sweat that started to bead at her temples, the heat of her thighs against Will's cool jeans. She pulled away and looked at him. His hands came up and pushed her hair right away from her face.

"Shit. We need to cool you down. Can you stand?" She shrugged. He stood with her in his lap. She wasn't quite sure how he did it but next thing she knew she was clinging to him.

He placed her on the counter next to the sink and he turned the shower on, fiddling with the settings until there was a cool jet of water. Not too cold, he didn't want her body to go into shock but cool enough to stop her from overheating. He took a hair tie from next to the sink and pulled her hair up roughly into a messy bun on top of her head. She made an involuntary moan when he'd tugged gently and he swore under his breath.

"I swear to fucking god," he gritted out. He shook his head and looked her in the eyes.

"You're pretty," she blurted out.

"Thanks princess. Get your ass in the shower," he said, pulling her off of the counter and towards the shower.

"No!" she said, stopping him. She reached behind her for the zip on her dress.

"Ella, what the fuck are you doing?" he asked.

"This dress is new and I'm not ruining it." She pouted as it finally came loose enough for her to shimmy out of it. She stood before him in a black bra and matching underwear. He swore again. Running his hands over his face, he let his eyes wander all over her body. The heat coursing through her meant that she didn't care if her belly wasn't flat. She grinned wickedly when she saw the fogged, lustful expression on his face.

"Tomorrow, we are going to be having a big discussion about your priorities." She giggled and he rolled his eyes.

"Okay. In," he said as he pointed. She stood in the shower and when the cool water hit her skin she almost lost consciousness, the relief was so immediate. The next thing she knew he stood in the shower with her, his chest pressed against her back, making sure she didn't crumple with an arm around her waist. She knew he must be getting just as soaked in cold water as she was but judging by the hard length pressing into her ass, he needed it almost as much as she did. She was filled with heat on the outside as well as the inside and she didn't know if it was because of whatever was going on with her fever but all she knew was there was a huge, beautiful man standing behind her and she could still feel his breath on her neck, even amongst the water.

"Will," she whimpered.

"I know princess, it'll stop soon I promise, just keep still. You're doing so good." She arched, brushing her ass against his length and a small moan escaped her. "Fuck," he said. She felt his head drop to her shoulder.

"Well, I'll file that under new things I learned about Ella tonight," she grumbled but pressed herself further against him.

"I'm sorry," he said, his lips ghosting over her skin. He wasn't kissing her, but speaking into her skin. "But I'm concentrating really hard on anything other than you right now. For both of our sakes."

"Why don't you want me?" she asked in a dazed voice. He stilled completely.

"You have no idea how much I want to turn you around, pin you against that wall and make you come until you can't see but the only reason you're feeling like this is because of that…" He huffed in frustration. "Because of what's going on in your body." She shook her head against his neck.

"Not just because of this," she admitted. There was a voice deep inside that hadn't been pulled into a daze that screamed at her to stop talking. That this was a road she did not want to walk with him.

"So you were jealous when you saw me with that girl... Tell me again in the morning princess." His hand went to her forehead and down her neck.

"Okay you're feeling a little cooler," he said. He shut the water off. "I'm gonna go to Leo's room and grab some sweatpants because I am soaked. I'm gonna put you back here," he said, manoeuvering her back to sitting on the closed lid of the toilet. He darted away and she let her mind wander to what could have been happening with them still in the shower, then she heard him rummaging in her room..

"Where's Leo?" she asked, her words slightly slurred.

"He stayed at the apartment tonight, he has more stuff to pack."

# CHAPTER NINE

H e entered the room again and with a t-shirt in hand.

"I wondered where this had gone."

He lifted a t-shirt and she felt herself blush. It was one of his. He and Leo had been led out in the sun in the summer and he had hopped back over the fence leaving his shirt behind. She had intended to wash it and give it back to him but she had ended up using it as pyjamas.

"I can explain that..." He grinned and rolled his eyes.

"Keep it, I'm sure it looks better on you."

"I doubt that," she muttered and he laughed. He pulled his own soaking wet t-shirt off of his body and she couldn't help but stare at him.

"I know you're enjoying the show sweetheart but if you don't close your eyes, you're about to get an eyeful." His hands had moved down to his belt and immediately she closed her eyes. She heard the thump of wet denim hitting the floor and she felt as though her temperature might be rising again.

"You can open your eyes Ella." He was hanging his jeans and t-shirt over the top of the shower screen to try and dry off. He was wearing a pair of Leo's grey sweatpants and nothing else.

"How are you even a real person."

"What?" he asked, looking around at her confused.

"Nothing!" she said, standing up and swaying a little. He steadied her with a hand again and goosebumps raced over her skin.

"Your hair is going to be a mess if we leave it like this princess." She felt the mass of tangled wet hair. She groaned. "Put this on." He passed her the t-shirt and turned away. She quickly took off her bra and underwear and found the t-shirt was handed over with a pair of shorts. She smiled at the thoughtfulness and tugged on the shorts. Not that they covered much but standing in only a t-shirt around Will when she was this hot and bothered, for whatever reason, was not a good idea. She pulled the soft fabric over her head.

"You can turn around," she said meekly. He turned

and looked her over. He seemed to tense for a moment and then cleared his throat.

"Okay hot stuff. Let's get your hair sorted." She laughed.

"You don't need to do that, I can manage." He placed a hand on her forehead.

"Yeah, I'm gonna stay till you're a little less warm." He led her to her desk and sat her down. He pulled the hair tie gently from her hair, fighting through the wet tangles. He picked up a nearby hair brush and got to work. Luckily it wasn't as bad as they had thought, not all of her hair was wet but it still took a little while to untangle the knots. She let her eyes flutter closed as his hands worked at her hair. She opened her eyes and realized that he was braiding her hair into a long plait.

"How do you know how to braid hair?" she asked quietly.

"My six year old cousin loves to play hairdressers. So I learned how to do it," he said quietly. "And if you tell anyone I can braid hair, I'll have to kill you." He tugged the end of the braid playfully and stepped away. She turned to face him. He was leaning back on her dresser.

"I'm feeling a little better." He nodded.

"I thought you might be." He walked over and opened her window and she stiffened. A feeling creeped over her and without even turning around he asked her, "What's wrong?"

She shook her head. She felt as though the heat that she had felt before was being replaced with icy fear.

"I don't know. I just feel anxious." His eyes softened.

"Go to bed sweetheart. You can yell at me for turning up at the bar tomorrow." He went to move towards the door.

"Wait," she said, and he stopped. She couldn't ask this of him. Not when she had just come home from a date with Lucas, not after everything that happened in the shower.

"Nona is out of town," she said and he turned to her nodding. "And Leo is at his apartment." He nodded again. She glanced down to Ruby. "I... don't feel like you have to but..." She swallowed. "I don't feel safe." She seemed to be trying to find a way to ask the question.

"I don't think I can stay." He swallowed. "I'm sorry Ella." She shook her head.

"No, I get it, it's okay." She wrapped her arms around herself, the anxious feeling crawling up her spine.

He stood watching her and she gave herself a little

shake. She stamped down on the anxiety forcing it back. She wouldn't crumple in front of him. Not after everything that happened tonight. She wouldn't ask him to stay again. With great difficulty she peeled her arms from around herself and placed them at her side and her spine straightened. When she looked at him, he was looking at her with such pride and affection on his face that she was a little startled.

He walked slowly towards her and stood directly in front of her.

"You are extraordinary Marcella Romano." She smiled and he looked down at her lips. She saw something in his eyes snap and she thought she heard a whispered, "Fuck it," before he crashed his lips to hers.

She was unaware of her body responding. As far as she knew, she should have been stood straight with eyes open in shock, because that's how she felt. What she did however was meet the kiss with as much ferocity as he did. His hands were at her waist, pulling her flush against him and her arms had crawled around his neck, she was slightly on tip toes to reach him. There was no tentative kisses, from the moment his mouth was on hers there was a firm demand, he was in control and he chose the pace. She opened her mouth and his tongue immediately brushed against hers. She moaned slightly in the back of her throat at the feel of it. She was pushing herself up further to meet his mouth and he snarled slightly, breaking the kiss for his hands to run down over her ass. He lifted her and without thinking, she wrapped her legs around his waist. She felt him walk and the next thing she knew her back was pressed against the wall. She grunted in pleasure and shock and he ripped his mouth away from hers to kiss down her neck. Her hips bucked and she found the much needed contact but it didn't last long enough. He span around and lowered her onto the bed, his mouth covering hers again and she pulled him heavily on top of her.

"I'll crush you," he mumbled against her lips.

She gave a huff of annoyance. "I don't care." She took his bottom lip between her teeth and pulled gently. A guttural moan stuttered from his throat and his hands found her waist beneath the t-shirt. She gasped at the skin on skin contact and pushed her mouth harder against his. The feeling low in her stomach was filling her with an aching need and if they didn't stop soon, they were going to reach the point of no return. He seemed to realize it at the same time as she did and slowed down his kisses. It felt like he kept trying to pull away but not able to stop himself from keeping his mouth against hers. What the fuck was she doing, she was kissing Will! And earlier that night she had been on a date with Lucas. He stopped kissing her but his forehead rested against hers.

"And that's why I shouldn't stay," he said, his eyes closed.

"Oh," she said stupidly. He laughed into her neck, pressing kisses into her neck and jaw. "Will, unless you plan on doing something about it, you really need to stop kissing my neck." He stilled and she felt his hand grip her waist tighter.

"Sorry." He moved off of her and sat on the edge of her bed, with his head in his hands. She stared at the large expanse of skin across his back. How had she never realized just how massive he was. Wide shoulders, broad chest, thick, perfect neck, hands the size of shovels.

"Will, it's okay." She moved behind him and put her hands on his shoulders.

"I can't do this to you Ella," he said quietly. She frowned. If he meant he couldn't kiss her, it was a little late for that.

"Can't do what?" He looked up into her face, a pained expression flitting across his perfect features. She knew he was attracted to her but the fact he stopped before it went too far told her that he actually cared about her. "I get it," she said and he turned to look at her. She slid off of the bed and stood in front of him.

"It's okay. It's been a weird day, really weird." She thought back to the date with Lucas. A twinge of guilt hit her.

"It was a moment of madness." He made a noise that barely sounded human but nodded.

"I was on a date a few hours ago." He squeezed his eyes shut.

"I'm so sorry," he whispered.

"Why are you sorry?"

"For kissing you, it's not fair to you after what happened tonight." She put a finger under his chin and forced it up so she could look him in the eyes.

"I could have stopped it, you didn't see me pushing you away."

"Yeah but you've been through something really weird and I took advantage." She let out a noise of frustration.

"My mind is clear, it has been since you braided my hair and stop being so fucking sweet or I'm gonna kiss you again." His head snapped up and her heart squeezed at the look on his face. She didn't think she had ever seen someone look so conflicted.

"We can't do this Ella."

"I know," she said. "Let's agree that tomorrow morning this never happened." He nodded.

"Okay," he said, nodding again. He went to stand but she placed a hand on his shoulder. Just a hand. She didn't push him down. She simply placed a hand on his shoulder and he stopped.

"There are hours before tomorrow morning," she pointed out.

"Ella," he warned. His jaw ticked as he clenched it.

"I'm not talking about having sex with you." She rolled her eyes. "But we've already crossed the line tonight." She thought of her earlier promise to herself that she wouldn't ask him to stay again but after what just happened... "Just stay with me. Hold me, sleep next to me, kiss me if you want to. Then tomorrow we pretend this never happened." He shuddered.

"This is not a good idea." He bent his head forward, resting his forehead on her chest.

"You don't have to stay, if you don't want to."

"I want to," he said, pulling back and looking up at her again. "You have no idea how much I want to." She looked down at the hard length pressing against the fabric of the sweatpants he was wearing.

"Hmm I can take a guess." He laughed.

"You're my best friend's little sister, you've just been

out on a date, alright he ended up being a douchebag but still." He traced his thumb down her neck and she could feel her breath start to quicken. "My job is dangerous and you're my friend, I don't want to lose you. I can't loose you," he said, looking into her eyes.

She crawled into his lap and with both hands on either side of his face, kissed him again. His hand went to her backside to keep her in place and he kissed her back with enthusiasm.

"This is kinda going against everything I just told you princess," he said into the skin of her neck.

"Well now I know that you don't hate me." He rolled his eyes.

"You know I've never hated you, you also know that I'm attracted to you, what you don't know is... well, that doesn't matter."

He brushed a piece of hair that got loose from the braid behind her ear.

"Okay, so we're friends. We look out for each other." He nodded.

"I'm just happy I got my friend back." He smiled up at her. A real smile with his gorgeous white teeth and the dimple that didn't make an appearance very often.

"You never really lost me, sweetheart."

"I know, no matter how much you annoyed me

and I was a bitch to you, I knew you'd be there when I needed you." He pressed a kiss to her forehead.

"Are you going to keep seeing Lucas?" he asked. She stilled in his lap. "Ya' know, after what happened tonight? With him I mean, not with me." She shook her head.

"No, I have no idea what happened but I am not getting a good feeling off him from it. I don't feel safe with him." She shifted forwards more into his lap and he groaned lightly.

"This is a bad idea."

"I'm serious if you want to go home just push me off of you." He laughed and squeezed her hips slightly.

"I don't wanna be anywhere but here." She kissed his forehead this time.

"So for now we have tonight. Future us can worry about our futures," she said, leaning forward and catching his lips in a kiss.

"And from tomorrow we're friends, right?" He nodded.

"Okay," he said. He barely had the chance to finish nodding before her lips were on his again. He chuckled against her lips.

"You've had a long day princess. You should sleep."

"My one night with you and you want me to sleep it away?" she asked innocently.

"Ella, my self control is good but don't fucking push it. I'm so hard it literally hurts." She wanted nothing more than to help him get rid of the ache. "Give me a few minutes to try and think about something other than your hands or lips on me okay?" She nodded. She moved from his lap and went to stand at the window. She looked out at the line of trees.

Something caught her eye. There seemed to be something or someone standing in the tree line. She moved closer, kneeling on her window seat.

"Will?"

"Yes princess?"

"I think there's someone in the trees." The thing was already moving back into the trees but before it went out of sight completely, the moonlight illuminated auburn curls.

He turned to face her and his eyes locked with hers.

"It's Lucas." She sucked in a breath.

"Ruby, stay with Ella." He had already left the room by the time Ella turned around and Ruby placed her mouth over her wrist and gently pulled her away from the window. She was now sitting on the edge of her bed, shaking. She felt her mind slip into darkness.

# CHAPTER TEN

By the time Will had returned to the bedroom, she had moved to curling up on the window seat looking out of the window, trying to catch a glimpse of Will.

"I saw him, but I couldn't catch up to him to find out what the fuck was going on." He crossed his arms over his still bare chest. "Ella?"

She turned to face him with strangely blank eyes. "It's okay. It wasn't him."

He narrowed his eyes. "I saw him. I just told you it was him." She shook her head.

"You must have got it wrong." Will lowered his arms. He went and stood next to her and placed a hand on her hair. She brushed him off. "I need to go to sleep.

You need to leave." He pulled his hand away like he had been burned.

"You asked me to stay." He gritted his teeth and she snorted in laughter.

"Why would I do that?" Will knew then, he knew that they weren't the only ones with access to magic and whoever Lucas was working with had enough power to be able to mess with her mind without even being in the same room as her.

"My mistake," he said, crossing his arms. "How'd your date go?"

He ignored the feeling of someone crushing his heart in his hand. He saw her face light up and it was at that moment that he knew he was in love with her. The agony he felt that the look on her face was because of the date that she had apparently had with Lucas and she couldn't even remember anything with him.

"It was amazing, well, until you showed up." He swallowed hard. "But it doesn't matter, I had a wonderful time. I'm definitely going to be seeing him again." Will nodded and forced a smile.

"I'll be in Leo's room if you need anything," he said quietly.

"Night Will," she said, climbing into bed. He nodded to Ruby who took a protective stance and he walked into her bathroom, gathering his clothes. All of the evidence of what happened the night before. He put her dress over the back of her desk chair and left the room without another word.

When he got to Leo's room and rifled through his drawers, he got changed into his own, less tight sweatpants and a plain black t-shirt that he knew he'd hidden in the drawer. He pulled his phone to his ear. Magda answered on the second wring.

"Boy, you better have a good reason for waking me up in the middle of the–"

"It's Ella," he said simply.

"We can't mess with her head again Will, you heard what Elena said." He sighed.

"Someone else is messing with her head. She just spotted the guy she had been on a date with tonight lurking at the edge of the forest. Now she doesn't appear to have any idea what happened from the moment she got home from the date." Magda was quiet for a beat.

"How do you know?"

"She walked in with a burned mouth, it was the fallen that she had a date with. He tried to give her an ash kiss but she was fighting it." He felt tiredness wash over him.

"I stayed with her while she went through the stages, distracted her so that she wouldn't go to find him." Magda hummed in amusement. He rolled his eyes.

"He must have realized it hadn't worked because she spotted him in the forest. She sounded terrified but I couldn't get to him fast enough. By the time I got back to Ella she had forgotten everything. Said it couldn't have been Lucas and sent me away." Magda sighed.

"Okay, this isn't good." He huffed.

"I will send a message to Elena in Astridia, she will be home by morning. We will wait for Ella to go to work tomorrow afternoon and we will have a meeting at the house. Are you still there?"

"Yes, I told Ruby to watch over her and I'm in Leo's room." She seemed to be moving around, picking things up and putting things down.

"Try and sleep Will, it sounds like they got what they wanted. We will deal with it in the morning."

"I'll try. Thanks Mags, see you tomorrow." She tutted.

"Boy, if you were not so handsome you'd be in big trouble calling me that." Her no nonsense voice made him chuckle lightly.

"Good job I am this handsome huh." He grinned and she said something in a language he didn't know.

"Goodnight child."

"Night." He put the phone down. It warmed him slightly to know that Magda referred to him as child and boy. He may be twenty-three but being treated like a cheeky kid sometimes made him feel almost normal.

The muscles in his back shifted, reminding him that he was very far from normal. He set an alarm for a few hours and let the exhaustion of the last few days flood over him. He closed his eyes, led on his friend's bed and all he could think about was the feel of her in his lap, her hands on his skin, her lips on his. He balled his fists. He would kill Lucas for taking this night away from her. For taking it away from him.

E lena and Leo both arrived earlier than expected, finding Will sat in their kitchen with his hands around a cup of coffee.

"Did you sleep?" Elena asked him at once before even saying hello.

"Yeah, I got a few hours in. Ella is still asleep." Leo sat next to him and thanked Elena when she placed a mug in front of him and brought her own mug and the refilled coffee pot to the table.

"Magda wasn't very clear, what exactly happened?" Elena asked. Will blew out a breath and explained as best he could. He didn't mention the conversation in the shower and the kissing, for obvious reasons but the way Leo was staring at him made him think his friend knew there was something he wasn't telling them, but he didn't press him.

"I called Blake earlier," Leo said. "He said that she told him and Sam about the date when they met her for lunch the other day. She seemed to be toying with the idea of inviting him to her birthday party." Elena huffed.

"We need to put an end to this before it starts. The fact he attempted to give the ash kiss means he's not pursuing her for any genuine reason. He knows what she is." Will nodded in agreement.

"He definitely knows, but how are we going to stop Ella from seeing him if that's what she wants?" Leo's eyes met his friends.

"We ask Magda to remove the glamour that they weaved to make her forget about last night."

"No," Will said before he could stop himself. "I mean, I don't think she will be able to. Whatever did this, did it without being anywhere near Ella. It's gonna take a lot more effort to undo it than anything else we've done before and we can't risk it."

"Agreed," Elena said as Leo opened his mouth to

speak. He shut it again and paused for a moment before nodding.

"We keep an eye on it, we put barriers up if needed. Even if she ends up hating us for now, she will thank us later." They all stopped talking as they heard movement upstairs. Elena rose from the bench and went over to the stove to start making breakfast.

Ella came down just as Elena was putting the eggs and bacon on the table.

"Morning sweetie," she said.

"I wasn't expecting you home so early!" She went and kissed her Nona on the cheek.

"I wanted to be here to help Leo move back in." Ella beamed at her brother and the smile on her face made Will's heart ache in his chest. He knew that she was still reeling from her apparently perfect date. He didn't know if he could bare to be in her presence for another minute.

He was waiting, leaning against the counter. Ella slid into the booth next to Elena and Will considered leaving when Elena raised a thin eyebrow. He was to stay for breakfast. He sighed and slid into the booth next to Ella. His thigh brushed hers and he moved so fast he almost fell off the damn seat. He put as much distance between them as he could while still being seated and let

Ella fill his plate with food. Leo shot him a questioning look, he'd noticed Will's odd behaviour and he shook his head slightly. Leo seemed to understand that it mean Will would discuss it with him later.

"I'm surprised," Ella said to the room at large as they started.

"At what?" Leo asked around a mouthful of food.

"None of you are giving me the third degree about my date last night." Leo looked at Elena and Will paused with a fork halfway to his mouth.

"Of course, I almost forgot," Elena said in a breathy laugh. "How'd it go?" she asked. Leo shot an apologetic look at Will and he shook his head slightly. He placed his fork back on his plate.

"It was great! He called me this morning and we're going out again next week." Leo cleared his throat.

"That's great." He smiled at his sister's happy face.

"But don't think I've forgotten about you turning up Will," she said coolly.

"I told you I was there on business." He gripped his glass and took a swig of orange juice.

"I don't care." His hand clenched and the glass cracked. The room went silent.

"I have to go." He stood and walked towards the door.

"We need to discuss this Will!" Ella said rising from

her seat too. Leo said something to her as she stormed after him but he didn't hear what. His heartbeat was pounding in his ears. He had to get away from this house, from her. He had reached the front door when a hand on his arm stopped him and he turned to her.

"We need to talk about it."

"Not now Ella," he muttered. Her hand slackened and travelled down to his hand, pulling him around to face her fully. He looked down to see concern etched over her beautiful face. Her grey eyes narrowed slightly, as if trying to analyse him. Her button nose was wrinkled and her full mouth parted slightly. The memories of all the kisses they shared last night welled up inside him. The fact that she would probably never remember them was making him so angry that he wanted to find Lucas and rip him apart piece by piece.

"What's wrong?"

"Just... not today Ella, I can't fucking do this today." He pulled his hand from hers and walked out of the door. He didn't look back to see if she was watching him go.

# CHAPTER ELEVEN

Ella didn't bother going back to the kitchen. She went out into the back yard with Ruby and stared at the line of trees.

"Ella." Leo came to stand next to her.

"Don't go blaming me, it's him that seems to have a stick up his ass today," she snapped.

"I know, but I just wanted to tell you, don't take it to heart. He's had a really bad few weeks. I think last night was a particularly bad one for him. Nona shouldn't have made him stay for breakfast." Ella looked at her brother's kind face.

"Well it's not my fault, why is he being an ass to me?" she asked.

"That's something Will needs to explain. I'm not

excusing him but he really did have business at the Rose last night and I don't think it went according to plan." She felt a bite of shame crawl up her throat.

"Okay, I'll apologize later."

"Thank you." He put an arm around her shoulder. "I have the day off today."

"Why is it when you're off I'm working?" She leaned into him and rested her head on his shoulder.

"Come on, let's go into town and grab a coffee and I'll walk you to work." She smiled.

"Ruby, you can come too," he said to the dog who barked and raced into the house.

They heard a motorcycle start and her head whipped around as she heard it going extremely fast down the street.

"I wish he wouldn't ride those things so damn fast. He's going to get himself killed." Her heart gave a squeeze at the thought. She may have had an amazing date with Lucas last night, but it was Will who she thought of when she first woke up this morning. She swore she could smell the scent of him on her, as though he had been wrapped around her. When she saw him in the kitchen there was a rush of lust and something more. She was on cloud nine with Lucas and had enjoyed a light and flirtatious conversation with him on the phone that morning, promising each other another date but seeing Will so angry and sad looking had made her want to pull him to her and hug him tightly. They hadn't hugged since they were children.

"He's a better rider than anyone gives him credit for. Don't worry, he knows what he's doing." Leo looked at her and gave her a little grin.

"So you're really not gonna let him take you out for a ride?" Her eyes widened at the teasing nature in his voice.

"I wouldn't have been able to get on that bike in that dress and I don't know. Maybe one day, when I'm more appropriately dressed." Leo nodded.

"You wouldn't be worried about me being on the back of his bike when he drives like a lunatic?" He shook his head.

"If there is one person on the planet that you could do any dangerous thing with and not have me worry, it's Will." Her heart fluttered. Will in himself was dangerous to her. However, he had a point.

"Me too." He squeezed her shoulders a little and they heard an indignant bark from inside the house. They both laughed and retreated into the house. Ruby was waiting impatiently next to her lead.

When they got to the coffee shop down the street from the café, which didn't open on weekday mornings they slid into a booth and ordered. She ordered a large iced coffee with whipped cream and sickly sweet flavourings. Leo was rolling his eyes at her with a smile. She had a sweet tooth, she liked to drink her sugar as opposed to eating it though.

"What do you want for your birthday?" Leo asked her and she raised her eyebrows at him.

"Not long to go now brother, you're leaving it a little late aren't ya," she teased and he grinned.

"I already have some of your smaller gifts, but it's you're twenty-first birthday, you deserve something special," he said seriously and she reached out and squeezed his arm.

"I appreciate the offer Leo but I don't want you to feel like you have to. I know you like to do the things that a dad should do, like spoiling someone on their big birthdays but you're under a lot of pressure. You being there, spending the day with me, having been present my whole life. That is the only present I've ever needed from you," she said kindly and his shoulders sagged.

"I've been wondering if he would send something in the mail for you." She snorted and took a sip of her drink through the straw.

"Well, he didn't for any other birthday. I'd rather he didn't." Leo nodded.

"I know you don't know any different because you never knew him." He sighed heavily. There had been something weighing on her brother for a while now, whether it was the weight of his job and studies or something more.

"Leo, you knew Dad, for a few years at least. I'll never resent you for wanting more from him than I ever did." His shoulders sagged a little with what she thought was relief. He pushed a hand through his dark blonde hair and his ocean blue eyes crinkled slightly at the corners.

"Mom would be proud of you Ella. You're a kind, beautiful, funny human." She laughed.

"She would be proud of you," she emphasised. "You helped raise me that way." She felt a burning in her eyes at the look of appreciation in his face at her words.

They chatted about Leo's work, him moving back into the house and his lack of a love life.

"Yeah well, having a love life isn't all it's cracked up to be," she said, crossing her arms slightly. He raised an eyebrow at her.

"I thought you had a perfect date with Lucas?" She uncrossed her arms.

"I did. Well, yeah, I did it's just..." She paused. She didn't know if she could confess to her brother, the knowing look and I told you so's enough but not only that, she felt a burning lump of guilt in her stomach.

"It's just... Will," he said knowingly and she looked over his face. There was no trace of 'I told you so's' there.

"How awful am I?" she asked, putting her head in her hands.

"What're you talking about?" She looked up at her brother through her hands.

"I had a really great date with a really nice guy and yet I can't stop thinking about the asshole who infuriates me all the time, your best friend! Stop laughing!" she said, throwing a sugar packet at him.

"Sorry," he said, trying to stop himself from smiling. "Ella, you're a beautiful young woman who has the right to date whoever she wants. Until you and Lucas become exclusive or you actually tell Will how you feel you have nothing to feel guilty about." She bit the inside of her cheek, thinking hard.

"It's so stupid. Nothing is ever going to happen with Will, it's a disaster waiting to happen," she said, turning another sugar packet over between her fingers.

"Don't write him off just yet," he said, signalling the waitress and asking for the cheque.

# CHAPTER TWELVE

L eo pulled up outside of Sam's house and was not surprised to see both him and Blake waiting in the front yard.

"So what happened?" Blake asked the moment they were in the car. Sam had sat in the back with Ruby and Blake was sat in the passenger seat.

"Honestly, I'm not sure. Will was very vague this morning and I think there is a lot that he's not telling us, but from what he said Lucas gave Ella an Ash kiss." Blake raised his eyebrows and Sam swore.

"You think something happened with Will and Ella?" Sam asked.

"I think so, but then this glamour kicked in and as far as Ella knew, she'd had a wonderful date with

Lucas, she'd got home and gone to bed. So if something did happen, she wouldn't remember a minute of it." Blake swore.

"That's fucking cruel," he said, folding his arms.

"I assume we're going to the ring?" Leo nodded at Sam's question. They pulled up on the drive and Elena was stood at the front door.

"Take Ruby with you," she said, waving at the other two boys. "Magda and I will meet you there."

Leo nodded at her and entered the side gate, going straight through the garden. When they reached the low wall at the end of the garden Leo took off the lead and Ruby ran, jumping over the wall. As though they had done it thousands of times before, the three men followed suit, jumping over the wall as easy as if they'd merely stepped over a kerb. They penetrated the first few layers of trees, following Ruby who was leading the way. The canopy of trees got thicker overhead and they walked into darkness. They'd been walking for a little over twenty minutes when the trees above started to thin again and speckled light displayed the path ahead.

They stopped at the edge of the clearing. There were small wooden huts in groups all around the edge. Half of the space in the middle was taken by a campfire with logs around to sit on and the other half was a make shift training area. In the centre of the training area was Will. His shirt was off, sweat pouring down his skin and his hands were bloody from the continuous punching of the wooden pole in front of him. Leo and Blake stood back as Sam approached him.

Will and Leo might have been best friends, but Will had known Sam the longest, before Sam and Will even came to live here, they'd grown up together. Trained together.

---

Will felt the body move beside him but he didn't stop punching until he felt Sam's hand on his shoulder.

"Will," Sam said in a stern voice. "Stop." It took him a great effort to stop. He turned to look at his friend's startlingly clear eyes and he felt all the fight leave him. He didn't stop Sam from taking a hand in his own and healing the damage he'd done. As he felt the bones pop back into place and the cuts close, he looked over at Leo.

"We need to know what happened last night," Sam said calmly, working on his other hand. He nodded.

"But first, you're going to spar with me and get your ass kicked." Will couldn't stop the smirk.

Sam was a very skilled fighter, his whole family came from a line of Angels of Mercy that were stronger than any other. Sam had broken the mould however, when his wings had come through blue and green like a peacock. Will had been almost as surprised as his family. Sam hadn't been surprised at all. As skilled as he was, he only fought to train or when it was necessary. His lean muscled body was better for spying, detecting and his even temperament for giving guidance. So he had embraced his calling to become an Angel of Solace. Without that, Blake wouldn't be standing here with them today.

"You're talking real big there Sam."

"Oh please, you may be the chosen one William, but we both know I'm faster." His teeth flashed with the challenge. Will hated the name the chosen one. Especially when, at first, no one was able to explain what had happened to him. He was a bastard brat who was taken in by Tony, one of the angels of armor's trainers. The Order had always looked at him as if he was less than nothing, an annoyance. So they didn't know why he had received his wings at the age of nine instead of twenty-one.

Not until that day a few months later when they had the news of the guardian of the gate being murdered. Then the order seemed very clear that he had received his wings to watch over and protect the next guardian in line and he and Tony were to protect the gate in the interim. What he didn't expect was for the order to bond him to her, so that her pain was his pain, getting warnings when she was in danger. He also didn't expect to fall in love with her. He gave himself a mental shake. Since he'd admitted to himself that he was in love with her, he couldn't stop himself thinking it every time he thought about her. He'd done so well at denying it to himself since she split with David. That the joy he felt to find that she was finally free of that moron and the enjoyment that he experienced as he watched her confidence grow and start to love herself again. He was honor bound to protect her, he needed to take a step back.

This didn't take away from the fact that Will was the most lethal angel there was. Possibly that there ever had been. Faster, stronger and gifted in their powers. The downside was the responsibility that came with it. He grew up being able to be a kid, as long as his job came first. If she was protected, he was free to do whatever he pleased. As long as anyone that was a threat was taken down before they got close to her.

"Challenge accepted," he said as he moved forwards. The little son of a bitch dodged right out of the way and got a lucky shot in his ribs. He gave himself a little shake and stilled his mind. He let himself forget about Ella, forget about Lucas, the Order. He concentrated solely on Sam.

The others had started to spar next to them, although Leo didn't need to technically be battle trained, he liked to help Blake by sparring with him. He liked to make sure he would always be able to defend himself. If shit hit the fan he would be expected to fight and with Ella being what she was, he didn't care that he was only an Angel of Oblivion, he would protect his sister. Always.

Once Will and Sam were finished their sparring session, Will had explained what had happened. He left out some of the details but the boys knew that something had happened between him and Ella. He wandered over to Leo while Sam and Blake moved closer, talking low.

"If you wanna swing at me dude, you can," Will said and Leo looked at him like he'd gone insane.

"What?"

"I made out with your sister." Leo laughed and Will grinned at him.

"I've been waiting for this to happen since we were fourteen. It's literally your job to keep her alive and keep her safe. I'd rather she was with you than most." Will smiled sadly.

"Thanks bro, that means a lot. Shame it will never happen now." Leo grinned.

"I wouldn't be so sure about that." Will looked at him with a questioning gaze.

"Let's just say her mind may have forgotten what happened last night, but there's something in her that knows. If my conversation with her earlier was to be understood correctly." Will mulled over this information and opened his mouth.

"I swear if you ask me what she said about you like a teenage girl I will never let you live it down." He snapped his mouth shut and glared at him.

By the time Elena and Magda had joined them, all four men were shirtless, sweating and drinking from bottles of water. Magda smiled at the boys and Will tried not to laugh.

"We need to discuss the issue of Lucas," Elena said, without preamble.

"I vote I go ahead and kill him," Will said. Blake

nodded his head in agreement but Leo and Sam both sighed.

"And how are you going to explain that to Ella right now?" Sam reminded him. He wasn't sure he much cared. He would not be satisfied until he held that little asshole's heart in his fist.

"We need to keep her busy, the less time she can spend with him, the less opportunities he has to try and get whatever he needs from him," Elena said, glancing around the circle of people.

"Magda is going to do some spells that protect her when she is alone with him but I want us all on Ella duty." Blake grinned.

"Interrupting her whenever she's alone with him? Consider it done." Leo chuckled.

"I can't do that," Will said. Elena's eyes met his and there was a level of understanding that told Will that Elena guessed what his feelings towards her granddaughter were. She nodded.

"I understand, we will need you and Blake to be out on the hunt anyway. The amount of demons and fallen that are being sent after her are upping every single day. The rest of the angels in the area are reporting back to me daily but you two are the best that we have." Will caught the little gleam of pride in Sam's eyes as he looked at Blake.

"Sam," she said and he jerked his back to her, his face back to serious. "I need you to find out what you can about Lucas, what he's up to, who he's working for." He nodded.

"There's only a few weeks left until her birthday, they're getting desperate."

# CHAPTER THIRTEEN

The next few weeks seemed to fly by faster than Ella could keep up with. Elena was spending more and more time out of town and while Ella didn't begrudge her Nona the break that she clearly needed, she was always grateful for more money. Although it did cut into the time that she could spend with Lucas. She smiled to herself as she remembered a beautiful date they had shared, taking a stroll around the edge of the forest, talking, laughing, kissing. It had ended with a pretty heavy make out session against a tree that had freaked her out slightly. She felt as though he was always on the edge of snapping whenever he kissed her. Perhaps he did want her that badly but the thought of it made her not want to take the relationship any further.

"C'mon Ella," he'd whispered into her ear. "You know what I want to do to you." She'd gulped and placed a hand on his chest.

"I don't fuck on the second date," she said, pushing past him but grabbing his hand to pull him along with her.

Another date had been spent in a fancy restaurant but Ella had feigned illness to go home early. He'd been as nice as he could be to her, he said all the right things, complimented her to high heaven, flirted to within an inch of his life but he was rude to the staff, scathing of the other patrons and the whole date left her with a sour taste in her mouth.

Although she tried to keep her mind open, there were little things that he said that made her feel a prickle of fear or a feeling that he was lying about something. She had gone into the library only once to return the borrowed books and he was there again, standing between the shelves, looking gorgeous but he didn't seem to be doing much. Whenever she spoke about books he seemed uninterested in deepening the conversation and when she tried to press him he just said he worked with books all day, he didn't want to talk about them outside of work too.

Will had barely spoken to her since her first date with Lucas, she still hadn't discussed him showing up there but she didn't even care about that anymore. She missed him and that thought scared her more than anything Lucas had said. She got home and was in the middle of dumping her bag in the kitchen when she heard a knock on the door. She opened it and was shocked to see Lucas standing in the doorway.

"Lucas!" she exclaimed. She was about to move back to allow him in when Ruby appeared behind her, hackles raised, growling and snarling.

"Ruby," she said in her low commanding voice but it did nothing to sooth the canine.

"Sorry Lucas give me a minute." She pushed the door to and backed Ruby away, out into the back yard and closed the door.

She didn't know what to do. She knew Ruby's instincts were good and this was the first time she had seen Lucas. Was she really going to end something because her dog didn't like him? She ran a hand through her hair. It wasn't just Ruby though, she was having doubts herself.

"I'm so sorry about that," she said, opening the door back up and stepping aside to let him pass. He walked into the house and through to the living room. She followed him in.

"I've been wanting to do this all day," he said, capturing her lips in a kiss and she was too stunned to pull away. He pushed her roughly against the wall and his hand went to the hem of her t-shirt. She managed to pull away then.

"Lucas," she said, placing a hand against him.

"What?" he asked. "We're alone."

"I know, but we're in the middle of the living room and you've barely even said hi!" Lucas huffed in frustration.

"I didn't realize you were such a prude Ella." She glared at him and pushed him hard enough that he stumbled back a step.

"I didn't realize you were only after one thing."

"I've been open and honest with my feelings from the start," he countered. In all honesty, she wasn't usually this conservative with men she was dating. She didn't like to string people along; if she liked them, she showed them. If she didn't she cut them loose. Lucas was different, she seemed to not be able to make her mind up. She would be lying if she said Will may have been the reason she had held off getting physical with Lucas. That and she had no idea what she felt for the auburn haired man.

"Is this because of that dumbass of a mountain who lives next door?" She looked at him.

"Huh?"

"Don't play dumb Ella, he shows up on our date

and sounds like he's here more than his own house. He's the reason you won't go all the way isn't he. Are you fucking him?" he asked.

"No, I'm not. And I certainly won't be fucking you either Lucas. Get out of my house." He moved forward half a step and Ruby jumped against the door. She felt terror grip at her heart, if she didn't get him out of the house she really felt as though she could be in danger from him.

"Leave now before she breaks through that door," she warned. He gave the dog a look of loathing and stalked to the door. She waited for the door to slam shut and once it did she went and opened the back door. Ruby had gone to the front door and continued to bark. She was half tempted to open the door and let her chase him but she didn't want the hassle. Someone hammered on the door and Ella froze but Ruby wasn't barking anymore. Instead, she was on her hind legs, scrabbling at the door knob. Ella opened the door and saw Will. His eyes flicked over her and then behind her around the room.

"What happened?" he asked stepping in as she stepped aside.

"Nothing." He looked at her and rolled his eyes.

"Please don't insult my intelligence Ella, I heard Ruby going bat shit and I saw that boyfriend of yours storming down the street." She'd winced at the venom in his voice.

"Well, he's not my boyfriend, let's just put it that way."

"Did he touch you?" he asked immediately.

"No, not really."

"What do you mean not really?" he snarled.

"Oh calm down Rambo. He kissed me and tried to take it further but I stopped him. Let's just say he didn't appreciate it." His fists were clenched and his eyes were fixed on the front door.

"I'm sure if you left now you could catch him but he's really not worth it." He sighed.

"So you're okay?" She nodded.

"He's not your biggest fan though," she said. He had a questioning look on his face.

"What did I do?" he asked, bewildered.

"You exist, you're close to me and you look like... that." She waved a hand at him. He looked particularly good today, he'd obviously been outside working on a bike as there was motor grease on his hands. He was wearing navy colored overalls that were tied around his waist and a black t-shirt that was maddeningly fitted.

His work boots shifted as he crossed his arms and she felt a ripple of heat flow through her, landing low in her stomach. She didn't regret not sleeping with

Lucas but she needed to have sex soon because this man in front of her was driving her insane. How was it fair that he looked like he'd just walked off of a set of a grease monkey calendar shoot?

"Huh?" he asked, truly confused.

"He thought the reason I wasn't sleeping with him was because I was sleeping with you," she explained. He opened his mouth and closed it again. She smiled, it had been a long time since she had rendered him speechless.

"So, you and him haven't ever..." She rolled her eyes.

"No," she gritted out and his eyes flicked to her in amusement. He had understood the frustration behind her words. Not that she hadn't had sex with Lucas but that she hadn't had sex in a while and she was frustrated. She picked a magazine off of the table with every intention of throwing it at him but he was in front of her, his hand around the wrist that held the book. She was backing into the wall for the second time this evening and she couldn't have felt more differently about this situation than she had half an hour ago.

"Now now, princess. I know you're... frustrated." He smiled with a wicked grin at her and she huffed. "But you can't go round throwing things at people."

His other hand was on the wall next to her head and she could feel her chest heaving. She was embarrassingly aroused and she knew that he could tell. She chanced a look down to his lips and the deadly grin widened.

"You know, I'm sure I'd be able to help you with that," he purred into her ear and her gulped response was audible in the deadly quiet room.

"In the meantime princess, you're not going to throw books at me every time you get riled up?" She sighed and dropped the magazine from her hand. It thudded on the floor and he looked down at it and back up to her eyes. She couldn't look away from his golden eyes, blown wide with desire. Holy shit, she thought, he was just as turned on as she was.

"Good girl," he said and she whimpered. She fucking whimpered! She was cursing at herself, too busy to notice that he had moved away.

"See you later princess." He grinned as he backed out of the room and finally turned away. She groaned and she heard a chuckle.

"Fuck you," she called.

"Here's to hoping." She bit down another whimper and slid down the wall. That stupid, gorgeous man was going to be the death of her.

# CHAPTER
# FOURTEEN

S he'd showered, long enough that the aching need had subsided into a dull annoyance and dressed in a pair of sweat pants and a tank top. She was still feeling all too warm. She had decided to sit in the garden and read for a while, to try and quiet her mind and the warmth still peppering her skin. She had been trying for the last few hours to forget about everything that happened with Lucas and everything that had followed with Will. She brought the beer to her lips and felt her vision blur for a moment. She was surrounded by a strange feeling. She moved her hand in front of her face and it was as if she had no control over her limbs. Her hands danced in front of her vision and her beer clattered to the floor, the liquid flowing from the almost full bottle. She couldn't hear much, everything was muffled as if someone had stuffed her brain and her ears with cotton wool.

Lucas. She had to find Lucas, she had to get to Lucas. If she made it to him, she would feel better. Lucas, Lucas, Lucas was a drum in her head. She pulled a pair of sneakers on and styled her soaking wet hair into a bun on top of her head.

She felt herself flying down the hall as quick as her feet could carry her. She heard a growl from Ruby but she picked up her keys and pocketed them, running out of the door before pulling it closed behind her to stop Ruby from following her. Will was stood next to his motorcycle, a toolbox on the floor and engine grease still on his hands.

"Hey! Ella!" he called after her but she ignored him. She noticed in the back of her mind that she had heard him and wanted to stop but her feet carried her forwards. She was running after Lucas. What she planned on doing once she found him she didn't know, she didn't know why she was going after him at all but this was the only thing that stopped the panic from hitting her completely. Footsteps were thumping behind her but she paid them no attention as she reached the main road. She didn't even know where Lucas lived, or where he was going to be but her legs kept going, feet pounding on the cement. Then a lot of things happened all at once. Ella's feet turned her to the edge of the side walk, and she noticed a car that was coming down the street. It was going extremely fast and there was something in Ella's head that was telling her to stop, wait for the car to pass but then another feeling of bile crept up her throat and she couldn't stop herself from putting a foot out onto the road.

Internally she was screaming at herself to stop, she could feel herself pushing out against her skin, whatever force it was that had control over her but it was adamant. It would not be moved. She flinched, as if she could feel the impact before it came and felt an arm wrap suddenly around her waist before she was hauled backwards. Herself and the person whose arm it was fell back onto the sidewalk with a grunt. She felt whatever it was that made her feel so strange leave her body, like something was being yanked from behind her navel through her skin. The sensation was so strange that if left a churning in her stomach and bile rose in her throat. She rolled and turned her head, vomiting into a bush.

The sound of her own retching was the only thing she could hear, her thoughts were suddenly silent. When she had emptied her stomach she turned to look at Will who was now on his feet, one hand on her back. She wiped her mouth on her sleeve and let him help her up to stand on legs shaking so hard she thought they were going to snap.

His eyes looked her over, checking every inch of her and Ella realized he was looking for signs of any injuries.

"I'm fine," she choked out, her voice shaking almost as much as her legs. He threw his arms around her and pulled her close to him. She couldn't help but let out a sob the moment his skin made contact with hers. He pulled away slightly so he could look into her face. The startling difference between the contact earlier in the living room made her cling to him tighter.

"Why didn't I stop? Why couldn't I stop? I wanted to stop, I didn't even want to go, I could see the car. Why didn't I stop?" She could hear herself saying this over and over again until he put his hands on her cheeks and she stopped talking, looking reluctantly into his hazel, golden eyes.

"You're safe Ella. You're with me, you're safe." His voice was slow and steady and each word washed over her in a wave of calm, helping to relax her. She nodded. He let go of her face and swept her into his arms, one arm supporting her back, one underneath her knees and he lifted her as easily as if she weighed nothing. She wrapped her arms around his neck.

"Let's get you home," he said, starting to walk back in the direction of their homes. When they got to the end of the street they could hear Ruby barking and whining and Ella signalled to be put down. Will placed her on the ground and steadied her for a moment before she rushed up the steps and opened the front door as fast as she could. The dog came racing out of the door, almost crashing into Ella and whimpered again, sitting at her feet breathing hard. Ella knelt down on the floor and wrapped the dog in a hug.

"I'm sorry Ruby." She sobbed again into her dog's soft fur. Ruby broke out of the hug and licked away a tear. She then walked over to Will who had caught up with them and jumped up at him, licking his face. Ella, despite everything managed to smile.

---

When they had got into the house Ella had immediately excused herself to brush her teeth and freshen up. Once she reappeared back downstairs, Will had pushed Ella towards an arm chair, gave her a blanket and made her a cup of tea. She settled into the chair. Ruby was led at her feet and she was flicking through the TV channels absentmindedly. She was trying to figure out what on earth had just happened. She had been angry with Lucas when he'd left. Furious even. Yet she found herself running after him and hours after. Not even seeing Will had broken her out of it. But when it came to stepping out in front of that car, she felt as if she had absolutely no control over her body. Like she was a puppet and someone else was pulling her strings. Rationally she could not get her head around it, was she going crazy? Was she having a break from reality? Was something seriously wrong with her? That she was doing weird things without thinking she had no control over them. And most importantly, why was Will not at all surprised when any of this happened? Why did this not freak him out? Then again, she thought, maybe he was just as freaked out, but was tactful enough not to act like it in front of the crazy person.

"Ella?" Will was stood in front of her, his eyebrows furrowed. She'd guessed this was not the first time he had tried to get her attention.

"Sorry, I was spaced."

"Can we talk about it? Are you... okay to talk about it now?" he asked, sitting in the armchair beside hers, a cup of coffee in hand. She angled herself in the chair so that she was facing him and she nodded.

"What... What exactly happened?" he asked. She looked down into her tea cup.

"When, when you left..." She swallowed, chancing a look up to his face and was thankful to see that he didn't react, he was just waiting for her to continue.

"I had a shower, got changed, went out into the yard to read my book with a beer. I felt my vision go blurry, something came over me. Like that feeling you get when you miss a step on the stairs. But it lasted a really long time." She stopped and cleared her throat a little bit.

"So what made you run out of the house?" His voice was calm and soft still, it sounded like he was at the bedside of a sick relative and she felt her face flush in embarrassment. He must think that she is incapable of looking after herself.

"I don't know. I had a feeling like I had to run after him. That bad feeling would go away if I could just get to Lucas and before I knew what I was doing, I was running down the street after him." She wiped another tear away.

"You didn't even hear me call your name?" he asked. She shook her head.

"Not really, I vaguely remember a noise and hearing footsteps behind me but I didn't know you were there till you... pulled me back." Will was staring at his fist, which was clenching and unclenching in front of his face. His knuckles turned bright white every time he clenched.

"I thought so."

"How did you know something was wrong?" she asked him, also watching his hand now too. He noticed and stopped. She shook her head a little and looked at his face.

"You'd never ignore me unless there was something wrong, plus I haven't seen you run since you were eleven." He grinned at her and she smiled slightly. "And, my spidey senses were tingling."

"Your what now?" she asked, looking incredulously at him.

"My spidey senses! I knew something wasn't right so I followed you." She smiled slightly.

"Thank god for spidey senses," she muttered before taking a sip of tea.

Will wouldn't leave.

Not that she had tried very hard to persuade him to go but even so, he had insisted that he didn't want to leave her alone. Turns out almost dying does wonders for your social life she thought as she watched him on the phone to the pizza place. She looked at his dark, messy hair that was messier than usual, as he had spent a lot of the afternoon running a hand through it in frustration. His neck moved as he spoke and she couldn't help but watch and follow every movement with her eyes. The contrast between the terror that she felt with Lucas earlier that day and the raging lust at the way Will had held her and spoke to her just moments after was paramount. It didn't matter how dangerous he felt, with Will was always the safest place to be. She could enjoy feeling like she was doing something incredibly dangerous, flirting with the beautiful man who could break her in two if he wanted but she knew he would rather break himself apart than her.

She was still reeling from what had happened earlier. She knew that what she felt today, running out of the house isn't normal but if checking out Will gave her a moment's peace from her endless questions and anxiety then she would take it.

He turned and caught her staring. He smirked slightly as he gave her address but she had already zoned out, eyes slightly unfocused back to thinking about what happened and how close she had been to, if not death, then certainly bad injury.

He frowned slightly and walked towards her. He put his hand on her head, stroking her hair and she jumped at the contact, and then relaxed under his touch. He put the phone down and knelt down beside her. His arm rested on the arm of her chair with his chin resting on his arm.

"Ella, you went through something horrific today and I know you probably don't want to talk about it but I need to tell your Nona and Leo about it." She sighed and looked at him.

"Do you have to?" She groaned as he nodded.

"They trust me to watch out for you, if I don't tell them about this... they need to know."

"Okay, I think it will be easier you know, for you to tell them. I don't really know how to explain it." He smiled at her.

"You did a great job explaining it to me." That god damned praise again.

"You're sweet." She touched a finger to his face. "But I know you're just buttering me up so I don't hate you for telling on me." He grinned and she smiled back.

"I'll ask them not to bug you about it when they get back." She nodded her head.

"Thanks." He stood and once again pressed his phone to his ear but this time, he wandered out to the kitchen.

# CHAPTER FIFTEEN

The pizza arrived just as he had got off the phone to Leo. Apparently both Leo and Elena wanted to come home immediately, but Will had somehow convinced them to stay until tomorrow, that he would stay here with Ella and she will be better off speaking to them about it tomorrow. Ella was grateful that Will had taken the brunt of the shock and was pleasantly surprised he had managed to convince them to stay.

"They really must trust you with me. The last time something like this almost happened Leo almost got thrown out of the hospital because he wouldn't leave when visiting hours ended." Will smiled.

"I remember, I was there with him." He laughed.

"Yeah you were. One day, you're gonna need to

stop saving my life," she said jokingly, remembering what Leo had said about the inhumane noise he had made when she wasn't responding to CPR.

"Never," he said, so seriously that Ella had to look away. She took another bite of pizza, throwing a piece of ham down to Ruby.

They watched TV for the rest of the evening, Will choosing to watch TV quiz shows and then admitting he just liked watching Ella get frustrated when people didn't get the correct answer to easy questions. She was starting to feel extremely tired. This was the first time she had properly relaxed since the incident happened and exhaustion washed over her so quickly that she almost fell asleep there in her armchair.

"Bed time young lady," she heard a voice close to her ear say and she realized that she was being carried out of the living room.

"M'not sleepy," she mumbled and the chest she was leant against shook in a little laugh.

"Sure you're not, princess." They made it up the stairs and Will put her onto her bed. She pulled her jumper off. She thought for a second that she should brush her teeth but as it had been one of the first things she had done once she got home to get rid of the vile taste in her mouth and decided that the next lot of brushing could wait till morning.

Will came into the room. he had clearly just washed his face and brushed his teeth if the little droplets of water were anything to go by and he was dressed in sweat pants and a plain t-shirt.

"I'm staying in Leo's room, so if you need anything just shout out, okay?" She bit her lip.

"Will?" she asked before he had the chance to walk away.

"Yeah?"

"Can you lie with me? Just at least until I fall asleep. I'm scared if I sleep I'm going to dream about ... you know." She knew she sounded a little pathetic but her dreams had been bad enough lately. Will looked conflicted. He bit his lip but then he nodded.

"Sure, scoot over." She shuffled over to the side of the bed nearest the wall and he led down next to her.

"Thank you," she said, curling into him slightly. He sighed and put an arm around her. She moved her head so she was lying on his chest.

Just before she fell asleep she found herself wondering if his heart always beat that fast.

When she woke up the first thing she noticed was how she wasn't woken up in a drench of cold sweat like normal, then she realized that was because she hadn't had any nightmares. She couldn't remember dreaming at all, good or bad. Then something that wasn't her moved and her eyes shot open. She was facing the wall but there was a hard chest pressed against her back and an arm slung around her waist. She remembered that she had asked Will to stay with her until she had fallen asleep and she smiled to herself, realising that he must have fallen asleep too. The room was still dimly lit so she knew it was far too early to really be awake so she closed her eyes with a content smile and let the steady rhythm of the heart on her back and the breath on her neck lull her back to sleep.

When she woke again it must have been hours later as the room was filled with a dim sunlight that was straining to be seen through her dark curtains. She still felt the press of him against her but now she was facing him, her face buried in his neck and his arms wrapped tightly around her. One under her neck and one again wrapped around her waist. She breathed in deeply, letting herself enjoy the moment before real life came and ripped him away from her. As she pulled back slightly she felt Will pull her closer, trying to stop her from moving.

"Stop wriggling, I'm comfy," came a voice from above her head and she grinned again. His voice was heavy with sleep and she settled back in, wrapping her arm around his waist also. She would usually have been extremely embarrassed and nervous in a position like this, but it was Will. The person who, although annoying, she felt the most safe with, the one person who she knew would go to the ends of the earth to protect her. Her Nona and brother would too, of course but Will was just her friend, her neighbor. He didn't have to watch out for her like he does.

"You're thinking too loudly," he said again, his voice sounding slightly more awake, making her believe that she wasn't the only one who couldn't get back to sleep.

"I didn't have any nightmares last night, I thought I would..." He squeezed her slightly and she inched even closer.

"I am a human dreamcatcher," he said and she laughed. At the sound of her laugh Ruby decided it was time to be awake. She stood from her position led at the end of the bed and squeezed herself between them, forcing Ella out of the way and lying down, her head between theirs.

"I think someone wants breakfast," Ella said, stroking the dog's head.

"Good idea, I'm starving," Will said, rubbing his eyes. She laughed again and waited for him to get out of the bed. Then he gently nudged Ruby.

"Come on girl, breakfast time." Ruby jumped off of the bed in a bark and trotted out of the room.

"I'll be down in a sec," she said to Will who was making to follow Ruby. He nodded and followed the dog.

By the time she got downstairs, having brushed her teeth and changed, Will was flipping pancakes while on the phone and Ruby was eating out of her food bowl. There was a cup of tea already waiting on the kitchen table and he pointed to it with a spatula and mouthed at her to go and sit down. Doing what she was told for once, she was too tired to argue, she sipped on her tea. She watched him move effortlessly around the kitchen, wearing a joke apron that she had bought for Elena for Christmas one year that says "kiss me I'm Italian," flipping pancakes like this was the most normal thing in the world.

"That was Elena, there's no need to open the café today, she's called the guy from the shop next to it and he is putting a sign in the window for her."

"You don't have to babysit me you know," she said, biting her lip. She didn't want him to be here if he didn't want to. He sighed. He went to retrieve the tray with the stack of pancakes and the toppings and put it down on the table between them.

"Is that what you think this is? That I'm babysitting you?" She shrugged.

"I'm fine here alone if you have better things to

do." He stabbed a pancake onto his fork with more aggression than Ella thought was strictly necessary.

"You're an idiot sometimes." She glared at him and stabbed her own fork into the next pancake in the stack with equally as much force.

"That's just rude."

"I'm here because I want to be here. I'm here because you scared the shit out of me yesterday and being here looking at you reminds me that what almost happened didn't happen." He was staring directly into her eyes and she could feel the blush creeping up her neck.

"I'm here because if I take my eyes off of you I feel sick and I panic that I'm dreaming all of this and I didn't reach you in time." His voice wavered and it was this that made her put her fork down and stare at him back.

"Will..."

"I was terrified Ella, as terrified as I was that day at the lake. I saw your foot move about to walk out into that road. I thought I was going to lose you and the look on your face when you did it... will haunt me for the rest of my life." A tear rolled down her cheek and his eyes too looked watery.

"I didn't think you'd feel that way," she said, a little dumbfounded at his confession.

"Well, I do," he said.

"Thank you William, for saving my life. Again." His eyes squeezed shut at the sound of his full name and he let out a breath. She looked down and set about adding syrup to her pancakes. When she chanced a look up at him he was looking at her, watching her while she moved around the assortment of items he had placed on the tray. She smiled at him and he swallowed and smiled at her too. They ate their breakfast in silence and when they were done, they cleared up in silence too.

---

Mal walked into the café and Ella's head whipped up.

"Nona, can I go on my break now?" she asked. Elena nodded with a small smile on her face.

"Sure my love, the lunch rush is over, I can watch the counter."

"Thank you." She kissed her Nona on the cheek and pulled her apron off. She grabbed two bottles of diet coke from the fridge and went to join her best friend.

"Thanks," Mal said, taking the bottle she was offered and twisted off the lid.

"You okay?" Ella said, sitting down and appraising her friend. She looked stressed.

"I'm fine, just school." She shrugged.

"How's it going with your bar girl?" Mal's dark cheeks deepened in color and Ella took a moment to appreciate how truly beautiful her best friend was.

"Good. I mean, we've got passed the cocktail sex." Ella laughed and lifted her own bottle to her mouth, taking a long sip.

"It's hard, she's so gorgeous, everyone wants to speak to her, everyone wants to flirt with her. I feel like I'm wasting my time." Ella was surprised her friend sounded so downtrodden.

"So what you're telling me is, this really hot woman who gets offer after offer every night, ignores almost everyone but she engages in lewd conversations about cocktails with you and just so happens to appear when you walk into the bar. How exactly do you think you're wasting your time? Sounds like everyone else is," Ella said, looking confused. She watched as her friend worked out the truth of what she said and a grin spread across her wide, beautiful mouth. Ella grinned back triumphantly.

"So, Lucas turned out to be an ass, huh?" Ella nodded, swallowing.

"Major asshole. I haven't heard from him, even

when I text to tell him he's not welcome at my party tomorrow." Mal paused.

"You don't think he would just show up do you?"

"No, well he might, but he wouldn't get very far. I'm pretty sure Will would rip him apart." Mal grinned and Ella couldn't help but smile with her.

"Do you believe me now, that Will is totally into you?" Ella rolled her eyes.

"Maybe, I know he cares about me and I know he finds me attractive." She thought back to the incident in the living room a few days ago. What happened after had meant they'd never spoken about it but she couldn't help but let her mind wander to it. She had never been made to feel that way. Like she was truly desirable.

"Oh please!" Mal said quietly. "I'm pretty sure you could kick that man to the ground and he would thank you for it." Ella's eyes widened in warning and she looked around to make sure Elena hadn't heard but she was on the other side of the counter.

"My life was much simpler when I thought he looked at me like an annoying little sister," she admitted.

"Simpler maybe but don't tell me you're not enjoying every fucking minute of it," she teased and Ella grinned wickedly.

"Maybe just a little. But it's Will!" she said.

"Exactly, he's a walking masterpiece Ella, he could be a model and he's hot under the collar for you. Embrace it." Ella nodded.

"I am, it makes me feel sexy as hell." She blew out a breath. That was an understatement.

"But it's more than the attraction. Why do you think we've pushed each other away for so long? He's the one who could obliterate me into tiny pieces if I let him. You don't fall for guys like Will and come out with a happy ending." Mal rolled her eyes so hard that she looked truly annoyed.

"You don't see the way he looks at you when you're not looking. So, excited for your party?" she asked and Ella brightened up again.

"Very," she confirmed. It was going to be a standard party in a bar; nibbles, booze, dancefloor.

"Good, I'll be round yours by 5 to start getting ready, I think Blake and Sam said they would be meeting us at Phoenix later." She nodded.

"I'd better get back to work." She nodded towards the counter.

"I'm going to go on home anyway, I'll call you later." She hugged her friend and watched her walk out of the door.

# Chapter Sixteen

Elena had to leave before closing so Ella had locked the door behind the last patron and had moved to start cleaning up. She heard a knock on the door and turned. Someone must have left something behind. She unlocked and opened the door and stared out into an empty street. She looked up and down the street but there wasn't anyone there. She felt a slither of something like fear crawl up her spine and she closed the door and re-locked it, thinking she must have imagined it. She had almost finished cleaning up an hour later, the cash had been locked in the safe and she was gathering her stuff ready to leave when there was another knock on the door. This was a hammering on the door that made her freeze for a second.

"Ella?" she heard a voice calling through the door.

"Will?" she said, moving to the door to open it. It was Will who was standing in front of her but instead of his usual smirk, there was a grimace of pain across his face.

"Are you okay?" he asked her, looking her up and down.

"Yes I'm fine, but you look like shit!" she said, pulling him into the café gently.

"Thanks princess. Lock the door." She locked up behind him and turned to see him falling into a chair, a hand over his left side. He moved the hand and it was stained red. She went into auto pilot, moving behind the counter and pulling out the first aid kit.

"You should go to hospital," she said sitting on the chair opposite him.

"If you thought for a minute I would agree to that then you wouldn't have picked up that." He nodded a head towards the red box in her hands.

"It was worth a shot." She pulled the lid off of the box and pulled out the things she thought she would need.

"Well you're still an asshole so it can't be too bad. Shirt. Off." He let out a breathy chuckle.

"Didn't even offer to buy me dinner first." He grunted peeling the shirt away from the wound. He lifted it so far but couldn't get it any further without hissing in pain. She moved forward and helped him take his arm that was on the opposite side to his wound out of the arm hole. She lifted the rest over his head and down the arm that he was using to press his hand onto the wound. She got a wad of bandages and held them out to him. He lifted the hand from the wound long enough for her to pull the shirt down the arm and off completely and he pressed the wound with the bandage.

"What happened?" she asked. His jaw tensed and she predicted his answer before he gave it.

"Nothing for you to worry about."

"You're bleeding all over my cleanly mopped floor, I'd say I do have to worry about it."

"You're a menace woman." He moved the wad away again and the bleeding seemed to be slowing right down.

"Ready for me to clean it?" she asked.

"I can do it."

"William," she muttered and he huffed out a laugh.

"Fine." He lent back in the chair, his torso stretched and he moved his eyes to the ceiling. She opened the antiseptic wipe and got rid of most of the blood, the size of the wound was small, considering the amount of blood. He hissed when she got closer to the opening.

"I know, I'm sorry," she whispered gently. She was bent forward concentrating on his skin, it would take a couple of paper stitches to hold it closed so she moved backwards to root through the box. She caught his eye as she moved back. He was staring at her.

"It's gonna scar," she said, moving back to him with the paper stitches in hand.

"I know," he said quietly. She thought he probably didn't care, his tanned skin was littered with the pale lines that she tried not to think about.

She applied the bandage over the stitches and moved to stand, ready to clear away the rest of the blood and bandages. She felt a hand on her arm and she looked down into his handsome face.

"Thank you." She nodded and set about clearing away. When she was finished she held the trash can in front of him. He was looking at his white t-shirt with a sad pout.

"This is why I usually wear black." He tossed the shirt into the garbage and took the zip up sweat shirt she held out to him. It was one of his that he'd left behind at the café a little while ago. He grinned.

"Why does this smell like you?" he asked, pulling it

gingerly over his arms without moving himself too much.

"It's comfy," she said, giving him a glare. "And maybe instead of just wearing black, you could try not getting stabbed." He bit his lip, fighting a grin.

"What would be the fun in that?"

"You're a psychopath," she said moving forward. She pulled the zip carefully up, stopping halfway up his chest.

"You're not complaining," he said, grinning down at her.

"Why are you here?"

"I thought that would be obvious, I wanted to play Doctors and Nurses," he said, pushing a large hand into her hair.

"I should have left you to bleed out in the rain."

"Don't be cruel, princess." She'd moved closer to him without really realising what she was doing. "It does wicked things to me." She chuckled and brushed her thumb over his jaw. His golden hazel eyes met her steel grey ones and then they broke apart, both jumping with the sound of his cell phone ringing from his jean pocket. He grunted, the shock of jumping had jarred his wound and he answered the phone with a growl.

Ella couldn't stop her grin as she walked behind

the counter to collect her bag, making sure everything was switched off. By the time she was ready to leave he was off the phone.

"I'm walking you home." She rolled her eyes.

"You're the one with a knack for getting stabbed. I think you'll find I'm walking you home." He glared at her walking out of the door and waiting for her to lock up. The moment she turned he threw an arm around her shoulder, the one on the opposite side to his injury and they started to walk.

***

They'd been only a few streets away from home when the heavens had truly opened. They were in the rain for only seconds before Will had tugged her into a closed doorway.

"We're almost home!" she countered.

"Give it a few minutes. It'll settle down." They were very close together, his skin was glistening with the rain and his wet hair fell in front of his eyes. He pushed it back with a hand.

"Any excuse to pull me into a dark corner huh," she said and he looked down at her.

"I don't need an excuse princess. We both know you enjoy these cozy little moments just as much as I do." She was pulling a hair band out of her pocket and pulling her wet, bedraggled hair into a ponytail. He stopped her.

"Stop." Her hands stilled.

"Why?"

"I like your hair when it's down." He ran a hand up her spine, pushing it into her wet hair. Gripping it lightly, his calloused fingers scraped slightly on her scalp and she let out a little whine that she wasn't sure she could repeat if she tried.

"Will." She let out a warning and he chuckled somewhere near her ear.

"What's the matter princess?" She made another little noise. "C'mon, use your big words."

He moved his face closer and closer and then he went deathly still. His hand in her hair loosened.

"Stay here," he told her as he moved out into the rain.

"What the fuck?" she hissed after him.

"Stay. There." He sounded so terrified that she didn't argue. She slunk further back into the shadows of the doorway when a man approached Will.

# CHAPTER SEVENTEEN

"Where is she William?" The man seemed to be bald, broad shouldered and older than them by at least a decade.

"You're not going to get to her before it happens. You may as well crawl back into the hole that you came out of and go back to the drawing board." He took a fighting stance and Ella noticed at least four people start to encircle him.

"Lucas may have failed, but the time for tricks and mind games are up. I have my best soldiers looking for her and you're never far away, like the faithful lap dog you are so where is she hidden?" He looked around, past where she was hidden twice. She felt a hand cover her mouth. She was about to scream when a familiar voice whispered into her ear.

"It's Sam, don't make a sound, don't move." She nodded and he moved his hand but continued to pull her against him. There was a crash like a thunderbolt and Blake appeared next to Will, as though he had just fallen from the sky. Ella had no idea what was going on or what these people were talking about but she couldn't tear her eyes away.

"She's not here," Blake growled at the man.

"Get lost newbie, I'm talking to Rover over here." He nodded to Will but Blake pulled a huge sword from his back and the man looked a little wary for the first time.

"Which one of my boys got you Rover?" he asked Will, gesturing to his side.

"I didn't catch their name before I ripped them limb from limb," he said with a feral curl of his lip.

One of the men moved towards Will and Ella had to fight all of her instincts to stop herself from crying out to him but he had whirled around and thrust a hand into the man's face. He stumbled back and gave a roar of pain. Will thrust his hands into the man's mouth. Sam was trying to pull Ella away so she couldn't see but she pushed him away.

With one hand on his bottom jaw and the other on his top jaw, Will pulled the man closer to him, pressed him down to his knees and then ripped in opposite directions. Ella felt a scream rise in her but it didn't come out. The man had fallen to the ground almost completely split in half but by the time he had reached the floor, he had completely turned to embers and ashes, flying up into the wind.

Ella turned to Sam. "What the fuck is going on," she hissed at him and Sam shook his head.

"Later." Ella wanted to scream at him but she nodded. Her friends were still in danger from whatever the fuck was happening out there. As they'd been talking Blake had taken on the other three men, his sword glinting in the dark was thrust through the chest of one man who turned to ashes a moment later and he swung it up and around to chop the head of another approaching him from behind. Ella's mouth was bone dry, these were her friends, they were ripping people apart, appearing out of nowhere. These people they were *killing* were turning into ash before her eyes.

Will had stalked towards the bald man.

"I know you're not the top of the food chain. Who is doing this?" Will demanded, almost nose to nose with the man.

"As if you don't already know."

"Dominic." The man smiled.

"Of course, I'm only one of many soldiers that he has working for him. There is going to be a war,

William. Would you like me to send a message to my boss? Maybe how the pretty little thing is standing in that doorway with the angel of solace?" Will straightened.

"If I need to send a message to your boss, it will be this." He stepped slightly closer, eyes full of dark promise. "Anyone who touches a hair on her head will die the same painful way you did." The man smiled for half a second and then his eyes widened as black blood pooled at the edge of his twisted smile. There was a sound that Ella could not bear to hear, it sounded like the tearing of muscle and flesh. Will turned and held what was unmistakably a spine in his hand. His fist closed as the body behind him crumpled to the floor and both the body and mass of bones and nerves in his hand both turned to ash.

Will's eyes found Ella's in the dark and she did not recognize the stare that bore into her. She had seen Will angry before but he was murderous with rage.

"Will," Blake said, moving towards him but he held up the hand that was still covered in black blood and Blake stopped.

"Is it clear?" he asked and Blake nodded. "Leo is searching the skies but there's nothing else here that I can detect." He paused but he seemed unable to stop himself. "What the fuck were you thinking coming out here with no fucking weapons?" Will turned to him. The rain had settled to a light shower and it was helping to wash the black blood away from both of their hands and faces.

"It's not like I needed them," he snarled back at him, no gold in his eyes now.

"No but you were injured in the first fight. You should have called us in sooner."

"Don't tell me how to do my job." Sam took her hand and pulled her out of the doorway.

"That's enough," Sam said looking at Blake as he looked as though he was going to argue.

"Are you okay?" Blake asked Ella instead. She was staring at Will.

"Explain. Now," she demanded but it was Sam who spoke.

"Not here."

"You two get Leo and get back to the house. Tell Elena."

"If there's more of them..." Blake said.

"Then kill them. That's *your* job, remember?"

"Stop being an ass," Sam said rolling his eyes. "She's safe and you two butting heads isn't helping anyone. I will get Leo and tell him to go home and then Blake and I will patrol the rest of the way, making sure there's nothing on the way. Then once we are home all of us will speak to Ella." Sam had a finality in his voice that no one seemed to want to argue with. Except Ella, apparently.

"If you idiots think I'm taking another fucking step without being told what the fuck is going on here then you're deluded." She rounded on Will. "They were after me by the sounds of it and right now I am angry enough to rip off all of your heads so..." There was another crash and Leo appeared in front of her. She took a step backwards. Her brother seemed larger than usual, like there was a presence around him.

"Not here Ella." She had meant to argue but she closed her mouth. His voice sounded not of this world. It was low and gritty, it had a resonance behind it that suggested an echo but there was nothing around them to cause the reverberation but what made her truly stop was his eyes. They glowed a color that should not have been there in his ocean blue eyes. Oranges and reds danced around his black pupils and she had never seen anything like it. It looked like hell fire.

"Not here," he repeated. Ella faltered. He pulled her against him in a hug and she wrapped her arms around him too. They broke apart after a second he nodded to Sam and shot into the sky.

Ella felt dizzy. She didn't notice that Sam and Blake had disappeared until Will was stood in front of her. She looked up at him and couldn't bring herself to get angry. He looked terrified. He placed his thankfully now clean hands on either side of her face, inspecting every inch of her. Knowing what he was doing she sighed.

"I'm okay." He shushed her and she shot him an incredulous look that he completely ignored. He didn't move and she went to speak again.

"I really need–" His mouth was on hers before she could finish her sentence. It turned out that what she really needed was his lips on hers. She pulled him closer and opened her mouth, meeting the kiss with as much enthusiasm as he gave her. This kiss was a desperate, needy kiss, he needed to make sure that she was here and she wasn't hurt. She took hold of one of his hands and placed it on her chest so that he could feel her pounding heart. He broke the kiss and rested his forehead against hers, staring down at his hand.

"Take me home," she whispered and he nodded. He moved back and took his hand away from her chest, the place where it had lay feeling instantly ice cold. He wrapped his hand around hers and they walked quickly and silently back to the house.

The house was quiet when they entered. Not even Ruby came bounding into the hall to greet them. Will closed the door behind her and pointed to the kitchen.

"They're in there," he said, his voice empty and hollow. She strode towards the kitchen but Elena came into the hall before she could reach it.

"Go and get changed and dried off first. Both of you." Her arms were crossed and Ella knew better than to challenge her, even if all she wanted was answers, she didn't care that she was freezing cold.

"There's clean, warm clothes for both of you on Ella's bed," she said to Will and nodded to the stairs.

"Thank you," he said numbly and Ella felt him follow her up the stairs.

She threw her bag with probably unnecessary force on the floor and grabbed the pile of clothes meant for her on the bed, passing Will his.

"You can use the bathroom," she said quickly. He nodded, took the clothes and disappeared into the room. She pulled off her wet clothes and threw them into her hamper. Pulling the soft underwear and sports bra on she was trying to think about nothing that happened that evening. Not even the fucking kiss. She failed miserably, pulling on the leggings, thinking about the heat of his mouth on hers she jumped.

"Are you decent?" he asked and she laughed, she couldn't help herself. She wasn't thinking very decent thoughts right now.

"Yeah." She hadn't pulled her jumper on yet but she didn't want to until her hair was brushed and up. He walked into the room as she was attacking her hair with a brush. He rolled his eyes and came to stand behind her.

"You're gonna rip your hair out you psycho." He held his hand out and she handed the brush over to him.

"Why does this feel familiar to me?" she said quietly. He was braiding her hair.

"Because I've done this before, you just can't remember it." She stiffened.

"Why don't I remember it?" He sighed.

"Because of Lucas. It'll be easier to explain this later, after you've spoken to everyone else." There was pain in his voice that made her heart squeeze uncomfortably.

"What else have I forgotten?" He sighed and she looked at him in the mirror. His eyes were shining as he fixed the end of the braid with a hair tie.

She stood and turned around to face him.

"Will..." She reached out for him but he took a step back.

"Don't." His voice wavered and she grimaced.

"Please," she said, her voice breaking a little as she went to him and dragged him so that he was sitting next to her on her bed.

"They're waiting for us," He said, gulping.

"They can wait," she snarled and he gave her a weary smile, stroking a thumb across her cheek.

"You might not like me very much. After this conversation," he breathed into the dark. They hadn't bothered to turn the light on.

"You just ripped a man in half to protect me," she said and he let out a barking laugh.

"It's my job."

"Oh," she said, moving back slightly but he put a hand on her face to stop her.

"It's my job and a fucking privilege Ella. I get to defend the person that means the most to me in the world, I get to rip anyone who even threatens her into shreds and get told I'm doing a good job because of it." She sucked in a breath but he kept talking. "I was made to protect you, I was bonded to you to know when you were in danger or in pain but I was not forced to feel about you the way that I do." She felt far too hot considering she had been out in the freezing cold less than an hour ago.

"Before you hear the conversation downstairs I

need you to know that I did everything I had to do to protect you. All of the fights and pushing you away was to keep you out of harm's way. You won't like some of the things I did Ella, but I had no other choice." Her mind was racing. She stood. He still sat at the edge of her bed, watching her.

"Did you have to push me away for so long? Did you have to make me feel like I meant nothing to you?" She swallowed back the burning in her throat. He closed his eyes.

"I did what I thought was best. Do you think it's been easy? Every time you challenged me with that stupid glint in your eyes, you think I didn't want to drag you up here? When I see you master your emotions or do something so inexplicably brave, do you think I don't want to just walk right over and kiss your stupid—" She moved and launched herself into his lap and smothered the end of his sentence with her mouth. She needed to be as close to him as physically possible. Their tongues clashed and teeth snapped, fingers clawing at each other's skin. She felt as though if she stopped kissing him she would fall apart completely. He was the glue holding all of her confusion and emotions together. Their kisses slowed until finally they broke apart.

"We need to go and have the conversation Ella. You

may not want to do this after it." She let out a sob and he wrapped his arms around her.

"Then I don't want that conversation." He shuddered a breath loose and ran a soothing hand along her back.

"You need to. Just remember everything I did was for you. Some things I did because it was my job, some things I did just to keep you safe and happy. Even if you hate me for it. It was worth it cause it means you're here, safe." She kissed him on the mouth again.

"I'm not going to hate you. I'm expecting to be so fucking pissed at all of you but I spent half of my life being pissed with you." He smiled and kissed her forehead.

"Time to go princess." She sat in his lap for another minute, wondering what would happen if she simply refused to move. He stood up with her still clinging to him and he laughed.

"I can carry you into the kitchen like this if you really want me to." She huffed and slid herself down his body. He hissed.

"Sorry," she said, her hand going to the wound on his side.

"Huh? Oh that's gone." Her eyes widened. She pulled his shirt up and she barely noticed when he said "Easy tiger." She gently pulled the bandage away and sure enough the paper stitches fell away, the wound was completely healed. A red line was in its place that would no doubt turn to a silver scar in a few hours.

"So why did you make that noise? And why did you let me patch you up!" she hissed indignantly, ripping the rest of the bandage off with a lot less care.

"Fuck," he said as she pulled. "Because I had the girl I've wanted for longer than I cared to admit sliding down my body like a god damn stripper on a pole. I'm a guy for fuck sake and I let you patch me up because you looked so concerned and at the time, it fucking hurt." She rolled her eyes at him but couldn't help a grin.

"If we don't get down to that kitchen soon, they're gonna come in here looking for us," she said, smirking because he looked like he was about to throw her on the bed, conversation be damned. He huffed in annoyance but nodded.

"After you princess." She strode past him and out of the door.

# CHAPTER EIGHTEEN

When they entered the kitchen Will went and stood next to the counter and Ella sat next to Leo on the bench at the table. Leo had his head in his hands.

"Leo," she said gently and he looked at her. Tears were swimming in his thankfully ocean blue eyes.

"I'm sorry if I scared you Ella," he said, a tear escaping and she threw her arms around him. He wrapped his arms around her and shook into her shoulder. She gripped him as tight as she could. Elena was preparing tea and the hall clock chimed midnight. It was like they'd all been waiting for it. Leo pulled back, wiping a hand cross his cheeks. Everyone squeezed in around the table except Will who had hopped up onto the counter facing them.

It was Elena that spoke first. "This isn't going to be very easy to hear Ella, your instinct will be to go against what we're telling you, to tell you that it's not logical, that it can't physically be possible but if you listen carefully and fully, you'll see that this isn't a trick or a prank. I need you to understand this Ella, to fight those instincts." She nodded.

"Nona, I just saw Will rip out a man's spine and tear another one in half for them to disappear into ashes. I think my instincts are already fucked." She frowned at her granddaughter's use of the curse word but didn't say anything.

"Ella, angels are real." Ella sighed. She had heard the man mention an angel of solace and she worked out that he had been talking about Sam. Elena continued.

"I am one, everyone in this room is one, including you." Ella looked around the room. Ruby who was sitting under the table placed her head in her lap, asking her nicely to stay and hear the conversation.

"Right, okay. I mean, yeah. I mean, what?" Leo smiled a little and Elena gave him a stern look. He shrugged and folded his hands in front of him. She carried on.

"There are different kinds of angels and they live all over the world. We have more in Elk Grove because this is where the portal to Astridia is. There's a few others all over the world bu–" Elena was interrupted.

"I'm sorry, a PORTAL? To WHERE?" Ella asked. It felt as though someone kept pulling the seat from under her.

"Astridia is the place where a lot of the angel population live. You can only get there through a portal and there are only 20 over the world." Her head felt like it was going to explode.

"Elena, maybe you should explain the most important part next, before she spontaneously combusts?" Sam asked, looking at his friend with a worried expression.

"There are many different kinds of angels but usually someone will get the choice to accept their angel gifts, if they choose not to, they will lose any memory of the angel world and will continue to be human. I'm sorry Ella, you do not have that choice." Ella's head snapped up then.

"Why would I not have a choice?"

"You are the Guardian of the Gate. You are here to protect the portal in Illinois. I was a Guardian of the Gate. As was your mother." Ella's hand went absentmindedly to her chest at the twinge of pain she felt cutting into her chest.

"Mom was one?" Tears stung at her eyes but she

held them back. "Is that why she died?" Her voice was shaking but it was loud. Leo reached and held her hand.

"Yes," Elena choked out. She couldn't stop the tears that started to stream down her cheeks.

"Someone murdered my mother to try and get into some different world?" she all but whispered. A tear splashed on her hand that didn't belong to her and she looked at her brother who had tearstained cheeks too. She squeezed his hand.

"And now you want me to do the same thing that got her killed?"

"We don't want you to do anything, it's not about wanting, it's about what we can and can't do. I'm sorry Ella but you can't refuse this," Will said from his perch on the counter.

"Watch me," she bit at him.

"Do you think that everyone around this table wishes it wasn't the case, that it had to be you?" he spat back.

"Do you know how hard it has been for Leo and Elena to know that you were going to have to shoulder this burden? They know it's not fair that you don't get a choice and the rest of us do." Ella chanced a look at him and regretted it. There was pain and anger written all over it like an open book.

"Who killed her?" she asked Elena.

"Dominic Quinn. We don't know if he killed her himself or had someone else do it." She wasn't sure what she had expected from her grandma, she should have known her well enough to know that if she knew the answer she would tell her without sugar coating it. She remembered hearing the name Dominic earlier this evening.

"Why did he do it?" she followed immediately.

"Ella, I will explain everything that happened with Dominic and your mother but right now I need to explain more about the Angels and what we do." Ella completely ignored her.

"Where is he now?" She heard Will sigh.

"We can tell her the quick version now Elena, she's got months of training ahead of her to learn everything else." Ella's eyebrows rose at that.

"Training?" It was Sam who answered her.

"As the Guardian of the Gate, you need to be trained in different areas. Most angels have one or two areas of expertise. You'll need to be trained in hand to hand combat, weapons, healing, magic, magic defenses and that's just the ones I can think of off the top of my head." Ella looked at the boy who she thought she knew so well.

"Is this why you're so good at reading people?" Blake shuffled in his seat as Sam nodded.

"That is one of my... gifts, yes." Ella was processing the new information a lot quicker but she hadn't forgotten what Will had said.

"Can I please have the cliff notes version of what happened to Mom and then I promise I'll hear whatever you have to say about anything else." She looked at her Nona who simply nodded.

"Your mom and Tobias were very good at their jobs. Yet somehow, Dominic managed to get past all of the defenses around the house. Dominic is a fallen angel. He fell a few months before it all happened. When an angel falls, they try to keep hold of their angelic powers but we can usually separate the most dangerous of them." Ella nodded as if she had any idea what she was talking about but she would save her questions about fallen angels until later. She did not want to get side-tracked from the details of her mom's death again.

"We still don't know how he managed it but he, or one of his minions got into the Nerium in Astridia, this is a prison that we put angels who attempt to fall but get caught or we keep the powers that we manage to extract as an angel falls. He got into Nerium and stole back all of his powers, he even stole some powers that don't belong to him so he is incredibly powerful."

"Do you know where he is now?" Ella asked, the feeling in her stomach getting heavier and heavier with every answered question.

"Ella," Leo said, looking at Elena then back to Ella. "It's not just angels that are real." Her eyebrows furrowed again and he went on.

"When an angel falls instead of descends it drives them mad."

"Descends?" Elena clarified this for her.

"If you decide you no longer want to be an angel and choose to become mortal instead." Ella's head was spinning again but she encouraged her brother to continue with a wave of her hand.

"So if an angel falls, he can be sent insane with the angelic powers they still have trying to rebel against what they're doing, whatever it was that made them fall. There's only two ways to stop the madness. You either give up your powers and become mortal again." Something about that sentence triggered a thought for Ella.

"Mortal? Are angels not mortal?" Sam gave a little chuckle.

"We're not immortal, but we age a hell of a lot

slower than humans." She was starting to feel a little sick now.

"Or..." Leo said, bringing himself back into the conversation. "They can steal a witch's power and turn themselves into a demon."

"A demon? Are you telling me that the person who murdered Mom is a demon?" she said with her mouth so dry she swiped her mug from the table and took a long sip.

"Yes. Different angels turn into different demons but Dominic is something completely different. He stole so many different angels powers from the Nerium, he is now the most powerful demon that has ever lived."

"Great. He killed mom when he was a fallen angel who was a bit crazy. Now he is the most powerful demon to ever live and I have to fight him off?" Will growled.

"He has no reason to come after you himself. He can't get into Astridia even if he did fight his way through it. He's not an angel anymore. Demons who attempt to cross through the portal are eviscerated," he explained.

"Well, at least there's that," she muttered to herself and she saw Blake give her a grin.

"So we have no idea what he's up to now?" Sam

and Blake looked at each other and then at Will and Leo.

"Actually," Sam started. "I think we do. They all want to get to you before you go through your gifting ceremony. They've tried a bunch of things over the last few years that we've managed to hide from you. But there's one that we didn't. Lucas, he is a fallen angel." She clenched her fist. After what she had heard and what Will had told her she assumed that Lucas wasn't good.

"What?"

"He's a fallen angel, probably sent by Dominic to worm his way into your life to sabotage your gifting or trying to find a way into the portal to steal more angel powers to give to Dominic and his soldiers." Ella was definitely feeling sick now.

"Of course he didn't actually want to be with me," she muttered and she saw Will stiffen.

"Don't do this to yourself short stack," Blake said. "You weren't to know, you don't know what his orders were if he was supposed to seduce you or harm you. Either way he showed his true colors that last time you saw him, it was the madness taking hold of him. He would have needed to descend or turn into a demon by now." Blake looked straight into her eyes and she nodded.

"So why was I drawn to him? That day after..." Her eyes flicked to Will.

"He's used a number of different tactics to try and get you under his control. We believe there was an angel of fortune working on his side that caused you to do what you did that day," Elena said.

"So, are all demons evil?" she asked. She thought it was a dumb question because obviously they were evil, they're demons.

"Weirdly enough," Will said who had seemed to be relaxed again. "No. A lot of demons just didn't want to be crazy but didn't want to give up their powers. There are a few who are loyal to Dominic who fell and turned demon for him but there are those who after the turn... you have to kill a witch a turn into a demon. After they do that and turn they never harm another human again. They like to play with humans but they won't usually hurt them and they definitely won't kill them. If they do, they are free game for the angels of mercy to hunt and slaughter them." Ella's eyes widened.

"Witches? Hold up, what's an angel of mercy?" Elena smiled.

"Ella, you're going to have questions. Lots of them and we can sit here all night and talk till the sun rises but there's too much to go into. You'll need to learn as you go." Ella sagged a little.

"I thought my education would finish with senior year," she grumbled and Leo laughed.

"Where's Mal?" she asked suddenly, realising who was there. Sam and Blake looked at each other. Mal had turned twenty-one the previous month.

"She wasn't chosen Ella," Sam said cautiously. "Not everyone is offered the gifts of the angels." She chewed on her lip for a second. His eyes met Elena's and she nodded.

"Mal comes from a long line of witches. Her grandmother has been the one to help this family for years. Her daughter, Mal's mom refused to use her powers and she refused Magda from telling and training Mal. Mal knows nothing of the angel world or that she is a witch and her mother has explicitly asked us to keep it that way."

Ella's hand clasped over her mouth to cover her gasp. She couldn't tell Mal. The one person in her life who she always told everything to and she wasn't allowed to tell her the most life changing thing that had ever or would ever happen to her.

# CHAPTER NINETEEN

E lla had removed herself from the table and went to the bathroom. She stood at the mirror and looked at her own pale face. Her thoughts strayed to Will. What kind of angel was he? She didn't know what to make of all of the information that she had been given so far. Why did it seem like Sam was some sort of authority? Blake had only turned twenty-one a few months before her. Is this why he and Sam fell out? What kind of angel was Sam? And Blake? Leo? Her heart was racing. What kind of angels are there? She thought back to the conversation about demons. Witches are real? And to become a demon you have to kill them and steal their power? And then she thought about Dominic and her blood began to boil under her skin. The most powerful demon there has ever been and he sent people after her. How did Sam know that he was a fallen angel? She would need to ask him that. There was a soft knock at the door followed by a voice.

"Ella?" It was Blake's voice. She opened the door and he squeezed almost comically into the bathroom. He sat down on the closed lid of the toilet and looked at her.

"I know you're freaking out, I bet your head's a mess of questions." She nodded.

"I was the same, I got angry with Sam when he told me and I ignored him for a few days and it was the worst thing I could have done. I almost sent myself crazy having all these questions and not asking them. So ask me any question you have that you might think sounds dumb." He looked at her expectantly.

"What happened with you and Sam? Why did you fight?" Blake rolled his eyes.

"I'm offering you enlightenment and you go for gossip?" he asked and she flipped him off.

"Answer the question."

"Fine, I found out why Sam came into my life. After my parents died and I went completely off the rails, I was fighting and drinking." Ella winced and the casualness of his tone but she remembered the time vividly. Blake had been an absolute mess. She hated seeing him go through that, her and Mal had tried everything they could to help him but he just wanted to be left alone to wallow in self-pity and hit the self-destruct button.

"Then Sam showed up and he helped me. I listened to him when I didn't listen to anyone else. If I wanted to start a fight, all it would take was a look from Sam and I'd rethink my decision. He centred me. So as you can imagine, after being friends for all these years, I get told that he was an angel and it was literally his job to get me back on the straight and narrow." He laughed to himself at the pun and Ella couldn't help smiling.

"He said that to you?"

"You know Sam, straight to the point." He shrugged. "Also, he is not twenty-one," he added and her mouth fell open with a comical pop.

"What?" she squealed.

"They told you angels age different. He's twenty-eight years old." Ella's head was spinning again and she braced her hands on the counter top behind her.

"It must suck," she said looking at her friend earnestly. "That the guy you're in love with was sent to you as part of his job." Blake chuckled but it didn't sound very cheerful.

"Why do I think you're trying to deflect this about you and Will?" She shot him a warning look.

"How long have you known?" he asked.

"Since the first day when you saw him punch Barnes in the face, the look on your face. You were a goner." He really did laugh this time.

"Well, sorry to disappoint you Ells but Sam doesn't feel the same way about me. We're just friends. When I got over myself and we made friends again, he was the one to help me train." Ella nodded.

"What kind of angel are you?" she asked. She didn't know angel etiquette yet. Was it considered rude to ask someone what type they were?

"I'm an angel of mercy." She looked at him blankly and he sighed. "I'm a soldier. I'd be on the front lines in a battle. I get sent to deal with demons that have overstepped the line and killed a mortal." Her eyes widened.

"That's dangerous. Blake!" she scolded him.

"You don't get to choose what you are Ella." He laughed at her look of incredulity.

"I'm big and strong and emotionally equipped to deal with death. I have already killed demons Ells. I struggled at first because at one point they were an angel just the same as you or me but then I think back to few months ago when none of us were angels and I think what if it was Mal that they'd killed? I got over my guilt pretty quickly once I started using that sort of logic," he said and Ella had felt a flare of rage at the mention of Mal being anyway hurt let alone...

"But I won't go through all the rest of the different types. We can save that for your training." Ella nodded.

"Hey, Blake?" she asked as he stood from the toilet, looking much too large in the small downstairs bathroom.

"Yeah?"

"Our lives are weird." He laughed.

"Yep, and this is just the beginning of it."

When she re-joined the kitchen Elena and Will were stood at the counter talking and Sam and Leo had gotten the cards out and were playing go fish.

Ella sat down beside Sam and he put his arm around her, hugging her into his side. She paused for a second.

"So you're really old, huh?" He laughed and squeezed her.

"I'm not that old." He sulked.

"No, you're just practically angelic royalty," Leo said, who was losing at the card game if the look on his face was anything to go by.

"What!" Ella said.

"My family goes way back to the first head of the

Order, a lot of my ancestors have become head of the Order. I grew up in Astridia so I knew all about angels before my twenty-first birthday, that rule only applies to angels living in the mortal realm." Ella was gaping at him and he gave a dazzling smile and continued.

"I still had to wait till I was twenty-one to be offered my gifts though, and I could have turned them down but it's very unlikely for an Astridian raised child to deny their gifts and even less likely if they're in my family." He threw his last pair down on the table in triumph and Leo poked his tongue out at him and stood, wandering over to Elena and Will.

"And besides, I may be royalty, but it's Will who has got the special gifts." Ella looked up to Will who was watching her with his arms crossed. He sighed and sat next to her at the bench. Their legs touched and she felt a huge relief flood over her.

"My gifts came to me at nine years old," he said without pre-amble. "They didn't know why until a few months later when your mom was killed. They realized that the new Guardian of the Gate would be a child so they sent me and Dad. We would guard the portal while you waited for your twenty-first birthday and I was given every gift that was possible to give an angel, trained up to be the best and within a year we'd moved here. My job to protect you started at age ten

Ella." She was staring at him and her mind had gone blank. She struggled to think of the question that she wanted to ask.

"So, you've had no choice but to look out for me for the last thirteen years?" He nodded. "How can you even stand the sight of me?" He laughed then, loudly.

"What did I tell you earlier princess? It's a job and a privilege." She felt the blush creep up her neck.

"That's no life for anyone. Will, I'm so sorry." He shook his head.

"Don't. There hasn't been a single moment where I wished my life had gone any differently." He paused. "Except when I had to made shitty decisions for you, because you didn't have the knowledge to be able to make them for yourself. Me being an overbearing asshole and telling you what to do wasn't because I didn't think you could choose for yourself. I just couldn't give you all of the information you needed to make it." She nodded her head.

"I get it, if I had known how much danger I was in I wouldn't have fought you so much on it."

"And we both know how much of a shame that would have been." He winked at her and she rolled her eyes. She turned back to Sam who released her and she found herself falling backwards slightly into the arms of Will. She felt exhausted.

"So what was it like living there?" Ella asked.

"The place is beautiful Ella, you'll love it. There's plants, flowers, trees and grass everywhere, but I spent most of my childhood training."

"Training?"

"Yeah, my dad is one of the schools best teachers in hand to hand combat and weapons. Even though I didn't get my powers until I was twenty-one, I was training from the age of six." He shrugged, as if this was of no importance whatsoever.

"Can I ask you, what kind of angel you are? I heard that guy say angel of solace?" she said hesitantly.

"Oh sure, yeah, kinda like a guardian angel, we help steer people in the right direction. You know, once we get your gifting ceremony done and your training started, you won't need to ask. You'll be able to tell by the wings."

"Oh really? That's cool, I didn't know if it was– wait a minute..." The room watched her process what Sam had just said.

"You know, you're taking all of this better than we did," Leo said pointing between himself and Blake.

There was a stiffness in his shoulders that made her think that she should wait until she was one on one with her brother to ask him about his experience. Then her brain caught up to the conversation.

"What do you mean I'll be able to tell by the wings? WE HAVE WINGS?" She felt Will's shaking laughter behind her and she felt a kiss pressed into her temple. She flushed red and sighed.

"Ella, I think you should go and get some rest, we can talk more tomorrow. Your gifting ceremony will be the day after your party." She nodded.

"Will?" she asked as the rest of them set about clearing the table and Sam and Blake stood to leave.

"Can you... stay with me tonight?" He nodded and she smiled. He stood to let her out and she stood on shaky legs. She hugged Sam and Blake and watched them leave. Then her Nona kissed her goodnight.

"I'm so proud of you Marcella," she said with watery eyes.

"I love you Nona," she said as he watched the older woman climb the stairs.

"I assume you're staying with Ella tonight?" Leo asked his friend. She felt her ears burning as he nodded.

"I'm going to stay at the apartment."

"You okay?" Will asked, his hand on his arm.

"Yeah," he spoke to Ella. "I'll be round in the morning with your gifts. Happy birthday short stack." He squeezed her gently and she hugged him back.

"Love you," she said quietly.

"Love you too, sis." He nodded to Will and he left.

Her head was spinning with information and worry for her brother. Will seemed to sense her panic and steadied her.

"Come on princess." He turned and crouched in front of her. "Hop on." She laughed and climbed up onto his back. She clung to him as he moved through the house, pressing quiet laughs into his neck. When they got to her room he crouched and she climbed off.

He turned to face her and smiled at her.

"Happy birthday Ella."

# CHAPTER
# TWENTY

"Do you want your present?" Her head whipped to face his.

"You already got me a present?" she pointed out, eyes narrowing. "A very expensive present." His smile widened at the look of incredulity on her face.

"I'll be back in a few minutes." He pressed a kiss to the top of her hair and disappeared. She sighed, watching him go and she pressed a hand to her mouth. She had so many questions rolling around in her head that she couldn't put them in any semblance of an order. Her exhaustion rolled over her and she sat on the edge of her bed. Ruby had clambered up onto the bed behind her. She hadn't heard Will come back into the room. All she felt was someone pushing her knees apart and a large warm body fitting between then.

"You okay?" he asked, pushing her hair away from her face. She nodded.

"I have so many questions but I can't even start to think about them." He nodded.

"It's gonna take you a few days for it all to sink in and for you to get used to what the fuck is going on, then after your gifting ceremony... You're gonna need about a week to deal with everything that comes with that," he muttered. Her eyes found his.

"I'm scared," she admitted.

"I know sweetheart."

"You said something earlier, about being bonded to you... what does that mean?"

"Before your gifting ceremony, so since I moved in next door, to now, Magda bound my soul to yours." Her eyes widened. "So that I knew when you were in danger, or when you're feeling scared or worried. So that I would be able to know exactly where you are and get there in time." He swallowed.

"That's why it was always you who saved me." He nodded.

"Do I feel this... bond?" He shook his head. "But you do?" He paused.

"Kinda. It only really kicks in when you're in

219

danger or scared." She nodded. This must be the reason he felt about her the way that he did. It was his job to protect her and he had to be around her all of the time. She had made up most of the last thirteen years of his life.

"But after your gifting ceremony that bond will be broken." Her eyes whipped up and took in his handsome features that were twisted in pain.

"Does that mean... will you not need to protect me anymore?"

"I'm still your angel of armour princess. I'll still be the one to protect you and help you protect yourself." She let out the breath she had been holding.

"But you won't be able to feel me in danger or anything anymore?" He shook his head.

"Unless you accept my birthday gift." Her eyebrows knitted together in confusion. He pulled a velvet box from his pocket and handed it to her.

"Open it," he whispered. His voice was calm but his hands shook. She took the box from him and prized it open. On a black velvet cushion she saw a silver necklace. It was like a silver cage around a clear sphere. She looked up at him and he was staring at her face.

"When you get your gifts..." He swallowed. She couldn't pull her eyes away from his face. "The bond will be removed. You'll remember everything that we needed to hide from you. Once you get your gifts, the only way we can be bonded is if we agree to a bonding ceremony. The magic that binds us together will live in this necklace." He nodded towards the box in her hands. "You have one and I will have one." She swallowed.

"Will, I..."

"Just so you know, I won't hold it against you if you choose not to be bonded with me. It doesn't mean like we're married or anything, it's nothing to do with how we feel about each other. It means that we're true partners. We trust each other with our lives. Instead of me being bonded to protect you, we will both be bonded. To protect each other. Only a few Guardians of the Gate have ever bonded with their angel of armour once they were gifted. But I know that Elena was one of them. If you'd like to speak to someone about it." A tear fell from her eye and he wiped it away with a thumb.

"What's the matter princess?" She shook her head, taking in a big breath to try and steady herself.

"You've been bound to me since you were ten years old, you have the choice to be free, at least in that sense." He smiled at her.

"I will never be free of you Marcella Romano." Her eyes squeezed shut.

"You don't have to decide just yet," he muttered. "Wait until you've started your training, you've got your head around things. In the meantime." He picked up the sphere of the necklace and held it in his palm. There was a faint purple light shining beneath his finger tips and when he opened his palm she gasped.

There was what looked like a purple galaxy sitting inside the sphere.

"What is that?"

"Magic. Just a spark, we angels have some basic magic. We have to rely on the witches for the big stuff. It won't do much, it just looks pretty." He smiled as he took in the awe on her face.

"Thank you," she whispered. She removed the necklace from the box completely, the chain was long enough that she could put it over her head and the sphere rested on her chest between her breasts.

"You're welcome princess." He had moved closer so that his face was inches away from her own. She pressed a kiss to his lips and it was a stark contrast to the feral wanting need of their earlier kiss. She felt her chest expand with a feeling of warmth, the scent of his skin filled her and she let herself drown in the sweet vanilla and spiced aroma. He smelled like a sweet coffee, Christmas cookies, a warm cozy sweater. He smelled like home. She wondered if he could feel the shift between them. Nothing had to be said but it was understood that they were willing to explore whatever this is between them. Slowly, her world was going to be turning itself on its head.

He was still kneeling between her knees, kissing her softly with a hand on the back of her neck. He pulled away slightly.

"You should really get some sleep," he mumbled against her lips.

"You should stop talking," she whispered back and he broke away from her laughing.

"You're not scared of me, are you?" he asked, pushing himself back up onto his feet and dragging her to hers.

"Why would I be scared of you?" she asked. He looked her up and down.

"Ella... you just saw me rip out a guy's spine with my bare hands."

"Yeah?" He looked at her as if she had gone truly mad.

"And that didn't freak you out?" She thought for a moment. It had not. If anything it turned her on.

"Absolutely not." She stopped censoring herself. Will was now being honest with her, she had no reason to not be the exact same way with him.

"It was one of the hottest things I had ever seen."

223

He bit out a laugh and then looked at her, seeing the heat in her eyes and the heaving of her chest.

"Wait, seriously?" He hissed.

"Yeah."

"Ella! That is not something you should find attractive." She shrugged.

"Then you shouldn't be so fucking gorgeous, and huge and–" He was spluttering.

"Jesus Ella, what the hell has gotten into you?"

"I just found out that the guy I have had a crush on since I was twelve has been ripping demons apart to keep me safe and that he wants to be bonded to me for the rest of our probably lengthy lives. What and I'm supposed to be having some moral dilemma?"

"Well... yeah kinda." He was looking at her with wide eyes.

"Well. I'm not. Not about that anyway." He looked her up and down as though he was calculating all the ways that he would have his way with her and that made it much more difficult to say what she was about to say.

"What I am having difficulty with..." She sighed heavily and his eyes stopped roaming her body and met hers. "Is thinking that you being into me isn't just a by-product of most of your life having to revolve around me. That as much as I would like you to throw me on that bed and do all of those deplorable things you're thinking of doing to me, I can't let you. Until I know for sure that this isn't just some sort of weird Stockholm Syndrome from having to be around me for most of your life." He clenched his hands into fists at his sides.

"Do you really think I haven't tried not to feel this way about you?" She averted her gaze.

"I've had meaningless sex with more mortal women, angels and even some demons than I care to admit. No matter how gorgeous or good in the sack they were, they were an hour's distraction from you that didn't even work. Ella. I've wanted you for months, maybe even years. Plenty of angels of armour are bound in the same ways we are to the Guardian of the Gate and they haven't been anything other than platonic! I feel the way that I feel, the job and the bond are just a bonus."

"I thought angels couldn't fall in love with

mortals?" She was sure this had been one of the things Blake had told her in private before re-entering the kitchen.

"You're not mortal."

"No but you said..."

"I said I fucked them. I didn't fall in love with them." She flinched at the harshness in his voice.

"You can fall in love with whoever you want though, you're exempt from the mortal rule," he said, crossing his arms over his chest.

"What? Why?"

"Because your family have had the firstborn female as Guardian of the Gate as long as the world has been here. It's imperative that the family line is carried on. You have more chance of having children if you're not limited to angels." He sighed.

"So I have to have kids?" she whispered in a terrified voice.

"Either you or Leo, but it's preferred for it to be you." She closed her eyes.

"Holy shit."

"Indeed." She looked up at him.

"Will... you know how much I care about you." He sagged slightly.

"Not really." She glowered at him.

"I assume that you no longer think I'm the most annoying asshole on the planet?" he said sarcastically.

"Keep talking like that and I'll sure as hell go back to thinking it." He laughed then.

"Sorry."

"I want you just as much as you want me," she said moving towards him. "But I've also just had the rug pulled out from under me and my life has been tipped completely upside down. I need some time. I can't give you everything you might need from a relationship right now." He nodded.

"I know." She squeezed his arm.

"I'm not trying to lead you on or keep you hanging on. If you need to go and put space between us while I figure this out, I get it," she explained, her voice hoarse with emotion.

"I'd rather there was less space between us," he noted, bending his head down to capture her lips in a kiss. She sighed and melted into his arms.

"I don't care if I have to wait, we go at whatever pace you choose." He moved his lips to her ear and his breath on the shell of her ear and neck was making her weak with pleasure. "I will continue to protect you, I will watch you, be around you." She tightened her arms around him and pulled his lips to hers with so much gusto that their mouths meeting should have hurt but she didn't care. She wrapped her legs around him and hauled herself up into his arms. Her throbbing centre pressed against his waist and she grunted as she rocked her hips against the impressive length of him.

"Ella." He moaned and she locked eyes with him.

"If you continue to do what you're doing, I'm not going to be able to hold back anymore. I can't fuck you until I know you're ready." She whimpered. "I'm sorry. I'm not trying to punish you but if I take you, I can't give you back." She nodded.

"I know, I get it. I..." She thought of seeing someone else's hands on him and she felt a fire of rage building inside her.

"After the gifting ceremony, after I've got some sort of order to my thoughts and what the hell is going on, then we will come back to this." He grinned at her and kissed her softly.

"I'll wait forever if I have to princess," he said, nipping at her earlobe. "But you really should get some sleep. You have a lot of gift opening and partying ahead of you tomorrow." Her heart fluttered thinking about the VIP booth as he lifted her from him, as if she was nothing more than a toddler and placed her on the floor in front of him. He pulled his t-shirt off and climbed into her bed. She found the t-shirt of his that she wore to bed and pulled off her leggings. He watched her every movement and she heard him swear quietly as she faced away from him, pulling the sports bra off and sliding the soft fabric of the t-shirt over her body. She watched Ruby moved from the other side of the room to the end of the bed, flopping down on the floor.

She slid into the bed next to him and he rolled towards her, pulling her back flush against him. He was still hard against her ass and she moaned slightly.

"This is torture," she said biting her lip. He chuckled.

"Go to sleep you menace." He snuggled his nose into her neck and she sighed.

"Will you dance with me at Phoenix tomorrow?" she asked, thinking how strange the question was in contrast to the conversations they'd been having earlier.

"Of course I will, princess," he spoke into her hair. She smiled to herself and despite herself and her racing mind, she fell into a dreamless and comfortable sleep.

# CHAPTER
# TWENTY
# ONE

W hen she opened her eyes she found a pair of golden hazel eyes staring back at her.

"Happy birthday princess." She grinned.

"Thank you, what time is it?" she asked, brushing the hair that had escaped her braid out of her eyes.

"Early," he replied simply. He leaned in and kissed her. She cringed at first, no one wanted to kiss in the morning with morning breath but her thoughts simply floated out of her head as she kissed him back. If she had morning breath he didn't seem to mind. Kissing her firmly but sweetly, she slid a hand up his bare chest to rest it on his neck and she found herself lost in him.

She didn't know how much time had passed when there was a knock on the door. She pulled away.

"It's Leo," he said with amusement in his eyes.

"William, put my sister down. I'm coming in." She sat and watched her brother poke his head around the door. He seemed very relieved to have not caught them in any scandalous position.

"Nona's waiting with breakfast. It's gift opening time." He grinned and Ella felt her annoyance drift away. "Happy birthday short stack."

"Thank you," she said simply. She looked back at Will who was led on his back, one arm behind his head looking like the epitome of male beauty.

Leo rolled his eyes.

"When you two have stopped eye fucking... if you'd care to join us." Ella whipped her eyes back to her brother but he was smirking at her.

"We were not..." she started but he held up a hand.

"I knew I'd have to get used to it one day," he said simply.

"You knew?"

"What? That my best friend and my sister were grossly in love with each other and would one day pull their heads out of their asses enough to realize it?" he spouted easily and her mouth opened in a gape. "Yes. I did," he said, grinning at her.

"We're not together, just seeing what happens," Will said rolling his eyes.

"You're not together yet," Leo said simply and he turned and left the room. Ruby followed him, clearly wanting breakfast herself.

"Your brother's annoying," Will said, pushing himself up into a sitting position too.

"Hey, I didn't have a choice, you're the one who chooses to be his friend," she said yawning. He laughed and pressed a kiss to her shoulder through the t-shirt.

When she had dressed herself back into the soft leggings, leaving herself in Will's t-shirt, she waited for Will to pull his own t-shirt over his head.

"Why do your t-shirts look so damned small on you and yet make me feel like I'm wearing a tent?" She gestured down to herself and indeed the t-shirt did fall to cover her ass.

"I'm big, you're small," he said smiling.

"I still think I could take you," she said, smiling and sizing him up.

"I'm sure you could, princess. Once we train you up a little." She rolled her eyes and glanced at his well-muscled body through his shirt.

"Why the tattoos?" she asked suddenly. She had never asked him about his tattoos.

"Some are angel with reasons, some are mortal, just because I liked them," he said, watching her carefully.

"These," he said, flexing his tattooed hands and

fingers. "They are angel tattoos, to help with strength and precision." He pointed to an intricate design of roses surrounding a sword.

"This one is mortal."

"Why'd you get it?" He paused and chewed the inside of his cheek.

"This one is for you." He saw the shock across her features and a faint dull pink colored his tanned cheeks.

"This is the sword that will be made specifically for you." She gulped.

"Jesus Will, are you trying to kill me?" she whispered.

"What?" he asked.

"Never mind. What about this one?" she asked, pointing to one on the side of his neck. "Hang on," she said, getting closer and peering at it. She pulled the chain out from under her t-shirt and examined the sphere. It was the exact same as the pattern on his neck.

"If you choose to be bonded to me, you'll have the necklace and I'll have the tattoo." He smiled at her.

"What color will it turn?" she asked, looking down at the purple spark of magic.

"I'm not sure yet, but it'll probably be green." Her eyes lifted to his and she smiled. "Come on princess, your brother will be barging in again any second." She laughed and pulled the hair tie from the end of her braid, pulling it apart and seeing the waves it made fall around her.

"Let's go," she said, walking from the room.

---

S he sat at the kitchen table and opened her presents from Leo and Elena and found an assortment of different types of tea, a few new books, and some gift cards for her favorite stores and then she opened what looked like another jewellery box. Inside was a ring, it was a silver colored metal but it didn't look bright or shiny enough to be silver, there was a bright, sparkling emerald sat in the middle and it was flanked either side by two smaller diamonds. She looked up at Elena in shock and found her grandma was crying.

"It was your mother's. I gave it to her on her twenty-first birthday, just like my mom had done for me. I don't know how far back that ring goes but it's one of the only heirlooms that the Romano's have." Ella was crying now too. She slipped it onto the middle finger of her right hand where it sat almost perfectly. It was a little loose but her knuckle stopped it from being able to fly off easily.

"It's part of the protection for the Guardian of the Gate. Wear it always."

"Thank you Nona," she choked out in a sob and Elena moved out of the booth as Ella stood to embrace her.

Then there was a knock at the door.

When Ella opened the door she was almost knocked over by a lemon colored wrecking ball. Mal had arrived in her trusty yellow rain mac, her hair left wild and free and she appeared to be carrying a bag that was almost as big as she was. She handed the presents to Ella as both girls righted themselves and then she hugged her properly.

"Happy birthday baby girl!" Ella grinned.

"Thanks Mal." She kissed her friend on the cheek and returned to the kitchen, Mal following behind her having taken off her mac and hanging it over the banister.

"Hey Mal!" Leo said, also standing to give her a hug.

"Hey." Mal squeezed in the booth next to Ella, there was almost no space when Will lifted her easily and dragged her onto his lap. Mal's eyebrows shot up and she gave her friend a look as she settled comfortably into Will's body. She gave her friend a look that said *later*.

"Open this one of mine," Leo said, pointing at the rectangular package. She picked it up and she guessed that it might be another book. When she opened it she saw that it was indeed a sort of a book, but more specifically, it was a beautiful journal bound in navy blue leather with golden stars and constellations imprinted into it. She had kept a journal since she started therapy. Her therapist had told her that writing down her feelings would help get them in order and allow her to see them from another perspective if she read them back. Her current journal was an old study notebook, as she hadn't got around to buying herself a new one yet. She flipped through the thick paper and felt the soft leather of the cover. It was gorgeous and she couldn't have picked herself a better one.

"Thank you," she said staring at him. He just smiled and nodded at her and Mal pointed at the huge bag of presents that were sat next to Ruby.

"You'd better get started on those, we haven't got all day." Ella laughed and it was the lightest sound she had heard from herself in what felt like a really long time.

Mal had kicked Will out of Ella's bedroom at 3pm.

"Out lover boy. I need a word with my best friend and we have to start getting ready for tonight." Will opened his mouth to protest but he saw the glare in Mal's eyes and raised his hands in surrender.

"Fine, I've got things to do anyway." He motioned Ella over and when she reached him, he pulled her into a kiss that took a small and not so subtle cough from Mal for them to break it.

"I'll meet you at Phoenix okay?" he said and she nodded.

"Sure, now get lost."

"You're a cruel thing, do you know that?" he said, amusement dancing in his golden eyes.

"I've been told." He waved goodbye to Mal and left. They waited for his footsteps to subside before Mal whirred on her.

"You have some explaining to do." Ella bit her lip. How was she supposed to tell her what happened between her and Will without telling her everything that she wasn't allowed to tell her. She opted for confusion.

"Honestly, I don't know how it happened or what's happening from here." Mal looked at her expectantly.

"We've been getting closer and closer. He walked me home and we ended up having a discussion about how we felt. We're just going to keep it light, no pressure and just go with the flow." She thought of the heavy sphere of the necklace between her breasts. How Will had wanted her to bond with him even after the gifting ceremony and everything else that had gone on between them. She felt ashamed of the butchered version she gave her best friend.

"I feel like you're holding out on me but fine, have your secrets. I just enjoy being right," she said, wriggling her eyebrows at her friend.

"Is he as good a kisser as he looks?" she asked unashamedly.

"Better." Mal grinned.

"Have you slept with him yet?" Ella choked slightly on the water she had just taken a sip of.

"No! I have not..."

"Are you insane? You have seen him right?"

"Yes. To both," she said and Mal laughed. "Neither of us want to rush this and ruin a friendship," she said and her friend's eyes softened.

"It sounds very sensible. You must have a willpower of steel though," she said and Ella grinned.

They spent some time talking and messing around before starting to get ready. Ella was soaking up the interaction with her best friend. She knew that her life was about to get really, really complicated and not being able to lean on Mal was getting her all twisted inside. She couldn't help but be furious with Mal's mom for taking the decision away from her whether she wanted to be a witch or not but it wasn't her place. She enjoyed her company with Mal today, every second of it. Not knowing the next time she would be able to spend so much uninterrupted, almost carefree time with her. Whether she would be truly care free ever again.

"You look amazing," Mal was saying, looking her best friend up and down. Ella cringed a little under her stare. Her hair was left down but it was curled to make it look as though it was effortlessly wavy. She wore the necklace from Will and the ring that her Nona had given her. The emerald matched the dress almost perfectly. She had let Mal do her make-up, eyes a little darker and more smoky than she would usually do for herself but she had left her lips nude in color. She had stared at herself in the mirror for a few minutes. She looked good. Hell, she looked beautiful and she looked like her mom. The emerald green dress looked as though it had been created specifically for her.

"Will is going to lose his god damn mind when he sees you in this," she said simply and Ella laughed.

They went downstairs and said goodbye to Elena who had taken one look at her granddaughter and burst into sobs. Ella had hugged her tightly.

"I wish she was here to see you Marcella, you look

so much like her." She nodded and swallowed, trying to keep her own tears from surfacing.

"She'd be so proud of you." Ella's lip wobbled and a tear made its escape down her cheek. Elena patted it away and smiled a watery smile.

"Go, have fun. Let Will take care of you and get as drunk as you like." Ella laughed at that and looked towards the door. Mal, in her gorgeous orange dress was already heading out of the door.

"Goodbye Nona."

"Bye sweetheart, have a good night." Ruby wagged her tail from beside Nona and Ella followed Mal into the cab.

# CHAPTER
# TWENTY
# TWO

I t was a short ride from her home to the bar but it was too long to walk and especially in the glittering silver heels Mal had insisted that she wore.

The doorman stopped them and asked for ID. When Ella showed hers they smiled at her and wished her a happy birthday, moving aside to allow them entry.

Ella felt a lot of things attacking her senses; there was music, not too loud but it was loud enough that you'd have to raise your voice to have a discussion. It smelled like sweat and stale beer and the floor was slightly sticky. She ignored all of this and followed Mal to the bar.

Ella saw a gorgeous looking woman, with blue eyes

and similar hair to her own, except this woman's was mostly blonde. She had spotted Mal and moved her way through the bar, ignoring the other patrons when they complained that they were first.

"Hey Mal," she purred.

"Lyra," Mal said in a business like voice. "It's my best friend Ella's birthday." She nodded her head towards Ella and Lyra spared her a glance, her eyes flicking over to another part of the room and then back to Mal. "What's your sweetest cocktail?" Ella was starting to feel a little warm from the sparks flying between her friend and Lyra.

"Leave it with me sweetheart. The rest of your guests are in the booth already, I'll bring them over." Mal cocked an eyebrow.

"I haven't told you what I want." Lyra smiled and it was a sinister, wicked smile.

"I know exactly what you want." Ella cleared her throat quietly and Mal broke the bar owner's stare.

"Okay, thanks." She moved away from the bar, grabbing Ella's hand and pulling her along.

"Holy shit Mal!" Ella said, stopping her. "She's gorgeous!" Ella admitted.

"She's dangerous is what she is." Mal groaned and tugged Ella back into movement. They approached the booth and Ella looked around for Will but she didn't see him there.

"Ella!" Blake exclaimed. "You look amazing." He spun her around, taking in her dress and long flowing hair.

"Thank you kind sir." She did a little curtsey and laughed. She followed Mal into the booth and Lyra was walking towards them with two of the most ridiculous looking drinks that Ella had ever seen.

Ella's was in a glass that looked like it usually held huge ice cream sundaes; it was slushy like a snow cone consistency, bright blue and bright pink, topped with cotton candy and what Lyra told her was bubblegum flavour candy.

"I love bubblegum," Ella said, looking at her amazed.

"Thought you might." Lyra set it down in front of her with a smirk. She really was a beautiful woman, she looked a little older than them but young enough that her owning the place was impressive. She had blonde hair that had darker slices running through it, a sharp pointed face with high cheekbones and expressive eyebrows. Her eyes were almost as light blue as Sam's but they were warmer in color. She was dressed in a plain black shirt and leather pants and she was still getting the most male gazes than anyone else in the bar.

"And this one is for you." She laid a glass in front of Mal. Ella wondered if it could be classed as a health drink for the amount of fruit that garnished the glass.

"What is it?" she asked warily.

"Taste it." Mal took a sip and made a noise that made even Ella flush a little.

"That is called paradise," Lyra said, the tip of her tongue running over her white, straight teeth.

"Coconut rum, pineapple juice, peach schnapps and..." She took another sip. "Passionfruit liquor."

"Almost," Lyra purred.

"Pineapple and mango juice."

"It's delicious."

"I was just thinking the same thing," Lyra said. She looked startled as she realized she had said it out loud. Albeit quietly. Ella think she was the only one who may have heard her.

"Enjoy, bye," she said quickly, rushing from the booth and wiping a hand over her face.

"Hey birthday girl," a voice spoke in Ella's ear and she jumped so badly she was thankful that she hadn't yet picked up her drink. She shivered at the breath on her neck and turned to see Will's face right next to hers.

"Hey," she said, looking at his face. It really wasn't

fair for one person to be so beautiful. She took in his golden hazel eyes that were like nothing she had ever seen, his long straight nose, cheekbones that should be illegal in most states. A mouth that said and could do such wicked things should not be that perfect. It was currently held in a soft smile. He'd noticed her staring. She grinned at him, there was no need for her to feel shame with him. So what if they were in a room full of other people? She wanted to stare into his arrogantly handsome face and she was going to do just that. Except his eyes had moved from her face down to her dress.

"You look…" He stopped himself, taking a long drawing look over her body. "Perfect," he said, swallowing slightly, his eyes traveling back up to hers. She spotted the tattoo on his neck, the one that was the double of the necklace that she now wore. This man a few months ago had annoyed her more than she ever thought possible and now all she could think about was how fast he would be able to get her out of the contraption of this dress. It had taken both her and Mal a number of minutes to fasten the many clasps and strings.

"Thank you," she said, finally moving her gaze away from him and scooting around, making room for him on the seat next to her. He slid into the space, placing an arm immediately around her shoulders. The steady weight of his arm felt like an anchor. The rest of them were looking at the two of them with knowing looks and teasing glances.

"Come on, get it all out of your systems," she said.

"What?" Sam said. He didn't often look mischievous but when he did, boy did it make you worried.

"The comments that I am sure are going to be thrown out there throughout the evening." Sam just winked.

"I can't believe you think so little of us Ella. It's not like we've got years' worth of 'I told you so's' to get out." Blake choked on his beer and Sam thumped him on the back.

"Maybe. Let's not go there, Mr. Huxley," Ella said with a pointed look at Blake.

"Besides." Will said, squeezing her slightly. A warning not to push them. "We're not dating."

"Yet," Leo said.

"Yet," Will agreed. Ella felt a flush of warmth fill her cheeks and there was a sinking feeling falling through her stomach.

"Hey, don't freak out. It's fine," he whispered in her ear. "You're going through a lot right now, they won't hold that against you and I won't either. But if reminding them of that makes them leave you alone to enjoy your night..." He kissed her temple and she let out a heavy breath.

"How do you do that?" she asked, turning her head so that she was facing him again.

"Do what?"

"Know exactly what's going on in my head?" He smiled and picked up his glass, taking a sip of the half full glass of warm amber liquid.

"I've spent most of my life watching you, closer than anyone else has." His eyes roamed over her face.

"Although, that was a lucky guess. Most days you still surprise me." She grinned at him and he winked, picking up his glass again.

She finally pulled her drink towards her and took a swig. It was delicious, sickly sweet and although there was a little bit of a bite to it, there was barely any alcoholic after taste.

"That looks truly awful," Leo said, laughing when Ella poked her now blue tongue out at him.

"Well, it's delicious," she said before taking another big sip and swatting Will's hand away as he tried to steal some cotton candy.

"Hey!" He said, pulling his hand back quickly.

"For someone who has watched me their whole life, you should know I am prone to attack when someone threatens my food. Especially candy." He rolled his eyes.

"You won't even share with me?" He raised an eyebrow menacingly.

"Not even kissing privileges get you a free pass to steal my food." She looked so serious that it didn't appear that he was going to argue.

She took a piece of the cotton candy and the moment she had put it in her mouth he kissed her. The cotton candy melted on both of their tongues. The sweetness of the candy and the spicy scent of him attacked her senses and she felt a fizz of electricity dance along her skin.

He pulled away and grinned at her, biting his lip.

"I might have found a loophole," he said.

"Are you not going to talk about how hot that was?" Mal asked the rest of the group, breaking the two of them out of their stare.

"No," said the other three boys who were all looking resolutely away from Ella and Will. Ella laughed and took another big sip.

The festivities were well under way in no time. Ella had moved on to drinking a much less sickly drink of rum and coke and Mal was pretending that she wasn't looking for Lyra every time she moved her head.

"Come dance with me," Ella shouted over the music to her friend. Mal scanned the area one more time.

"Sure, okay." Will stood so that her and Mal could leave the table. Ella stopped in front of him, pointing a finger into his chest. Holy shit, was there a slither of fat on that man?

"And you will be dancing with me later," she demanded and before he could reply she had walked away, following Mal onto the dancefloor.

She didn't know how long they had been on the dancefloor, possibly four or five songs had passed when she felt large hands slip over her stomach and she looked down to see the tattooed hands of Will. Leo and Mal were dancing together, not as closely as her and Will were now stood, with her back to his chest. Their hips swayed in time to the music and she was lost in the music and the movement of their bodies.

"I don't think I did you justice earlier. You look...

holy shit you look good." He bent his head, kissing her shoulder. She turned to face him.

"You don't look too bad yourself." She smirked up at him. He was wearing a pair of dark blue jeans and a fitted black sweater.

"High praise from you, vicious princess." She felt her breath fill her lungs and she knew her chest heaved. He looked at her as though he would like nothing more than to drag her out of the bar and into an alley and if they kept staring at each other like this, she might even suggest it herself.

"Well you certainly didn't dance like that with me." She froze and Will moved fast. Standing in front of her was a snarling Lucas.

"You were uninvited," Will spat.

"This is a public bar. I just can't join your little band of losers over there." He nodded towards the booth. The booth was now empty and Leo and Mal were still dancing. Ella looked around and spotted Sam talking to Lyra and Blake had completely disappeared. Will was looking around at the people who were standing around Lucas.

"Dina?" he asked. Ella tried to move to see his face, to see who he was looking at but he kept her firmly planted behind him.

"Hey Will," said a high and girlish voice.

"What have you done?" he gritted out.

"What do you mean? Oh, you mean falling taking a lot of angel's powers from the Nerium with me?" She giggled. "It was nothing."

"Why?" he asked.

"Why do you think?" she snarled. The sweet voice was gone. "You could have had me, every time you came back to Astridia you walked past me like I was nothing. So I decided to try and help Lucas." Ella managed a peek at the girl and saw she had black hair, a pretty face with a slightly upturned nose and bright green eyes.

"I told you every time that it wasn't going to happen Dina." His arms were crossed over his chest, and he stood resolutely in front of Ella to keep her from view as much as possible.

"I know, I got very upset until I had the chance to help Lucas and take away your little distraction." She flicked blood red nails in Ella's direction. "It's a pity you pulled her out of the way before that car could make her a little guardian pancake." Will stepped forward but Sam appeared in front of him.

"It's an ambush, there aren't any humans in this bar except Ella and Mal." Ella swivelled around to see a confused looking Mal being held back by Leo.

# CHAPTER
# TWENTY
# THREE

L yra appeared in front of Mal and grabbed Ella's arm, dragging them away. Ella heard the sounds of metal on metal and she knew the fight had begun. Lyra was keeping Mal in front, eyes averted from the carnage that was about to ensue. Ella caught a glimpse of Blake sneaking up on a demon on the edge of the dancefloor. Blake hadn't been present because he already knew what the rest of them didn't and he had already started hunting.

She was dragged into a corridor that was freezing compared to the hot, sweaty dancefloor and Lyra threw open a door to some stairs.

"Go." She nudged Mal who started to walk gingerly in her heels down. Ella's head turned back to the corridor.

"I know what you're thinking, you're not trained. You'd hinder more than you'd help." Ella whirred around to her.

"You know what I am?"

"Yes, and no I'm not going to explain right now. Get your ass down those stairs. I'll be right behind you." Ella stamped down the hundreds more questions that had arisen with the knowledge that Lyra knew who she was and that the bar was filled with fallen angels and demons. It wasn't until she reached the bottom of the stairs did she feel herself go numb with panic.

Elena. Ruby. What if they'd already visited her home? If Lucas was leading them he'd know she'd be here but what it they went there first? She had to find out if they were okay. She let out a frustrated grunt when she realized that her bag with her cell phone was sitting on her seat in the booth.

"Mal, have you got your cell with you?" she asked quickly.

"Yes but Ella, what the fuck is going on."

"I'll explain later please, I need to borrow your phone." Mal handed it over but she didn't look too impressed.

Ella dialled her home number quickly, she waited until the call ended itself with no answer and she bit down the bile rising in her throat, entering Elena's cell number now. She let out a sob when it went straight to voicemail.

"Ella, what the hell is going on?" Mal breathed as she rushed forwards and wrapped her arm around her friend, trying to sooth her.

"Those people are here because of me and now I can't get hold of Nona." Her hands were shaking as she wiped her cheeks.

"Why are they after you?" Mal looked horrified.

"I can't tell you." Lyra rolled her eyes and sat on an overturned bucket and started inspecting her nails.

"I'm sorry if were boring you." Ella hissed at her and she raised an eyebrow.

"Look sweetheart. I can see you're having a bad night so I'm gonna let that slide, but you need to calm the hell down." She went right back to her nails and Ella fisted her hands. She looked at Mal who was staring at her with a look of terror.

"What have you got yourself into? Is it drugs?" Lyra snorted with laughter and both of the girls gave her a venom filled stare.

"Of course it's not fucking drugs!" she said, folding her arms. They were silent for a few minutes when there was a shout from the corridor and Lyra stood, moving in front of both of them to stand in front of the door.

"Ella, you need to tell me what the fuck is happening." She could tell by her friend's voice that she was starting to get angry.

"I can't tell you! How many times do I have to say it."

"I'm your best friend!" she said, sounding hurt. "It seems like everyone else here knows what is going on and I'm scared and I'm freaking out. What is going on?" She almost screamed the last part.

"Oh screw this." Lyra turned and put her hand on her hip. With the other she pointed to an old bar stool. "Mal, sit there and I'll tell you."

Ella's eyes went wide.

"You can't! I'm not allowed."

"You're not allowed, I'm not one anymore, Ella." A wave of understanding broke over her. So Lyra wasn't an angel anymore and she didn't appear that deranged so she must be a demon. "The Order don't get to tell me what to do anymore." She winked at Ella who wasn't sure whether to be apprehensive that her best friend was having cocktail sex with a demon or whether to be grateful that the demon had found a massive loophole in the system.

"Do you want the abridged version?" she asked Ella. Ella nodded.

"Angels and demons are real, all of those boys you were out with tonight are angels, Ella will be an angel, the most important angel, like the Mother Theresa of angels in a few days." Ella huffed in annoyance.

"Keep it simple!" she snapped and Lyra rolled her eyes.

"One thing about angels, they're hardly ever fun." Mal looked as though she was going to vomit.

"Anything else?" she stuttered.

"Witches are real, angels can fall from grace and turn into demons, demons can turn evil and try and wage war with the angels, Ella's mom was murdered by the first ever demon to have more than one angel's power, now he's trying to get to Ella before she gets her powers..." She paused, counting things off on her fingers.

"How am I doing so far?" she asked and Ella sighed.

"Tactless but accurate." Her eyes met Mal's and she could practically see her friends beautiful brain processing the information that she had been given.

"Lucas?" she asked her friend.

"Fallen angel, wanted to get to me to stop me getting powers."

"He's not a fallen anymore," Lyra interjected.

"He's not?"

"Nah, he's gone full demon."

"What kind?" Ella asked fascinated.

"He's a reaper demon. Nasty creatures," she said shrugging.

"So what kind are you?" Ella asked with a raised eyebrow and Mal looked at Lyra for the first time.

"You're a demon?" Mal whispered.

"Very good little guardian!" she teased. "Impressive considering you don't have your powers yet." Ella crossed her arms and Lyra rolled her eyes.

"If you must know, I'm a siren," she said, curtsying slightly.

"If you have used some weird siren power on my best friend..." Ella warned.

"You can simmer down. I've never used any powers or influence over Mal." Mal looked relieved but still utterly horrified.

"How do I know you're not lying?" Ella asked, squinting at her.

"You don't. You either believe me or you don't. Hell if I care. I'm only protecting you both and helping your little angel boy band up there." She stood closer to Ella.

"I have nothing against angels, nothing against

humans, nothing against witches and nothing against demons. If they don't have a problem with me. However if they're trying to fuck up my bar. Or if they're pieces of shit in general, then we have a problem. Luckily for you, the asshole that killed your mom is on my shit list so me and you girlie are on the same side." Ella gave herself a moment to take in what she had said. Will and Leo must know what Lyra is and they appear to trust her enough to keep her and Mal safe. She nodded and Lyra dipped her chin in acknowledgement.

"Now you, my little pop tart." She approached Mal with caution. "Do you have any questions?" she asked kindly.

"Do I have any fucking questions?" Mal bit at her. "Of course I do, I have nothing but questions! I'm stood in the cellar of a bar with a demon and an angel apparently!" She was starting to breathe heavily.

"Why didn't you tell me?" she snapped at Ella.

"I found out yesterday," she responded warily. "And one of the first things I was told is that I couldn't tell you." Ella felt her eyes fill with tears. "And I'm sorry Mal, I know this is a lot but currently I can't get hold of Nona, her and Ruby are supposed to be at home. My brother and my... Will is up there. Blake and Sam are up there so I don't think I can answer all of your questions right now." Her voice broke on the last word and she let out a sob. Mal rushed forward and hugged her friend and Lyra looked a little uncomfortable.

There was a knock on the door and the girls broke apart. Lyra went and placed a hand on the door. She pulled it open before Ella could shout and Will filled the doorway.

Ella sagged to her knees in relief but before she could hit the floor Will was steadying her.

"Will what the fuck is going on? Lyra told me everything! What's happening?" Mal said and Will shot Lyra a look.

"What! None of you could tell her, doesn't mean I have to keep my mouth shut."

"Where's Leo?" Mal asked.

"Everyone is fine, they're all upstairs."

"What about Lucas–" Mal started but Ella spoke over her.

"Nona and Ruby, they're at home and they're not answering." Will shook his head.

"The minute you left they went into Astridia, they knew something was going to go down tonight, it's their last chance." The instant relief that washed over her made her feel light-headed for a moment.

"Where?" Mal asked. Will looked as though he was going to snap at any moment.

"Lyra, you answer Mal's questions as best as you can, you're the one who told her."

"Will, you need to tell me right now what the fuck is happening." Will wheeled around to Mal.

"Go and talk to your grandma, I have to get you and Ella out of here alive." Mal's eyes narrowed.

"What has my grandma got to do with this?" Lyra's eyes were wide.

"Well, you didn't tell me that part," she hissed at Will.

"You didn't need to know," he snapped at Lyra. "Mal, there's only so much we can tell you." He sighed. He looked conflicted and Ella could tell he felt guilty for snapping at her and for dropping it on her that her grandma knew things she didn't. Ella rubbed a hand over his arm.

"Right, Lyra, stay here with Mal. We need to get Ella out of here. If there's more it'll draw them away from the bar. Wait until it is completely clear. Leo will assist you. Once it's clear, bring Mal to the training camp with Leo." Lyra narrowed her eyes.

"I haven't been to that training ring in a very long time. I can barely go near that portal," she stuttered. She sounded scared.

"You've been seen helping us tonight, you're not safe until the morning at least."

"I can take care of myself," she pointed out.

"I know that, but Mal needs you." He nodded towards her. Mal's hair seemed to deflate slightly as she let out a breath.

"Come on." He tugged Ella towards the door.

"I'll see you soon," she said pointedly to Mal who nodded.

---

They walked up the corridor in silence. She had to keep reminding herself to breathe, that Elena and Ruby were safe, that Mal was being looked after. The best thing she could do was get out of there.

They came into the room and ashes and embers floated around the whole bar.

"Holy shit, how many were there?" she asked looking around.

"Not as many as it looks. We weren't overwhelmed which is good," he said. The rest of them came over.

"Where's Mal?" Blake asked Blake at once.

"Lyra's with her. Lyra told her everything." Blake and Sam shared a look that Ella thought looked a lot like triumph. Clearly they hated keeping the truth from Mal as much as she did.

"Leo, can you go wait with them? When the coast is clear get them out of here and to the training ring." He nodded and moved towards the corridor. There was a noise from the balcony. Two huge creatures leapt from the balcony above and directly into the middle of where they were stood. Sam pushed Ella to the ground and covered her body with his.

Ella could see everything that was happening; Blake was battling with one of the demons, his sword swinging impossibly close to the creatures face but never quite making contact. They were incredibly fast and vicious. Teeth snapping and claws swiping. Their grey skin looked stretched over their huge frames, their yellow eyes looked bloodshot and like they didn't properly fit in their sockets. Blake sliced the one he was fighting directly across the throat and something bright green that looked like bile spurted from the wound. It didn't kill the creature but it startled him long enough for Blake to swing a leg around and take it off of its feet. He drove his sword into the creature's chest, pinning it to the floor. He pulled a chain from seemingly nowhere and wrapped it around its still bleeding neck. He pulled hard and the demon's head parted company with its body with a sickening pop.

Ella's eyes slid to Will and she felt pure unbridled terror wash over her. Sam realized at the same time she had as she felt his weight shift. More of the creatures had crawled out of the shadows. Two were holding Will by the arms, one of them had moved towards Blake and another was holding a weapon that looked to Ella like a machete. She could see more of the creatures creeping into her vision from the shadows of the darkened room. Ella screamed as he swung the blade towards Will and something exploded from her chest. A blinding light forced her to close her eyes and her ears were ringing with the sound of her guttural shriek of panic. She heard a thud and a grunt of pain, metal clanging to the floor. The light appeared to dim from her closed eyelids and she opened them gingerly. Spots of light burst in her vision and she felt Sam move from her, pulling her into a sitting position.

"Ella, are you okay?" His face swam in front of her eyes and she blinked furiously, attempting to get her sight back to normal. There was a pounding in her ears but she stood with Sam's help on shaking legs.

"Will," she said suddenly, whipping around to where the creatures had hold of him but they were gone. Will was pushing himself up from the floor and Blake was putting down an arm that he must have used to shield his eyes from the blast.

Will moved towards her as quickly as he could but he appeared to be in a daze and there was blood coming from his hairline. His lip was also split open. He'd wrapped her in his arms before she could do more than let out a strangled cry of relief.

"What the fuck was that?" Sam asked the room at large. Ella pulled back from Will and pulled her necklace from the front of her dress. The sphere was empty once again.

"It was this." She held it up so they could all see it.

"You gave her the Votum?" he said, his eyes wide.

"Yeah, but I only gave her a spark of a protection spell." She narrowed her eyes at him.

"You told me it was just a spark of magic so it didn't look empty." He smiled.

"If I was going to give you a spark of magic, of course I would choose to protect you. But that spell should have only been strong enough for you, maybe you and Mal..." He looked around the room.

"It nailed every demon in the room," Blake said, looking around too.

"I've never seen anything like it, I've never even heard of something like that." Ella tucked the sphere back into the front of her dress.

"I don't care why it did it, I'm just glad it worked," she said, staring at Will. "Are you okay?" She lifted a hand to his cheekbone that looked a little bruised.

"I'm fine princess, all of this will disappear in a few hours." She nodded.

The door behind them opened and Lyra, Leo and Mal walked into the main room.

"What the hell was that?" Lyra asked, looking angry. "It felt like someone was trying to crawl out of my chest."

"Ella's necklace just pulverised an entire room of about fourteen Pugna demons," Sam said.

"So why did I survive?" Lyra asked.

"You weren't in the room and I think it was set off by Ella herself. She obviously doesn't see you as a threat." Lyra grinned at her.

"Then clearly she doesn't know me well enough yet, but thanks angel cakes, I appreciate not being blown to dust." She winked at Ella but put an arm around a very quiet Mal.

"Let's get out of here," Leo said. "We're taking Mal back to her place to get her some stuff but she's been seen with us, it's not safe. I'll speak to Magda about her and Mary going into hiding." He looked at Mal with a small smile.

"I need to find something else to wear," Ella said, looking down at her gorgeous dress, brushing some of the dust that she was pretty sure used to be a demon from her waist.

"I'll go ahead and check out the house, make sure it's safe," Blake said. Sam opened his mouth as if he was going to object but he closed it again and nodded.

Lyra closed down the bar behind her and picked up a duffle bag from a cupboard.

"You really have a bag prepared?" Will said, teasing her.

"Hey, when you've been alive as long as I have, you realize you need to be ready to disappear at a moment's notice." She swung it over her shoulder and followed Leo and Mal down the street towards Lyra's car.

# CHAPTER
# TWENTY
# FOUR

"Good job I was designated driver tonight," Sam said, ushering Will and Ella towards his own car. Ella got into the back seat and to her surprise, Will followed her.

"Why aren't you sitting up front?" she asked.

"I'm not letting you out of my sight until I have to," he said, placing a hand on her knee. Sam looked at them in the rear-view mirror.

"No getting hot and heavy in my car." Ella rolled her eyes.

"I'm not giving you a five star rating," she said and Will snorted a laugh next to her.

"You're insane."

"What?" she said.

"You were almost killed. I was almost killed and

you saved my ass, like less than 30 minutes ago and you're already cracking jokes," he said in disbelief.

"It's an ingrained trauma response. I'm sure I'll be having nightmares about those Pugna demons for years to come." She shivered and he put an arm around her shoulders, pulling her into his side.

"Who's Dina?" she asked quietly and she felt him sigh.

"She was an angel of fortune. They live in Astridia, they have this huge expanse of water called the Lilas pool. They use it to look down at their charges." He pushed the hair out of his eyes. "They are the karmic balance. They get to decide whether your luck is good or bad." She considered this for a moment.

"And she... she liked you?" He huffed out a laugh.

"She was obsessed with me. Even as kids, she was always nice and sweet but couldn't take a hint." She smiled at him and he continued.

"When I moved here, she kept doing things to try and get my attention. She was your angel of fortune. That day on the lake... she doesn't have the power to make that happen but she gave you the string of bad luck that led to it." His hand formed a fist and his knuckles turned white.

"I went back to Astridia and reported her to the Order. She was punished and you were removed from her." Ella's mouth was hanging open slightly. "She thought I was falling for you and she didn't care that you were the Guardian of the Gate, that millennia of your family being in that position could have ended with you if Leo didn't have children. She's been imprisoned in the Nerium. She had a few more hundred years of punishment before she was supposed to return to her duties." He looked at her. "Somehow she managed to make you take that step into that road." He swallowed and Ella saw his eyes fill.

"Hey. It's not your fault. She made me chase after Lucas, she was working with him. It's not your fault." She emphasised the last four words and Will blinked furiously.

"I'm going to send a message to Elena when we get near the portal so she can investigate what happened with Dina. She will be home in the morning for your ceremony." She nodded.

"What... what is the ceremony, what do I have to do?" She shifted nervously.

"Nothing really. In Astridia they're really lame and pretentious, loads of people wearing white robes and a platform where everyone can watch." He shuddered and she laughed.

"I haven't gotta wear a floaty white dress, do I?" she asked, still giggling.

"Not if you don't want to." He smiled at her. "It's probably just going to be Magda saying the words that unbind your powers and..." He bit his lip. "...And brings back your memories." He looked down at his hands.

"Will?"

"I'm sorry, I just know after tomorrow you're gonna look at me differently." He wiped a palm on his jeans.

"Whatever you've made me forget, you had a reason for doing so. If there's anything I'm not comfortable with, we will talk about it but I won't forget everything you've done for me, especially when I had no idea what you were doing, when I was a dick to you." He laughed then.

"You thought I was an overbearing asshole. I am, especially when it comes to you." He shrugged and she pulled away from him to turn and look him in the eyes. They were pulling into the driveway of her house so she closed her mouth and got out of the car.

Blake was stood on the steps.

"All clear. The garden seems disturbed so I think they did come and check here but they knew where she was going to be." Blake hugged Ella then, resting his cheek on the top of her head.

"How're you holding up you little fire cracker?" She chuckled.

"I'm fine, you know me. Trauma repression is my jam." They bumped fists and Sam rolled his eyes.

"It's cute that you can both bond over your unhealthy coping mechanisms but let's get this show on the road."

Ella and Will entered the house, while Blake and Sam circled to make sure nothing snuck in.

"Let's do this fast," Will said, climbing the stairs behind her. She pushed open her bedroom door and immediately started pulling clothes out of drawers. She threw a few shirts and a few pairs of leggings into a bag along with a hair brush and some hair ties before she pulled her hair into a bun.

"Crap," she said, standing still in the middle of the room.

"What?" Will was piling his own clothes into a bag. When had so many of his clothes found their way into her room?

"This dress takes about four years to get in and out of." He laughed.

"I could just rip it off." He smirked. "But seriously, I could." He moved towards her and she gave him an incredulous stare.

"Abso-fucking-lutely not." He rolled his eyes.

"We need to get out of here."

"Just undo all of the clasps and strings–carefully–enough so I can get it off." He huffed but made a start.

"This thing has more defenses than Fort Knox, you know that?" She laughed as he undid the last bow with a triumphant noise. Then she heard a groan.

"You're not wearing a bra, are you?" he asked.

"No," she said turning to face him. His eyes were bright with playful glee and he let out a breath.

"These assholes have the worst timing. You look so delightfully fuckable in that dress and holy shit." She let the dress fall before stepping out of it. She realized that she had yet to take her heels off, so she stood in front of him in nothing but a pair of underwear and a pair of glittering heels. He looked her up and down and she went to turn towards the comfortable and practical clothes she had found to change into but she was swung around by a hand on her wrist. He captured her lips in a kiss, her bare chest brushing against his sweater and her breath hitched as her hardened nipples grazed the fabric. A hand reached between them and he brushed a thumb over the sensitive peak and she moved her hips forwards to brush against him. The feeling of the zipper on his jeans brushing against her through her soft, thin lingerie sent a ripple of pleasure through her. Their kisses were fierce and heavy as they pressed themselves against each other hard enough to bruise.

"Hurry your asses up," called a voice from under her window. Ella pulled back, looking into the lust-filled eyes before her and wondered how long they had until Blake came storming up here to drag them out. Will growled. Not like a frustrated noise, a feral, canine growl. Ella couldn't help but laugh and Will joined her.

"When life has righted itself again and I have you for myself for any length of time, I can't even begin to tell you all of the filthy, deplorable things that I am going to do to you." She felt a slickness between her legs and was almost embarrassed by how aroused his words had made her. He seemed to sense it because he closed his eyes and there was a distinct air of trying to keep himself in control.

"But for now princess, the job comes first." With what Ella considered an applaudable effort, he moved back and returned to his bag. She gave herself a few seconds to catch her breath and dressed quickly.

Once she had been to the bathroom and collected her toothbrush and other necessities, they both rushed down the stairs into the back yard.

"Finally," Blake said and Sam rolled his eyes, grinning slightly at Ella who gave him a look that plainly said *thanks for cockblocking me.* They walked to the end of the garden and Ella was about to climb up over the wall when Blake lifted her and handed her to Will who set her down on the other side.

"I'm not completely incapable you morons," she said huffing, waiting for them to pass her so she could follow them. Sam laughed, linking his arm through hers.

"Don't mind them, they're in soldier mode."

They reached the clearing and Ella was looking around, wide eyed. There were small wooden huts, they looked a little like tents but sturdier. There was a fire which Mal and Lyra were currently sitting around together, talking quietly. The other side of the clearing held what looked like a gym but there were racks of weapons, different size targets and blocks that looked battered.

"This is where you'll be training," Will said, standing behind her.

"Who will train me?" she asked quickly.

"Me, for the most part. Sam will probably give you the boring lessons on the Order's rules and the different types of angels, the different demons." He gave a big fake yawn and she turned to give him a mocking glare.

"That sounds much more entertaining than my senior year of high school," she pointed out.

"True. I'll be teaching you weapons, hand to hand combat..." he said, his eyes roaming over her body again. She grinned maliciously.

"Please no cutting off any of my body parts princess, I think you'll find you like them, if you give them a chance." She flushed but laughed.

"Magda will teach you about angel magic and how to use it," he said, going back to his more serious tone. She nodded.

Leo arrived then with Magda and Mary. Mal stood in front of her mom and grandma with a furious look on her face, her arms folded across her chest.

"What have you done?" Mary sneered at Ella.

"Nothing. Your daughter witnessed most of it with her own eyes. I just filled in the gaps," Lyra said, coming to stand next to Mal.

"And who the hell are you?" Mary challenged. For a split second, Lyra's eyes changed to show pure white and Mary took a step back.

"Not someone who you should be taking that tone with." Magda pushed her daughter back.

"How dare you. Someone of your kind should keep yourself out of witches affairs." Mal looked as though she wanted to laugh. She clearly couldn't keep on top of all of the surprises.

"So we're witches? Is that it?" Mal asked. Mary swore and turned away. Magda frowned at her daughter and turned to her granddaughter.

"Yes, your mother chose not to accept her gifts and she decided that she did not want you to have them either. Both of your powers have been bound so you can't use them accidentally." Mal nodded.

"And were you ever planning on telling me?" she asked quietly.

"I don't believe so, no." Mary turned then.

"No, I was going to keep you safe. We do not need to be dragged in by the angels every time something goes wrong and we do not have to be an option for the fallen to slaughter to enable their transition to a demon." She looked pointedly at Lyra.

"You don't get to keep deciding what I need," Mal said. Not loudly, but there was a finality in her voice.

"I am your mother–" Mary started but Mal stood up straight and set her face in a hard line.

"You may be my mother but I am a grown woman. I am an adult whether you like it or not and I will not have anyone making decisions for me ever again. You took away too many of my choices. So I will be quitting school, I should have stopped studying years

ago and I'll be getting myself a job and my own place."
Mary looked furious but Magda put a hand on her
shoulder.

"Mally, you need to be sure of what you want
before making this choice. I have embraced being a
witch but it's dangerous and it's hard." Mal looked at
her grandma then.

"I want to do something with my life. Look
around Ma, all of the people I care about are here.
You're telling me I have the power hidden inside me
somewhere to help them. It's non-negotiable. I will
help them. I will unbind my powers and I will learn."
Mary was letting tears flow freely.

"But honey, you don't understand."

"No Mom, you don't understand. This was not
your choice to make and it's going to take a long time
for me to forgive you for keeping this from me." Mary
closed her mouth but let out a sob. "I love you Mom,
and I know you love me, but you love me too much.
You're snuffing out everything that makes me who I
am and I can't let you do it anymore." Magda smiled a
little sadly at her granddaughter.

"Well I can't stop you, you are an adult now."
Mary swallowed. "I'm going to go home. I understand
you'll be staying here Mother? Ready for the
ceremony?" Magda nodded and Mary smiled at Ella.

"Good luck and well wishes for tomorrow, Ella," she said politely.

"Thank you," she said smiling slightly.

Leo escorted Mary away and Ella turned to Mal but she was already looking at Lyra.

# CHAPTER
# TWENTY
# FIVE

"Is it true?" Lyra lowered her head.

"You killed a witch to become who you are now?" she asked in a clipped tone.

"Yes."

"Why." she said. Magda went to interrupt but Will shook his head at her once and Magda looked between Mal and the demon and something like pain flashed across her features.

"When an angel falls," Lyra started in a small voice. "They try everything to keep some of their powers. I fell in love, with a mortal. I fell and fought for my powers to make a better life for us and she..." She swallowed. "She left me." Ella's heart squeezed slightly for the siren.

"When you're a fallen you have a matter of months

to decide what you're going to do. You either get stripped of all your powers and become mortal or you become a demon. The person I was willing to give up anything for had just screwed me over and I was a few weeks away from becoming fully insane so I took the option. Yes, I killed a witch to become a demon. If I didn't, I probably would have slaughtered hundreds of mortals before the angels of mercy would have been able to stop me." She gave a little cough and her voice was stronger.

"So I'm not proud of what I had to do but I won't apologize for it. Not in the grand scheme of things and I've never harmed a human since." She shrugged. Mal looked like she was thinking through everything that Lyra had said.

"I don't like it," she said finally.

"No I don't expect you to," she said simply. Mal nodded. It went unspoken between them, this was something that would have to be ironed out over time.

Magda didn't look thrilled. She understood from the conversation that Mal had developed feelings for Lyra before she found out what she was and if what she said was true, then it could have saved the lives of many but it was as natural for witches to hate demons as it was for children to be scared of the dark but she watched her granddaughter and the demon a little longer and Ella could tell that if Mal decided to forgive Lyra, Magda wouldn't penalise her for it.

When Leo returned, he confirmed that he stationed an angel of mercy in the area to watch over the house. Ella wandered over to him and pulled him aside.

"I've been worried about you," she said bluntly and he laughed.

"Only you could go through something as mind-bending as this and come out of it worrying about other people." Her eyes narrowed.

"What kind of angel are you?" she asked and his smile faded.

"I had some trouble coming to terms with what sort of angel I am. It's better now but it's still hard. The one person who I wanted to talk to about it, I wasn't allowed. Because you weren't allowed to know yet." He offered her a small smile and a bubble of anxiety welled in her chest.

"What kind of angel are you?" she asked again softly.

"I'm an angel of oblivion," he replied carefully.

"That doesn't sound good," she said, her eyes watching him carefully. He looked tired.

"It's not. It's an angel of death, Ella." Her eyebrows rose and her eyes widened.

"Why?" she asked angrily. "Why did they make you an angel of death? Why would we even need them?" He smiled at her before he looked pleadingly at Will who she now realized was stood only a little way away.

"Angels of oblivion are necessary," he said, walking over to them. "They give help to those who are coming to the end of their life. They have powers to give peace in someone's last moments. They can try to stop people who want to take their own lives before their time. The world is about balance Ella, angels of oblivion are the best at helping us keep that balance." He had a grimace the entire time that he spoke and Ella wondered if he had been annoyed by the race of angel that had been bestowed upon his best friend.

"Fine, but why Leo! Hasn't he suffered enough?" Tears were threatening to fall and Will put a soothing hand on her shoulder.

"I was chosen because of how I dealt with what happened to Mom."

"And you're okay with it now?" she asked.

"I'm getting used to it. Most of it is helping to sooth people in their final moments, but when I get a charge wanting to commit suicide and I fail to save them, it still hurts but I'm still learning." He shrugged and Ella's annoyance flared again.

"I don't want you to become someone that doesn't

blink an eye at death," she said in an almost whisper. Leo looked at her for a few moments, thinking about the words she had just uttered.

"Me neither." He grasped her hand. "But at least now I have my baby sister to help keep me in check." She smiled and squeezed his hand.

"I think it's time we all call it a night," Will said. "It's been a long day and it's a big day tomorrow." Ella shifted nervously. "I'll take first watch," he said to the boys and they nodded. Leo went into one of the huts near the back, Magda and Mal went into one in the middle, Sam and Blake right near the front and that left three more. Ella wasn't tired yet, although she knew she should sleep. Her head was pounding with all the information that had been thrown around tonight.

"You need to sleep," Will said, standing in front of her.

"My head is too busy." He sat down behind her on the log and pulled her back against his chest.

"I know you have a lot of questions, god I think you've been incredible the last few days. I can't even imagine how scrambled that beautiful brain is." He kissed her temple and she smiled lazily to herself.

"I've had a good distraction," she said, walking two

fingers up his arm in front of her and she felt his chest give a chuckle.

"I know you're stronger than people give you credit for but you don't have to be... you're allowed to be scared. You're allowed to freak out sometimes." She would, she knew it would come sooner or later but with how fast everything happened, she didn't feel as though she could mentally process just yet.

"Do you think Mal and Lyra will work it out?" she asked as she watched the demon go into one of the huts at the back with her bag slung over her shoulder. He thought for a moment before answering.

"I don't know, Lyra isn't one for relationships. I've never seen her show an interest in anyone and I've been told that she hasn't since she turned demon." He squeezed her lightly. "Lyra is cynical about everything in the romance department and Mal... Mal loves hard. It's either going to work and be fantastic... or blow up in all of our faces."

"I don't want to see Mal hurt," she said quietly.

"Me neither," he agreed. They watched the sunrise together, lounging on the log, talking quietly about things that didn't matter. After what must have been hours, Blake came out of his hut.

"Ella, you didn't sleep?" She shook her head.

"My head is too full." He nodded.

"You know, I've always admired you for your strength and your courage." She looked at him in surprise. "Don't act like you don't know how much you're putting all of us to shame." She laughed and moved away from Will. She hugged Blake and stayed that way for a little while, his chin resting on her head.

"I'm going to try and get a few hours in before everyone else wakes," Will said, looking at them and smiling slightly. "You coming?" he asked Ella and she nodded. It was going to be a weird day, she didn't know how exhausting this process of the gifting ceremony would be. She said goodbye to Blake and Sam appeared out of the hut as they passed it. He nodded at her and carried a bottle of water and she watched him as he handed it to Blake. He took it from him with a smile and they stood side by side. Looking up into the morning light, Ella felt a squeeze in her chest at the sudden rush of affection she felt for her friends.

Ella walked into the hut behind Will and was surprised at how large it actually was. There was a small washroom and a room big enough for a double bed. She looked around.

"Do they all have double beds?" she asked, raising her eyebrows.

"No, most of them have two singles but there's a

few that have doubles." He ginned at her. "Don't worry princess, we both need some rest, I won't be dragging you into the bed for any reason other than to sleep."

"Damn it," she said quietly and he laughed, his eyes bright.

"My willpower only goes so far Ella." He smirked at her. She pulled off her jumper and stepped out of her sneakers. She crawled under the blankets and was pleasantly surprised by the softness of the mattress. She groaned a little and she heard a gruff sigh. Smiling to herself she rolled over to face him. He'd removed his shirt and was toeing off his shoes. She drank in the sight of him and couldn't quite believe her luck.

"You're literally perfect," she said quietly. He paused as he lifted the blankets to join her.

"I'm covered in scars," he said confused.

"Yeah, but that doesn't take away anything. I hate admitting it because your ego does not need encouragement but never in my life did I think I'd have a chance with you. You could have anyone you wanted." She averted her eyes as he climbed in beside her and led down on his side to face her.

"I think you're being kind but if I can have anyone I want, then that's great. All I've ever wanted is you." She rolled her eyes.

"Cut the crap." She laughed but his face was serious.

"Ella, I think I've loved you since I pulled you out of that lake." She slid her eyes to his and saw the pain welling in them.

"Then why have you never told me before?" He swallowed and she shifted closer.

"Because it took me so long to realize it. That and because my sole purpose on this planet is to protect you. To make sure nothing hurt you and to make sure you were able to do your job. Guardians of the Gates are like... angel royalty. Not literally but they're the highest ranking angel to exist."

"And?" He laughed at her flippant tone and continued.

"And... I'm not. My mom died giving birth to me, my real dad was nowhere to be found. I was a bastard orphan that nobody really wanted to deal with. I was pushed from family to family because the Order didn't know what to do with me and then Tony took me under his wing. He was part of the Order's personal guard and he trained me. It was less than a year later I got my powers. The Order gave a shit about me then but still treated me like a guard dog. I couldn't wait to come here and out of Astridia." She had a hand on her chest, pressing onto her own heart.

"Will, I'm so sorry, I had no idea." He half shrugged.

"I don't care about all that now but I grew up knowing that if I hadn't been the one chosen to protect you, I'd have been no one to anyone in Astridia, except Tony." He smiled slightly. "He might not be my real dad but he is to me." She slid one of her hands into his and she squeezed his hand gently. "So you see, princess," he said, looking at her again. "I may have been chosen to be your angel of armour, but I grew up believing that I'd never be worthy of you, not in any other way." She screwed up her face.

"Those assholes." He laughed again. "No Will, I'm serious. We haven't always agreed and I gave you a really hard time myself but there is no one in this world who knows you, really knows you, that would think that you're not worthy of anything. You're kind and funny, you do your job and you're good at it, you–" She was cut off by his lips covering hers. She threw herself into the kiss at once, only pausing to push him over onto his back and cover his body with hers. She kissed him again and he placed his hands lightly on her hips, which found themselves settled over his, her legs landing either side of his thighs. He moved forward slightly, pushing himself into a sitting position and she seated herself fully in his lap.

"We're supposed to be sleeping," he murmured against her mouth, sending shivering vibrations through her throat and chest. She pulled away and looked at him.

"I don't care what we should be doing." She ground her hips against his and he grunted. "I don't ever want to hear you say you're not worthy of me ever again." She ran a finger down his chest and held his gaze with hers. "I may be practically royalty, but you never have to get on your knees for me."

# CHAPTER TWENTY SIX

He watched her every move, mesmerised by her words and her actions as she moved herself down his legs, kneeling between them. She hooked his sweatpants in her fingers and pulled them down along with his underwear. He hissed as he sprang free, the cool air of the still morning hitting his hard cock. He looked as though he was about to say that she didn't have to do this but she silenced him with a look.

"I want to." She paused, waiting for him to say he wanted it too. He gave a nod and she grinned. She moved herself down and took in the size of him. She wasn't sure that she would be able to take it all in her mouth but she liked a challenge. She swiped her tongue over the slit of him and he fell back onto the pillows, cursing softly. She sunk her mouth around him and she growled in frustration as she realized that there was a lot more to go and wrapped a hand around the base of him. She moved mouth and hand in tandem, both going so slowly that she knew she was being cruel but she wanted him completely undone beneath her. She felt a sense of power of the world's most deadly angel completely at her mercy. She could feel that he was holding back and that just wouldn't do. She quickened the pace and heard his ragged breath working in time with her movements. She pulled her mouth off of him and glared up at him.

"Now is not the time to be utilising that steel willpower." He let out a shaking breath.

"I don't want to hurt you," he said and she smirked at him.

"So you like it rough, huh?" His eyes went slightly wide as she pushed her mouth around him again, more forceful this time and gripped him a little tighter. His hips jerked into her touch and she hummed in approval.

"Holy shit," he said, a hand fisting in her hair and she moaned around him. His hips jerked again and she rode through the feeling of him sliding deeper into her throat. She placed a hand on his hip and he stilled. She felt a sense of pleasure and something deeper in her chest that she knew if she wanted to stop, even though he was harder than she had ever seen anyone be, he would. She took in a big breath through her nose and pushed past the point of comfort. He swore loudly as she met her hand with her mouth.

"Ella." He moaned out her name in a way that made her shudder with pleasure. She pulled him out almost completely and took him in again just as deeply, sucking hard. "Shit Ella. I'm not gonna last much longer." She hummed, letting him know that it was okay. She rose to the tip again, moving her hand from the base of him to cup him completely and took him in as far as she could. He swore as she felt him come. She moved slowly to a point it was more comfortable for her as he rode through his release. When she was sure he was finished, she pulled her mouth from him gently and fell beside him. He was still facing the ceiling with his eyes closed and she couldn't help but chuckle slightly.

"No, no, no, you're not allowed to do that," he said, breathing heavily.

"Do what?" she asked and he opened his eyes to look at her.

"You're not allowed to do that, like that." She made a face that plainly told him how confused she was.

"You're Ella."

"Well I clearly didn't make you come hard enough if you still remember my name." His eyes flew open and he righted himself, pulling up his sweatpants.

"I don't wanna think about why you're so good at that." She rolled her eyes.

"I read good books," she said and he laughed now, pulling her close to him.

"What you said, before." He swallowed hard. "It meant a lot to me." She leaned up and kissed him. He pulled away after a little while and smiled at her sweetly as he looked between them, an evil glint in his eyes.

"No, it's time for sleep," she said sternly.

"That's not fair," he whined next to her ear, taking her earlobe between his teeth and nibbling gently.

"Life's a bitch, what're you gonna do about it." He took a breath and she placed a finger over his mouth. "Don't answer that." He laughed and pulled her tighter against him.

Nestled in his arms, breathing in the scent of his skin deeply, the taste of him still in her mouth, she finally fell asleep.

There was a persistent knocking on the door and Ella felt the bed shift beside her.

"Whatever they're selling we're not interested," she said, trying to get back into a comfortable position. She heard Will's soft laugh and heard him open the door.

"Ella's ceremony starts in an hour." Ella's eyes opened but she stayed where she lay.

"Thanks Mag's," he said. She heard the woman tut at him and Ella smiled. She heard his soft footsteps making his way back.

"She's gonna stop helping you soon," she teased and he stood against the doorframe. He took up most of the space; this small hut made him look even ridiculously larger than he did in a normal room.

"Morning princess." He gave her a lazy grin and she felt a wave of pleasure course through her. He rose an eyebrow, noticing either the glazed look of her eyes or the change in her scent but she heard a barking from outside and she shot out of the bed.

She rummaged through her bag, finding her soft, cream sweater and throwing it over her head, then quickly re-did the bun on top of her head.

"Nona and Ruby are here." She grinned at him as she ran past him and out of the door.

He watched after her from the doorway of the hut.

She ran to Elena, pulling her into a hug and Elena hugged her back as fiercely. Ruby was sitting patiently at Elena's side and it didn't take long for Ella to disentangle herself from Elena to fall to her knees and shower the dog with just as much affection. Tony, his dad, had joined them and he smiled at him from across the ring, raising a hand in hello.

He couldn't help but marvel at the woman before him. As much as he had very much enjoyed the attention she showed him earlier, it was her words to him that stuck in his mind. He had long let go of the resentment he felt at being passed around once he was orphaned, he'd come out of it rather well with a parent who loved him and the best job in the world. On top of that he was the fastest, strongest angel there probably has ever been but what had held him back is knowing that everyone in Astridia thought of him as an idiot who swings a sword, good for nothing except grunting and killing. He still didn't think himself good enough for her but he would accept her love if she was willing to give it. It may have been his job to put her safety first but it didn't feel like a job. It felt like a blessing. He knew that ultimately her safety came first, if he had to leave her to keep her safe then he would but there was no chance in hell that anywhere but with him is where she would be safest.

"How're you holding up kiddo?" Tony asked, coming to stand next to him.

"I'm fine, I'm just in awe at her." He nodded his head towards Ella.

"You always have been you goof." He ruffled Will's hair and he swatted the elder's hands away.

"I have not."

"You love her," he said. It wasn't a question.

"Yeah," Will said simply.

"Today is gonna suck for you then." Will couldn't help but laugh.

"Sure is. Any advice?" Tony turned and looked at Will.

"No, you've never needed me to tell you what you should be doing. You do the right thing on instinct." Will swallowed and smiled gratefully.

Blake came to stand beside him as Tony moved to speak to Magda. He passed him a cup of coffee and smiled at him. Will looked into Blake's face and smiled slightly.

"It bugs you, how fine she is with all of this, doesn't it?" Will said, blowing on his coffee before taking a sip. Blake's shoulders sagged a little.

"No, not really. I'm proud of her but hell if it doesn't make me feel a little ashamed of myself." He toed the dirt covered ground with a boot, kicking a small rock away from him.

"Your situation was completely different Blake. You had the option and you still chose to do it. That takes a lot of guts."

"Thanks." He shrugged.

"And she's proud of you, too." Blake nodded. "And you're about to tell me that if I hurt her you'll kill me, right?" He laughed then, kicking another rock.

"No. I see the way you look at her." Will followed his gaze and was not surprised to see it had landed on Sam.

"I've seen the way he looks at you," Will offered.

"It doesn't matter about me and him," he said quickly. "I will get over it."

"Have you two even had a conversation?"

"No, he told me that if I had chosen to stay mortal he would have to leave, he couldn't risk staying my angel of solace if I'd stayed mortal." Will cleared his throat.

"And we both know why that is," Will said simply. "Just give it time." Blake sighed.

"He feels guilty. He feels like he shouldn't have told me that. Like it swayed my decision."

"Did it?" he asked bluntly.

"No, being given the choice to channel all that rage in me into something not only productive but to do some good in the world? It was no contest. I couldn't stay a pressure pot of rage with no outlet." Will nodded.

"That's the conversation you need to have." He nodded and they both looked back at Ella. She was holding Mal's hand now and they were sitting on the log together talking quietly. As they watched, Ella kissed her friend on the top of her hair and went to speak to Elena again. She pulled her away to the side and they were talking quietly to each other. Ella showed Elena the Votum and Will pulled his eyes away, smiling slightly into his cup. Sam came and joined them.

"I asked Madga about what happened with the Votum in the bar. She said she's never heard of anything like that before but she's gonna subtly put some feelers out to see if anyone else has." Will nodded.

"Do you think she will want to be bonded?" Blake asked Will who shrugged.

"I don't know." He sighed. Sam and Blake looked at each other and something passed between them in that way they communicated without having to say a word.

"Share with the class," he said, taking the final sip of coffee, dumping the dregs onto the ground.

"She will bond with you," Blake said simply, patting his shoulder.

"We'll see."

Elena had braided Ella's hair away from her face. She was still in her leggings and cream sweater and Will couldn't take his eyes off of her. He watched as she wrung her hands nervously. She broke away from Elena and Magda who seemed to be discussing the order of what they would do and came over to stand in front of him.

"You okay?" he asked her, putting both hands on each arm. She nodded and bit her lip.

"What's gonna happen? Am I gonna feel different? Am I gonna feel weird? Will I still feel like me?" He melted a little at the sight of her panic and he pulled her gently into his chest and cradled her head.

"You'll be able to feel something like a light electric current. It won't hurt, it'll just feel a little funny at first." He stroked a hand up and down her back. "There will be a few minutes after that where you'll get back the memories that we had to change. It will feel like a long time to you but it'll only be a few minutes to us." He brushed a kiss down to her cheek. "You'll feel a lot of different emotions. While that's happening, the magic will start to undo the bindings on your powers. You might feel a little stronger or lighter, you'll feel different but you won't see any of the big differences for a few days yet. Your eyesight and hearing will improve. Your reflexes will sharpen." She nodded against his chest.

"Then what happens?" she whispered.

"Our bond will break. Then everyone else will go back to the house. You and I will stay here a few more nights. When you first get your powers unbound, your magic can react with your emotions. You're going to be going through a lot of different emotions with all of your memories coming back so it's better for it just to be me and you." She pulled back slightly and looked up at him.

"You said I might be angry with you." He nodded. "Then someone else should stay with me. I don't want to put you in danger." He smiled gently at her.

"I can't imagine anyone is going to be your favorite, princess. I'm the fastest and have the best defenses." She looked down at her hands again.

"Okay." She looked so small and scared in that moment that he put both hands on her face and brought his mouth gently to hers. It was a soft, reassuring kiss and unlike most of the others they'd shared it wasn't born from want or need. It came from comfort and reassurance. She relaxed in his arms and put her own around his neck.

"Finally!" Elena said loud enough for them to hear and Ella pulled away laughing.

"Are you ready Ella?" Magda asked who was smiling too. With one last glance at Will who nodded, she turned.

"Yes."

# CHAPTER TWENTY SEVEN

It took more than willpower to stop himself from walking to her while she went through the ceremony. He saw the surprised look at her hands as she experienced the electrical sensation on her skin, then he saw her eyes slip shut and the range of emotions flitting across her face. At one point she looked as though she was in agony and he shifted in his seat. Leo placed a hand on his shoulder and he looked at his friend. He hadn't told her about the feeling of the bond breaking because he knew there was no way to prepare her for it. Tony stood beside him, holding him tightly by the shoulders. Sam had moved to stand behind Ella. Will braced himself and then it happened. Ella sunk to the ground but Sam had already caught her. She let out a shriek of grief and Will had grunted.

It felt as though his skin was being ripped from his muscle, every fibre of his being felt like it was being cauterised and he couldn't concentrate on anything but Ella's sobs. He twisted in sheer pain. Tony yelled and Blake and Leo pinned him as best they could. Will roared in agony and Leo and Blake were both pushed away from him. He made it only a step or two and collapsed into a heap on the ground. Ella was no longer sobbing but had gone limp in Sam's arms. Leo and Blake ran to help up Will who was shaking all over.

The ceremony was over. Ella had opened her eyes after a few minutes. She was deathly pale and he knew he probably didn't look much better. Ella stood listening to Magda for a few minutes and Elena rushed over to him.

"Will, are you okay?" He nodded and looked away from the tears in her eyes.

"I've never seen a bond breaking that looked like that," she said, almost whispering. He had been told that it would be painful. He would feel the physical pain of the bond between them being ripped away from them and Ella would feel the emotional turmoil of what removing that bond meant. He had thought when it was explained to him that they just hadn't accurately described the agony.

"What do you mean?" She shook her head.

"When Glen and I had our bond broken, I sobbed and he had one friend supporting him through the pain. This, between you and Ella. This is the most damage I have seen it do." She was shaking slightly.

"Maybe because of how we feel about each other," he mused. Elena gave him a watery smile.

"That was my thought, too." He patted his shoulder and moved back to Ella. Mal, Magda, Blake and Sam had already hugged Ella and told them they'd see her in a few days. Lyra stood to the side and waved awkwardly when Ella caught her eye. He watched as Elena hugged her granddaughter and Ruby rubbed herself against Ella's legs. She unfolded an arm to pet her companion but she looked small, closed in on herself. He yearned to reach out and touch her but after the ceremony, he had felt more tired than he had possibly ever felt and he thought Ella must be moments away from either exploding or passing out. Leo hugged her the tightest and whispered in her ear. She smiled at him as he left and they all made their way out of the clearing. Sam and Blake would be patrolling around the area and Magda was casting a protection spell around the camp before leaving to make sure no one snuck up on them unawares too. He hoped that it meant he could concentrate on Ella for the next few days.

He waited for her to be ready to speak so he lit the fire and disappeared into one of the huts to grab a blanket. She jumped a little when he wrapped it around her shoulders. He immediately backed off and sat at the other end of the log. It was normal when a new angel got their gifts for them to be shouting and screaming. Blake's had hit him hard. Although he had no memories to be returned to him, adjusting to the new feelings, saying goodbye to his mortal life. It had been a lot for him to process. Leo had been manic, pacing up and down, asking more questions than Will knew how to answer. Plus he had the extra worry of finding out what Ella was to become on top of his own memories being returned to him, but the only memories they had removed from Leo had been the entirety of the scene of how they had found their mother when she was killed.

This was different. She was staring into the fire, those cold, steel eyes glazed, not like he had saw in her earlier with lust, no these were the eyes of someone who wasn't taking in any information in front of them, she had completely shut herself off from the present and was working through–knowing Ella–methodically all of the information that she now had to process. Will would not breathe easy again until she had made a joke. Ella making a joke was her way of signalling to those around her that she was okay.

They stayed sat on the log for a few hours. Will had passed her a tea that she barely drank and she had mumbled thank you, the first words she had spoken since the others had left.

"So..." She cleared her throat a little. "So the man who was in the kitchen, that... killed my mom. Could have been Dominic?" Will sat up straight and turned to her slightly.

"We don't know for sure. He was never caught but they think it was likely that it was someone who was working for him. They estimate that at that time he would have already been a demon for a very long time and that night they had a break in at the Nerium in Astridia. Any demon who passes through to Astridia gets eviscerated before they can step onto the soil. So they think it was a fallen who was working for him, to steal more of the powers."

"You said he wasn't a normal demon, because he had so many of the angel's powers?" She was still looking into the fire but he was glad she was talking finally.

"Yes, we don't know what would happen to him if he wanted to pass through the portal. There isn't anyone else like him, but they don't think he has ever attempted it, he's only ever tried to send others in his place since he left." He had his answers ready. He'd had years to think of what questions she would ask him and what he would need to say to her.

"So the asshole didn't even come and kill her himself." She tightened the grip on her mug handle and Will stopped himself from offering her a comforting touch. This was going to be much harder than he ever imagined.

"I'm sorry, Ella," he said and her eyes slid slowly to his.

"So you stopped that part of my dreams and a few conversations that could make me think that something weird was going on." She sighed. "Most of the moments through the last few years where you were saving my ass or looking out for me." She half smiled. His heart started racing. She didn't sound angry.

"I did it because if you had known earlier, before you were ready... you might have tried to reject it, tried to fight getting your powers. That would have left you with a whole load of shit from the Order and if you had left, you'd have been hunted down until you were dead." He swallowed and felt a prickle behind his eyes. "I hate that I had to take that choice away from you but I'd do it again in a heartbeat because it kept you safe." A tear rolled down his cheek and he wiped it away on the back of his hand.

"I know, I get it." His head snapped up to hers and she was still looking at him.

"I don't love the fact that my mind was messed with but as soon as I saw what was changed, I knew why you did it." She shrugged. "Thank you, for not taking everything about Mom's death from me. It may have hurt to go through it so young but I couldn't bare being lied to about that. Not about all of it." Will did reach out a hand but pulled it away at once.

"The bond," she said simply and he placed a hand over his eyes. "That was..." She appeared not to have any words for it.

"I didn't know it would be like that. I knew it would be painful but that was not what I was expecting." She looked at him then.

"You felt it too?" He nodded and then shook his head.

"Kinda. I felt the physical pain of the bond being ripped apart. You felt the emotional pain. Elena told me after she had never seen one like it." Ella had shifted and moved along the log towards him. "I thought you screaming was in my head," she said quietly and there was a slight wobble to her voice. He placed a hand over hers.

"No, that wasn't in your head." She let some tears fall into her lap.

"Something happened, when the bond broke. I had another memory come back to me." He cocked his head confused.

"The night I went on a date with Lucas, I thought it had been such a good date. I didn't understand why I was having such weird feelings about him and such strong feelings for you but after seeing that it makes sense." Will gaped at her.

"Lucas had someone, a warlock probably, make you forget that night, changed your memories. I thought." He gulped past a hard knot in his throat. "I thought you were never going to remember that night." She sobbed then as she flew at him, dropping her mug on the ground and the blanket fell from her shoulders as she threw her arms around him. He caught her and she squeezed him tightly.

"I'm so glad I got that memory back." She sobbed into his ear and he clung to her.

"Me too," he said thickly. They stayed like that for a little while, long enough that the sky had started to darken, the cold October evening creeping up on them.

"What was that, that he did to my mouth?" she asked after some time.

309

"The ash kiss." She pulled away from him, grabbing the blanket from behind her she moved so that she was huddled into him and wrapped the blanket around both of them.

"What was it supposed to do?" He made a disgusted noise in his throat.

"The ash kiss is what a fallen can use to make a mortal do their bidding. While the burning is taking root, it makes you feel weird and like you're high. If you were alone, you might have walked right out of your house to find him. Once it had taken you completely, if you kissed him again, it would have been sealed. He would have had a level of control over you." Her mouth was slightly open in horror.

"That's gross."

"Yeah, he saw me in your room with you through the window and must have known I'd let you ride it out with me. I can only imagine what he thought we were getting up to. So while I went after him, he had someone mess with your memory to make you forget the ash kiss. I think him taking away the memory of everything else that happened that night... with me, was more to spite me than help him." His hands balled into fists at the memory.

They stayed quietly wrapped up together for a while longer.

"Thank you, for staying with me. I'm going to get some sleep, it's been a long day," she said and he nodded, leaving her to her thoughts for a little while.

A few hours later when he crept into the hut he saw that she was still awake.

"Can't sleep?" he asked. Her eyes slid to his.

"You're an angel of armour, Leo is an angel of oblivion, Blake is an angel of mercy, Sam an angel of solace," she reeled off, ticking everyone off on her fingers. "You said Dina was an angel of fortune. Is that all of the different types of angels?" she asked.

"There are also angels of devotion," he said quietly. "They help people find love, true soulmates among the mortals. True mates among the angels are rare. In fact, I'm not entirely sure they exist." She nodded.

"And Mal is a witch," she said. This time he nodded. She was processing. She'd learned most of this information over the course of the last few days but only now did she have time to let it all sink in.

"Did Lucas die in the bar?" His eyes found hers again and he sighed.

"No, him, Dina and a few of their main cronies got away while we were fighting." She looked at him alarmed.

"I'm not going to let him get to you, Ella."

"I know." His chest tightened at her words.

311

"I think I'd like to kill him myself." Will felt a thrum of pleasure at the words. He could only imagine how magnificent she would look in combat.

"I'll try my best, princess." She gave him a weary smile.

"Get some rest." He turned to leave.

"You're not staying here?" He turned back.

"I thought you might like some time to yourself." She shook her head.

"I'm not angry at you Will, I'm not angry at anyone." He moved forwards and slipped off his shoes, pulling his shirt over his head and pulled back the blankets before climbing in beside her. Immediately she shuffled towards him and he pulled her into his chest. She gave a little contented sigh and he couldn't stop himself from feeling a fleeting moment of joy that maybe this wouldn't all end in tears after all.

# CHAPTER TWENTY EIGHT

S he had been sleeping for hours. Will had slipped out of the bed and met Leo at the edge of the clearing as he delivered the breakfast that Nona had prepared.

"How's she doing?" he asked.

"Amazing. She hasn't even attempted to use magic, nothing has come spilling out of her, no shouting and ranting and raving." Leo looked surprised.

"Is she giving you hell for messing around with her head?" he asked, wincing slightly.

"No. She just said she understands why we did it. Honestly, if it wasn't from the power I can feel running through her when I touch her, I wouldn't even think she'd gone through the ceremony."

"She's let you touch her?" Leo said alarmed.

"She flung herself at me and hugged me." His mouth fell open in an almost comical O.

"You're gonna have to try and get her to siphon off some of that magic before she comes home." He nodded.

"I'll think of something." Leo nodded.

"Tell her I miss her."

"I will."

There was a deafening blood-curdling scream and Leo went to move forward.

"Go, I got it." He pushed Leo back who looked furious but his orange and red wings flared behind him as he took to the sky.

He ran as fast as he could, flinging himself through the door to the hut and stopped dead. Ella was screaming engulfed in a layer of bright blue lightning.

"Holy shit," Will breathed. He'd never heard of a Guardian with powers like this, there hadn't been one for centuries. He gave a little prayer that he wouldn't burst into flames as he clambered onto the bed and touched her. There was pain but it was bearable. It didn't seem as though she could even feel him so he placed his body flush against hers. Her screaming stopped and he grunted in pain. Her eyes flew open and now it was only her hands that were encircled in the blue light. She shook her hands and watched as the lightning fell away from her.

"Will!" she screamed. He moaned. He could feel that his entire body was burned where it had touched hers.

"I'm okay," he gritted out.

"Are you fucking insane!" she screamed. She was sobbing but her cries became less as he pushed his healing magic through him.

"How do I do it, how do I help." She sobbed again.

"Place your hands over me and imagine all of the marks shrinking away." She looked at him as though he was crazy. He pulled off his shirt that was singed and she stared as the forked lines over his body withdrew one by one.

She placed a hand on his chest and closed her eyes. He stopped trying to heal himself and after a moment or two, he felt as though he was fine. He looked down and there wasn't a single mark on his body. No lightning marks and not even pale scars littered his tanned skin.

"Ella," he breathed. She opened one eye and he laughed.

"I was scared I'd made it worse you jackass!" she said, opening her eyes and giving him a once over.

"You look different."

"You healed everything. All of my scars, they're gone." Her eyes widened and she looked down at her hand.

"I didn't mean to!" she said and he laughed again.

"Quit laughing at me!"

"I'm sorry but you have no idea how extraordinary you are. I think I know why that Votum blasted an entire bar full of demons. Your power... It's big." She was wringing her hands together.

"What do you mean big?"

"I mean," he said, crawling towards her. "I've only ever heard stories as a child about a Guardian of the Gate that could heal every wound and produce lightning at their touch." She looked down at her hands. She narrowed her eyes in concentration and lightning sparked at her fingertips. She yelled.

"Shit!" She shook her hands again and it disappeared.

"Come on, let's go and eat breakfast and we can talk about whatever the fuck that was," he said and she went to open her mouth in protest but her stomach rumbled.

"Traitor," she muttered to her belly and motioned for him to go ahead of her.

He quickly changed into clothes that weren't

burnt and singed and sat down on the log next to her, dishing out the pastries that Elena had made for them.

"Is there any point us trying to make sense of what happened in there?" she said, brushing the crumbs from her hands the moment she had finished her breakfast.

"Parts of it. I need to know what set you off." She closed her eyes and he straightened.

"I woke up and you weren't there. I had a flashback of the man in the kitchen, Lucas lurking in the trees. It was like a waking nightmare..." She turned her face away from him. He could see her blush so he pulled her face gently back towards him.

"You've been through so much shit in the last few months, I'd be concerned if you weren't having these sorts of reactions. From now on, I won't get up until you wake." She looked at him questioningly.

"That means you would have to spend every night with me."

He nodded and let a feline grin slip into place.

"Will..." she said, half laughing. "I need to try and learn to master this by myself." He nodded in agreement.

"Yes, but right now, before you're trained, until you feel like you can take care of yourself, I'll be there." She bit her lip.

"If I had you in my bed every night, I'd never be able to sleep alone again," she breathed and he shifted closer to her.

"Then don't."

"Don't what?"

"Ever sleep alone again," he murmured and pressed his lips firmly against hers. It had been killing him, not being able to kiss her for so long and he wondered how he had managed so many years without doing so.

She kissed him back, wrapping her arms around his neck and not protesting when he lifted her into his lap.

They'd spent the rest of the day and the afternoon talking quietly. Will showed her little bits of magic she can use to get rid of the excess when she feels like it's gonna burst out of her. He watched her as she created fires with her lightning and then snuffed them out with her magic. She looked tired, she looked confused and wary but he kept staring and staring at her.

He jumped when she sat down next to him.

"Hey, princess."

"Will, why... why did you think I would hate you so much once I found out the truth?" He wasn't sure what he had been expecting, but it hadn't been that.

"As your angel of armour, a lot of the decisions

came down to me. I had to act like an asshole and tell you no because I was the one who made the decisions. You had just started feeling something for me and honestly, I thought that the moment you knew that I'd manipulated you, you'd want nothing more to do with me. That's why I never really acted on my feelings, I thought I was gonna get my heart broken when you realized what I was and what I'd had to do."

She took a moment to process.

"You need to come with me," she snarled and for the first time, she looked angry. She stalked off towards the hut that they had left earlier that morning and when he followed her in, he saw her with her arms folded in front of the bed glaring at him.

"How fucking dare you." He blinked at her.

"I'm sure I will have deserved it but you'll need to be a little more specific." He winced. He had been expecting to get chewed up and spat out ever since her ceremony but the sudden shift in her demeanour put him a little on the back foot.

"How dare you think so little of me that you would assume that I would hold any of this against you, or even worse, hate you when all you did is your job of keeping me safe." His mouth fell open and he barely had time to register what was happening before she hurled herself into his arms again and pressed her mouth to his. He was almost knocked backwards with the force of it but he caught her around the waist and her legs wrapped around his. He didn't care about anything else. She didn't hate him, she still wanted him.

# CHAPTER
# TWENTY
# NINE

It might have been a cruel thing to do, she thought, leading him to believe she was truly angry with him but the fact of the matter was that she was a little hurt by his lack of faith in her. Though she thought of the conversation about him feeling as though he was not worthy of her and that probably had something to do with it. She may be forgiving him too easily but she was tired. She was tired of fighting her feelings for him, tired of being sensible and she was so fucking tired waiting for the time to be right. If they kept waiting for the perfect time, nothing would ever happen. So she kissed him. He pulled away and she jumped down from him, yanking at the hem of his t-shirt and he quickly helped her lift it over his head. The moment he was free of the offending piece of clothing she was kissing his neck, before moving on to his chest. He slid his hands beneath the soft sweater and she lifted her arms, gasping a little when he slid her hands up the entirety of her body, gliding over her stomach and her breasts to push the fabric up, waiting until it reached her chin to pull it gently off of her. Her skin felt like it was made of flame and he was being so frustratingly gentle. Her hands reached down to his sweatpants and tugged them away from him again. He chuckled slightly.

"Slow down princess." She bit out a laugh.

"I don't think you understand how much I need you." He heard the strain in her voice and he grunted, stepping out of his clothes and reaching for her. He undid her bra and she pulled it away from her. The moment she had looked back at him he had picked her up and threw her on the bed behind her. Literally threw her. Like she was a piece of clothing he'd decided not to wear and she couldn't speak with how sexy she found it. He pulled her towards the edge of the bed and slid down her pants as slowly and frustratingly as he had done her sweater. She growled in annoyance but he chuckled, pulling them off completely. They were both bare now and he was looking at her like she was the most beautiful, glittering jewel he'd ever seen.

"I know you told me I'd never have to get on my

knees for you, princess," he said, kneeling down between her legs and tugging her closer still. She could feel his warm breath on the heat between her legs and she gasped. "But I think we can make an exception," he continued.

She moaned the moment his mouth was on her. His massive hands were pinning her hips to the edge of the bed and she writhed beneath him.

"So impatient," ge said before sliding his tongue up her center, the tip of his tongue catching that bundle of nerves and she moaned again, her breasts ached with heaviness, her nipples peaked. Every inch of her body was in need of him. He pressed himself deeper, slipping his tongue inside her and she bucked her hips despite the hands at her waist. He pulled his mouth away and she swore. The swear turned into a groan immediately as he replaced his tongue with a finger and focused his magnificent tongue on her clit. She was about to reach her release when he added another finger and she screamed in pleasure, clenching around his fingers. Her skin went from flame to ice as the force of her orgasm pounded through her. She had barely got her breath back before he was pulling her into his arms. He lifted her again and he carried her from the end of the bed to the middle and he laid her gently down amongst the pillows.

"You doing okay there champ?" he said with a smirk and she narrowed her eyes.

"Getting a little bored actually," she said and he stilled above her.

"You wound me, you evil little thing," he said, kissing up her bare stomach.

"I'm sure you'll get over it." He grinned up at her and carried on kissing up her body. He palmed one breast in his hand, the other he flicked his tongue over the hardened nipple and then moved his head to the other. Expecting him to do the same she cried out in pleasure when he took it lightly between his teeth and tugged. She was instantly slick between her thighs again and ready for him.

"Will." He raised his head and looked her directly in the eyes.

"Yes, princess?"

"I need you." Tears stung her eyes and she hoped to hell she did not cry. "I need to feel you inside me. The moment that bond was broken I felt wrong. I need to feel you," she breathed out. His eyes were so dark with lust that she couldn't see any gold in them. He let out a feral groan and he slid himself slowly inside her. He stopped part of the way in, letting her adjust to his size. It was safe to say she had never been with anyone as big as Will.

"You ready for more?" he asked quietly and she nodded. He pushed in deeper and grunted at the effort she knew it was taking him to not drive right into her. "You're doing so good, princess." She lost all sense of fear and pushed her hips towards his. He let out a chuckle but stopped her from going any further with a hand.

"I know you like being told you're a good girl but if you hurt yourself, you won't be a good girl anymore." He grinned wickedly at the effect his words had on her as she let out a whine of frustration.

He pushed himself in deeper and she knew he was almost fully inside her. He positioned himself fully over her and looked into her eyes.

"I need you to listen, sweetheart." She stilled and looked at him. "If at any point it hurts or you want me to stop, you're gonna need to say so. If you can't say so, you're gonna tap me right here," he said, pointing to the side of his neck. "Got it?" he asked.

As she nodded, he slipped a hand to the back of her scalp and gripped her hair, pushing himself fully into her.

"Atta girl," he whispered, before covering her mouth with a searing kiss. She was completely lost in ecstasy. He moved at a steady pace, kissing her slowly and tugging her hair slightly with every thrust. She was moaning into his mouth and moving her hips in time to his.

He pulled out of her completely and she barely had time to open her mouth when he whispered.

"It's time for you to get on your knee's again, sweetheart." Gathering his meaning she rolled over and he lifted her hips, whispering in her ear as her brain started to resume normal speed. "You might want to find something to hold onto, princess." He growled and she lifted her hips, although she wasn't quite aware of doing it. She felt like her body was taking its cue's from him now instead of her brain. She fisted her hands in the sheets before her and he chuckled.

"Why is it that the only time you seem to do as you're told is when I'm fucking you." She breathed out a laugh.

"The only time you can tell me what to do is when we're naked." He pushed into her fast and she cried out.

"You good?" She nodded and he started to move. He started off slower than she knew he wanted to and she pushed back into him to encourage him to go faster.

"I'm not going to hurt you, princess," he said, halting her slightly with his hands. She let out a frustrated snarl.

"Why the fuck not." He groaned and pressed his forehead into her back.

"You're gonna be the death of me." He ran a hand up her back and fisted it into her hair. He wrapped an arm around her waist and used the arm to haul her up, pressing her back to his chest and the change of the angle made her whimper. She started to move but he stopped her.

"Stay fucking still," he warned.

"Make me," she teased. He slid a hand around her throat and she stopped moving.

"Remember to tap out if you need to," he murmured into her ear but she shook her head. Her meaning was made clear as she felt her muscles clench around him still seated inside her. He moaned, his breath hot against her ear.

"You're incredible, do you know that?" he asked, his hand still at her neck but there was no pressure. He seemed to be able to tell that this was something new for her and he didn't want to overwhelm her but the feeling of his large hand at her throat made her feel like she was utterly at his mercy and she couldn't have been happier about it. He was thrusting in and out of her harder and faster now, using the hand on her throat to keep her where he wanted her and the arm still around her waist to keep them both steady. Ella had no idea that sex could be like this. She liked sex as much as the next girl but the few people she had been with had been more worried about getting their pleasure than her and she had more luck making herself come than anyone else but this was something entirely alien to her.

He released her throat and moved her back down so that she was kneeling before him again. She thought he must be close because he was thrusting harder and harder and she was starting to shiver and she could feel the building pressure in her abdomen. She fisted her hands into the sheets again and their moans mingled together in the silent air around them.

"Fuck," he muttered, his thrusts becoming more erratic and she clenched herself around him and he swore again. He shifted slightly and caught a spot that had her shouting out and seeing stars, she had never come this hard. It kept washing over her in waves but she felt his release barrel through him. Once they were both spent he pulled himself gently from her and scooped her into his arms. He kissed her cheeks, her forehead, her eyelids. He moved down to her throat and she smiled.

"You okay?" he asked.

"What kind of a stupid question is that?" she

asked. Her eyes were still closed and she was enjoying being in his arms.

"No need to be sassy, sweetheart." He nipped at her shoulder and she laughed. "I'm guessing we did a few things you'd not done before," he murmured against her skin. She nodded lazily.

"Anything you didn't like?" He pushed some hair away from her face and her eyes opened, looking directly into his.

"There was nothing that happened there that I didn't like," she said and he smiled and kissed her again.

"You go get cleaned up, meet me out by the fire." He went to release her from his grasp.

"Are you insane?" she asked, widening her eyes. "It's freaking freezing out there." He smiled a wide, charming smile and she couldn't quite believe that this moment was real.

"It is, but I have some of my biggest, comfiest sweaters for you to wear, blankets, thermals for both of us and..." he said, untangling their bodies and she shivered at the loss of body heat. He pulled up his sweatpants and turned to rummage in a box that was stored under the bed. She wrapped herself in a blanket and pulled her hair down, running a hand through it and wishing that she had unbound it before they'd had sex. Not only would it have made it easier for him to grab hold of but also she thought she probably had something akin to a bird's nest sitting on top of her head.

"This," he said, holding up a bag of giant marshmallows, some chocolate and some gram crackers. She paused for a moment stunned and then she let out a snort of laughter.

"We're making s'more's?" His face fell a little so she grinned at him and his face lit up like a firework. She went to the bathroom and looked in the mirror. The size of the smile that was on her face was borderline obnoxious. She saw to her needs and then rummaged in the bag that she had brought in with her and pulled out a hair brush. She brushed her hair as fast as she could. She came out of the bathroom and passed Will. He stopped her with a hand to her waist and kissed her softly on the mouth.

"I've left some warm clothes on the bed for you." He pressed his lips against hers softly once again.

"Thank you." She sighed and he moved aside, going into the bathroom himself. She pulled on the thermal undershirt he had provided and opted for a pair of her cosiest sweatpants.

She was pulling on some big woollen socks and she

noticed that he was now stood in the tiny doorway of the bathroom, watching her.

"They really didn't make this place Will size, huh?" she said, tugging an old pair of boots over the socks and turning to choose one of Will's ridiculously large hoodies. He came up behind her and pointed at a grey one.

"That's the warmest, and no, they did not think of us overly large giraffes when building these huts." She pulled the sweater over her head and was lost in the scent of him for a moment. When she opened her eyes he was biting his lip.

"What?" she asked, pulling a hat over her head.

"You look so small in my clothes," he said, nodding to the hem of the sweater that reached her mid-thigh.

"Hey, I am not small. You're just a giant."

"I'm six foot five," he said, narrowing his eyes. "I don't think I need to give up on human interaction and move to a cave in the mountains just yet." She paused and looked at him.

"Sam's tall... are Astridians usually on the larger side?" she asked. He nodded.

"Yeah, the angels that don't come from angel parentage but from mortal ones tend to be a more... regular height. Except Blake, he's just tall." He shrugged. She rolled her eyes and pointed towards the door.

"Come on, make me a s'more." He grabbed her hand and pulled her out of the door into the cold night.

# CHAPTER THIRTY

It was the next morning when they heard a noise from the camp outside. They'd spent the morning having lazy, slow sex and were just getting around to getting dressed. She had tried twice to put clothes on but it appeared Will had an aversion to them today, but finally he was actually letting her get dressed. They looked at each other and Will put a finger to his lips. He motioned for her to stay put and he pulled a lethal looking dagger seemingly out of thin air. A thousand more questions popped into Ella's head that she stamped down. He opened the door and peered outside. His body relaxed instantly.

"Leo? What's going on?" he asked. Ella moved forwards and followed him out of the door. Leo was pale and looked like he had seen a ghost. Ella went to repeat Will's question when Leo looked her in the eye.

"Dad's here." She stopped still. As far as she was concerned she didn't have a father. She'd never met him, he'd hightailed it out of their lives the moment their mom had found out that she was having a girl. She had to tell him then, about what and who she was and that it would be passed to Ella, so Will had explained to her at some point over the last day or so.

"He's no dad of mine," she snarled and Leo flinched slightly.

"He came back specifically for you." She clenched her fist and a bolt of lightning shot from her hand into the ground. It shuddered as it swallowed the impact of the magic. It was the first time that magic had come from her following a high emotion since she woke up alone, something that the rest of them had expected to happen pretty much as soon as she processed the ceremony.

"Ella." Will laid a hand on the bottom of her back and Leo flinched. Leo had found out the hard way that when someone was feeling that kind of emotion and couldn't control their magic, touching them was the last thing that you wanted to do. Ella breathed in and collected herself.

"I can't see him right now, Leo. It's too

dangerous," she said and he nodded.

"I know, but he's demanding it, he said it can't wait." Will snarled.

"I'll go speak to him."

"No," Ella said, holding her head high. "I'll go." Leo and Will looked at each other and she rolled her eyes but looked at Will. "Just stay close to me." Leo smiled at the sight of them and Ella tried hard not to roll her eyes again.

"Only if you're sure." Will sounded wary but she nodded.

By the time they got back to the house, Ella saw a pick-up truck that she didn't recognize in the driveway and she let the anger at the sight of it wash over her. There was a spark between her fingers but nothing more. Leo walked through the door first and into the kitchen. Ella followed, clutching Will's hand. The man standing before her looked vaguely like the old pictures she'd seen when she had asked Elena about her dad before but he was more lined, more grey and thinner. It looked as though the years had been hard on him and she couldn't help but feel a little bit glad at that. Blake and Sam were stood in the kitchen, too.

"Marcella," he said, taking her in, looking somewhat thunderstruck.

"My friends call me Ella."

"Ella."

"Not you, you don't get to call me anything." He closed his mouth and Blake and Sam who were standing the other side of the room nodded to Ella and left the room.

He looked at Will with a clear note of disapproval. Ella felt another spark between her fingers. Will squeezed her other hand and spoke low.

"Easy tiger." She took in a breath.

"Sit down," Ella said to him and he paused. She raised an eyebrow. "Sit or get out, you're in my home." He sat and had the common sense to look a little ashamed.

"Let's set a few ground rules. If you are going to be in this house, you will need to understand the following things." Leo was grinning wickedly at her and Will had moved a hand to her shoulder. "You will remember that I have never met you, you are less than a sperm donor. You are nothing to me." He went to open his mouth but she held up a finger and a flash of lightning sparked on the end of it. He paled and closed his mouth.

"You will also remember that I am a twenty-one year old woman, who can be where she wants with who she wants and if you ever look at my boyfriend like that again, you'll be out of this house faster than you can say deadbeat dad." She felt a squeeze on her shoulder and realized what she had said. They'd talk about that later. She snarled, moving a step closer to him.

"You will get exactly five minutes of my time to explain why you think you have the right to show up unannounced, twenty-one years too late and if it's to make amends and expect us to be one big happily family, I can save us all five minutes and tell you to get the fuck out of my house."

"Jesus princess, I said easy." She half smiled at him and turned back to the man sitting at the table.

"Your five minutes has already started," she said bluntly.

"Alright," he said, sighing. "I guess I'll skip the explanation. I've been sent to give you a message."

Everyone in the room seemed to look at each other with a blank, confused stare.

He clarified. "From Dominic Quinn."

---

Elena looked at than man in front of her.

"Michael, maybe we should go back to the explanation." Will was standing in front of her now and as much as she would usually have rolled his eyes at his alpha male bullshit, seeing her 'dad' looking up at him terrified made her forgive him, just this once.

"Maybe we should sit," Leo said, pointing towards the table. To save him from Will's wrath, probably. Elena and Leo made sure that they were sat either side of Michael.

"I'm not proud of what I did," he said, looking into Ella's eyes. "The woman I loved had just told me that she was an angel and that our daughter would be the next in line. It was... a lot." Will narrowed his eyes.

"The moment you bailed you would have had your mind wiped clean of the interactions by a member of the Order." The man's eyes moved from studying Ella's face to Will's.

"I did. I thought that we had argued, she had told me that she didn't love me, didn't want me around her or the kids. Up until recently, I thought I'd been forced out of their lives." He swallowed. "To now know it was my own decision to leave... that made me hate myself more than I thought possible." His eyes welled with tears.

"If you thought she had forced you to leave, why didn't you fight? Why did we never hear from you again?" he spoke quietly but there was an edge to his words.

"Your mother knew things about me, that if she wanted to, she could ruin my life."

"You thought that she was blackmailing you?" Ella asked, rage pounding through her like a pulse.

"Yes. I don't know why these Order people made me think this of her but it worked. It made me stay away." He seemed to be pleading with Ella whose hard features hadn't softened at all throughout the exchange.

Elena turned to look at the man next to her.

"Michael, why do you now remember everything?" Ella jumped slightly. She'd forgotten his name. She had trained herself so well to not think about him that everything she knew about him was buried deep, deep down.

"I was approached by a man called Lucas." Will stiffened and Ella grabbed his hand. The contact between them was enough for both of their rage to calm slightly.

"There's something I need to tell you all, before this story goes further," Michael said. He bit his lip and looked at Leo and Ella. Ella waved her hand to tell him to continue.

"I married a year or so after I left. I have two other children. One is eighteen and one is sixteen." Ella felt as though someone had thumped her hard in the back, all of the breath was knocked from her body.

"We have brothers or sisters?" Leo asked and Ella was shocked to see that he didn't look angry at all.

"Sisters. They're both girls." Ella squeezed her eyes closed. This was too much. Too much to process. A soothing hand ran up and down the length of her back and she took in a deep breath, pushing it out again as slowly as she could manage in time to the hand soothing her.

"Continue," she said, choosing to file the knowledge that she had two half-sisters away for her to freak out about later.

"Lucas started working with me in the factory, he was a nice guy, seemed like a good kid." Ella was definitely starting to feel sick now.

"When was this?"

"About 6 months ago." She squeezed her eyes shut.

"He didn't have any family so Maria, my wife, started inviting him to family dinners. One night he cornered me and told me that I'd been tricked, that he could help me. He was so... compelling." She couldn't help herself, she snorted with laughter.

"Yeah that sounds like Lucas."

"He took me to this dive bar downtown, a really

seedy looking place. I thought I was gonna have my head blown off but he just took me into this back room to meet with this guy called Dominic." Will leaned forward, both elbows on the table, his chin in his hands.

"What was the name of the bar?" Will asked.

"Lunar Wild," he answered instantly. "Dominic took away all of the false memories, I remembered everything. I told them I didn't want to get involved with them, that you guys were better off without me anyway." He took in a large breath. He seemed to be holding back tears but Ella was having trouble being sympathetic.

"They told me if I don't help them, if I didn't come back here to deliver the message, they'd hurt my family." He sobbed.

"Your other family, you mean," Ella shot back at him. Leo frowned.

"So what is the message?"

"Dominic told me that if you'd already had your gifting ceremony... that you'd better start training. War is coming." Will growled. A god's honest growl. For a moment Ella had thought Ruby had entered the room but the sound came from the man next to her.

"Well you've delivered the message, he can let your

family go," Leo said as Elena stood up and left the room.

"He's not going to let my family go. He wants to use us as messengers to you. He has armies, armies of demons, armies of hounds." Will's head snapped up again.

"Lunar hounds I assume?" Michael nodded.

"If you idiots tell me werewolves are a thing, I swear to god," Ella said quietly and Will smiled at her.

"Not in the sense of them being human turning into werewolves. But huge wolf hounds that can kill with a single bite, yes. Those were created by Dominic when he first became a demon." Ella sighed.

"Anything else I should be worrying about?"

"Sam will go through everything with you when your training starts. Tomorrow." She nodded.

"Are Lucas and Dominic still watching you?" Will asked Michael.

"Yes, I think so." He nodded. Elena had returned with Tony in tow.

"Michael, this is Tony. Will's father." Michael shook the man's hand and Ella's eyes narrowed. He'd never offered that courtesy to Will but then again, they'd both been more concerned with keeping Ella's rage at bay so she didn't fry him.

"Tony is going to arrange protection for you and your family." Michael looked panicked.

"No! There's no need. It'll only make things worse. They've already taken Marie and the girls to Lunar Wild, they've been there for weeks." He sobbed but tried to compose himself.

"I'm still at the house. They take me to them once a week where Dominic gives me his orders. I have to run errands for him." Tony and Will looked at each other and nodded at the same time.

"Okay," Tony said in his deep, calming voice. "Can you take a message back to him for us?" Michael nodded and Tony looked at Elena.

"We need to find out exactly what it is Dominic wants. If a war can be avoided, it should be." She nodded.

"Yes, agreed." They both turned to Michael and asked him to arrange a meeting between Dominic and us, to try and find out what Dominic wanted, if war could be avoided. Michael nodded and looked at Ella and Leo. He said goodbye to them and then looked as if he wanted to say something further but decided against it. He left the room and there was a few moments of silence that followed the sound of the front door being closed. They heard the sound of an engine and Tony looked back to Will.

"I'll need to go back to Astridia, warn the Order and gather all of the angels that are able to fight, put them through a crash course in battle training." Will nodded but looked a little sad.

"I'll be going back and forth as messenger from here to Astridia," Elena said and Ella looked at her. "Will, you're to stay in the house with Ella and Leo while Tony is away." Ella felt her face go hot and Tony smiled at her before turning to Will once again.

"If Blake and Sam wish to be closer, the house is open to them."

"That would be helpful, we need to get Ella trained as quickly as possible," Leo said, putting an arm around her shoulders.

"What about Mal?" she asked the room at large.

"There's plenty of room at our house," Tony said kindly and she smiled at him. He wasn't as fierce looking as his adopted son, he looked more like an approachable middle aged man than the lethal fighting machine that she now knew he was. He had a calming nature.

"She's currently back with her mother and grandmother. Magda has unbound her powers but Mal is insistent that she wants to move out. It may help having her so close. Magda can train you both together," Elena said to Ella who grinned. The fact that she didn't have to worry about not telling Mal anything anymore was a huge relief to her.

"Sam and I Will meet with Dominic," Leo said and Ella looked at him as if he had lost his mind.

"Absolutely not," she said. Leo laughed.

"Give me some credit, little sister. If Will goes the meeting would end in bloodshed." Will looked offended for a moment but relented.

"He has a point. Him and Sam are the least likely to lose their tempers. Plus..." he said, seeing that Ella was about to interrupt him. "He would be less threatened by an angel of solace and an angel of oblivion." Leo looked a little offended. Will grinned. "An error on his part, I assure you." Leo rolled his eyes but smiled.

"Why can't I go?" Ella asked.

"You're too important to be put within a mile radius of him. You're not trained and he's tried to kill you for months. Do you need me to go on?" Will said quickly.

"No, I get it." She huffed.

"I'm not saying you're not capable, Ella." He brushed his mouth over her temple.

"I know," she whispered, leaning into him.

# CHAPTER THIRTY ONE

The rest of the day was a flurry of activity. Will was packing up some things at his house to move into Ella's, she was clearing out some drawer space for him. It wasn't ideal to be moving in with someone after only dating a few days but apparently, when she had wished for a more interesting life, she'd wished a little too hard. Leo was all moved back into his room so was going to help Sam and Blake bring their things over next door. Mal would be coming in the next few days. From what Ella could tell, the atmosphere at Mal's house was currently very tense.

She'd watched a sweet moment between Will and Tony earlier as they'd hugged tightly, promising to keep each other updated on their progress before Tony ruffled Will's hair, having to reach up a little to do it and walked away. Will had watched him go, his back tight with worry.

"He'll be okay, he's only training," Ella had reminded him.

"I know, it's what he will do if there is a war that I worry about." He sighed.

"He'll fight? Even though he's an elder and technically retired?" Will laughed at that.

"I think Tony would rather be eaten alive than lay down his sword for good." Ella smiled up at him.

She stood up straight as Will walked into the room. He stood in the doorway, watching her and she could feel his eyes upon her.

"I can stay somewhere else if you'd be more comfortable," he said and she turned to look at him. He looked a little worried and her face softened.

"You will not be staying anywhere except beside me. I need my human dreamcatcher, remember?" He smiled at her and she reached out a hand to him. He took it and pulled her gently towards him.

"You called me your boyfriend," he said plainly and she felt her cheeks heat.

"Are you not my boyfriend?" she asked, with a slight waiver in her voice.

"I'll be anything you want me to be, princess," he said and she laughed.

"Boyfriend will do." He flashed his bright smile at her.

"And true partner. I want to be bonded to you again," she said and his eyes widened.

"You don't have to decide that now, there's plenty of time..." He started rambling and she silenced him with a look.

"We've just been told that war will probably be coming. I'm going to get my ass out into that ring every day and make sure that I am as prepared as I can be for what is coming but I never feel safer than when I'm with you." His eyes softened.

"It means that when I do stupid things and get stabbed you'll know," he warned.

"Good, that just means I can come and kick your ass faster." He dragged her body till it was flush against his and leaned down to press a hard kiss to her mouth.

"Don't worry princess, I have my all powerful Guardian of the Gate to heal all of my wounds." He bit her lip and she moaned into the kiss. Before things could get interesting, there was a knock on the door and Will turned around to open it. Leo stood before them looking tired.

"Nona wants us all at Café Ventuno tonight, all of

us are going to meet there for dinner at seven and to plan what's happening next." Will nodded and Ella bit her lip.

"Thanks Leo." He smiled at them both. They watched him go and Ella turned to Will again. Peering at the clock she saw that it was only five.

"Why does it feel like this day is never going to end?" She sighed and he stroked her hair.

"We're gonna sit down with your family, Sam and Blake, Mal and Magda and we're going to eat some good food and talk about what our next steps will be. If Elena's called a meeting, she's probably already heard from your dad and Dominic has been given the message." She hissed lightly at the mention of Dominic and at the use of the word Dad.

"Sorry princess. We'll call him Michael." She sighed.

"I hated him already but knowing that he just went and had a family a few years after completely abandoning us makes me want to..." Lightning zapped at her fingertips but she breathed through it. She really didn't want to set the house on fire. "Do that," she said glumly.

"Leo looked happy to find out he had other siblings," Will said carefully and a knot of unease curled in her stomach.

"A little too happy. I'm worried if we're forced to work with Michael while this whole thing with Dominic happens, that Leo is going to end up getting hurt again. He's gonna let him and his family in and then when the threat is gone, then what? Do we really think the Order will let them keep their memories?" she asked Will as she walked past him, sitting down at her dressing table. He sat on the edge of the bed and looked at her.

"Probably not, but it's up to Leo if he wants to try and get a relationship with him in the meantime." He shrugged.

"I know but I at least need to warn him, he needs to be careful. Him suddenly showing up after I just get my powers and yet his wife and kids have been taken hostage weeks ago?" she asked and Will smiled at her.

"Your brain works in just the right ways, princess. You're right that it's weird, he's only just arrived. Tony in particular feels it's suspicious as when we offered protection, he seemed genuinely scared. If that had not been offered, I don't think he would have told us that they'd already been taken. If they even have." She pinched the bridge of her nose.

"So Sam and Will are going to meet with Dominic to discuss what his demands are I guess, in an effort to stop a war. Mal and I will be training, all of the other angels in the area will be on high alert. So, who's going to be figuring out what Michael is up to?" she asked, her eyes locking with his. He seemed relieved that she didn't look upset that he'd accused her father of something untoward.

"That is for Sam to figure out when Leo is helping me and Magda with training. We have to be careful with Leo," he said lightly. "He's hanging on by a thread as it is and I wouldn't be surprised if he falls before long and goes back to being a mortal." Ella's hand flew to her mouth in a gasp.

"You really think he would do that?" she said.

"He's already asked Elena if he were to do so, would he have his memories taken away, would he be allowed to know what you and the rest of us are. As far as I'm aware, the Order have said he would have his memory wiped the same as any other mortal." She closed her eyes as a tear slid down her cheek.

"He won't do that, he won't put that burden on me," she said sadly.

"He's miserable, Ella. I've asked Tony to appeal directly to the head of the Order about his gifts. It's very rare that they would allow an angel to change their gifts, but it can be done. The last time I was in Astridia I asked and they told me they would consider it, but the look they gave me... I'm not hopeful."

"Shit."

"Yeah. He's fragile and if Michael is somehow working with or for Dominic, we need to keep Leo as far away from him as possible." She nodded.

"Did you and Tony tell Elena?" She looked at him and he shook his head sadly.

"Your Nona loves you both so much. Once we know something we will tell her." Ella cringed.

"It's really best not to have secrets from her." He studied her face and nodded.

"You know her best, we'll speak with her tonight." She nodded, smiling at the interaction. When he'd said before that now she would have all of the information to make the right decisions so that he wouldn't have to push her so hard but it was nice to see it, that this really was the way that he wanted it to be between them, coming to a decision together. That her opinion not only mattered but it counted, just as much as his did.

"I'm going to head to the café now and give Nona a hand with dinner. Care to join me?" she asked, standing and making her way to the back of the door to grab her jacket.

"Sure." He followed her out of the room, grabbing a sweatshirt from the back of the door also and Ruby was waiting for them at the bottom of the stairs. Ella pulled down her leash and attached it to her collar.

"Let's go." She said goodbye to Leo and let Will take her hand in his. They walked in silence the entire way, enjoying the darkness falling around them. When they reached the café they looked at each other. She let in a deep breath and he nodded. It seemed to impress upon them then that this was not just a family dinner, this was a plan of action, a board meeting to decide what jobs would befall to who. Ella had expected the few days after her birthday to involve left over cake and a two-day hangover. Instead, she got some cool lightning powers and the threat of war. She thought fleetingly of Lucas and Dina and a thrum of power washed over her. So what if she had a few hard months of training in front of her? She would work hard and she would be ready. If the war came she would fight, whether she was precious to the angels or not. If she was irreplaceable or not, she would fight. She knocked on the door and stood back, waiting to be let in to the dinner that might decide the rest of her life.

# About the Author

Andie lives in the southwest of England with her fiancé Matty and their bearded dragon Freddie. This is the first novel of the Angels of Series and she has now started writing the second. Angels of Oblivion.

When she's not working at her normal job, you can find her in the pub playing crib, tucked up on the sofa with a book, watching old TV programs, complaining that they don't make them like they used to or scrolling endlessly through social media to avoid doing anything else.

# ACKNOWLEDGMENTS

I would first like to say a huge thank you to my closest friends and family that have encouraged me, shown interest and praise since I started or since I finished this book.

To my wonderful fiancé for providing me with tea, snacks and ignoring me for hours while I worked on my book. Thank you for believing in me and letting me do this exactly how I wanted to do it. I love you.

Charlie, I'm grateful to you for reading it with the enthusiasm of an avid reader when you're not one and telling everyone and their dog about my book. You're the best PR a girl could ask for! Your comments about my writing mean the world to me.

To Abbie and Gemma, thanks for putting up with me constantly talking about it, getting your opinions on things and for letting me be excited!

Mostly I would like to thank my beautiful friend Jenna, who kept me talking about the idea for a novel I'd harbored for ten years, asking so many questions that this world created itself through our conversations in the pub while playing a game of crib. Your ideas, banter, gentle nudges have helped make this book what it is today. Thank you.

Thank you, Fantastical Ink for working with me to create the cover of my dreams, nailing it when I have you such vague descriptions of what I wanted! It's perfect.

Thank you to L G Campbell for being so kind when I asked for advice on how to start this whole process, giving me endless amounts of resources, pointers and being a lovely human being in general.

Thank you to Phoenix Book Promo for proofreading, dealing with my unrelenting Britishness while writing a book set in the states, my excessive uses of commas and then for formatting my drivel into a readable book.

Finally, thank you to you, whoever is reading this now. If you loved it or hated it, you gave it a chance.